The Amarantha Stories

From first memories to final breath...

By Laurie Otis

City Heights

PRESS

2007

City Heights Press - Ashland, Wisconsin
www.booktraveler.com
E-mail: cityheightspress@excite.com
Book design by *Glo Creations*, Ashland, Wisconsin

First printing

ISBN: 1-889924-12-1

In memory of Ma
Tills vi trafas ater I Himmelen

I.
Ma's Bedtime Stories
Gerton and Sigrid

Amarantha pondered, maybe more than a child ordinarily would, the *hows* and *whys* of her coming to be on her small farm in New Scandia, Wisconsin. Billy Curtis from her grade in school said his folks had been in New Scandia forever. And her friend Lynn knew her grandparents, but didn't even know what great grandparents were and, what's more, didn't care.

But Ma's tales of their adventures and tragedies made the ancestors live again for Amarantha, and she wondered how and where she would be if none of them had decided to immigrate to America? In Sweden? Ireland? And would she even be herself, or a completely different girl? These self-imposed questions nurtured a very analytical mind that listened and observed, traits that remained with her throughout life, for better or for worse.

She was most familiar with the Persons and Tulpans, Ma's side of the family. Her great grandparents, Gerton and Sigrid Tulpan, already in their early fifties, decided in 1878 to leave their grown daughter and her family behind in Sweden and immigrate to America, bringing their younger son Andrew with them. This was not a sudden whim on their part. Gerton had been thinking about it for thirty years, as he toiled away on a rented farm, but it had never seemed the right time to go. The children were little, Sigrid's parents were old and needy; there were always reasons to stay in the rut they had made for themselves.

But Gerton had already been to America. He was a seasoned world traveler due to his service with the Swedish Navy at a time when Sweden was considered somewhat of a power on the seas. His home village was in the county of *Blekinge*, located on the southeastern tip of Sweden on the Baltic Sea; and although his village was inland, they could smell the sea on a windy day and felt the North Sea storms and an almost imperceptible pull (more of the soul than body) of the tide. It was natural then, for many young, adventurous *Blekinge* men to gravitate to the harbor cities and make a living on the docks or sign up to sail the trade routes.

As for Gerton, he had always dreamed of more than a life on the sea and joined the Royal Navy hoping to improve his economic status enough to purchase some farm land back in *Blekinge*. His incredible odyssey began in 1851 with the passing of the then famous Treaty of Paris, which stated, basically, that piracy on the high seas was a crime punishable, in some cases, by death. With global trade increasing and European immigration in full swing, the privateers had become a serious economic liability. Sweden signed the treaty, along with most of Europe, and as a way of enforcement, each nation's signature also bound them to send three ships to patrol the world's major waterways in search of pirates.

The politics of this Gerton neither knew nor cared about and was initially unaware of the far reaching influence it would have on his life and the lives of his family, until his wooden sailing schooner, the *Ringaren*, was slated for pirate patrol. And so he left his young, pregnant wife in the care of her parents to spend two years circling the globe.

They set sail from *Karlskrona* naval base and sailed across the Atlantic Ocean to the West Indies; around the horn of South America; back to California; west to the Hawaiian Islands, the Phillipines, Japan, and China; back around by Italy, Spain, France, The British Isles; then home to Sweden.

The *Ringaren* didn't encounter any pirates, but the impressionable and intelligent farm boy from *Blekinge* had encounters of his own that changed his outlook on life forever. The world opened to him with its strange languages and cultures; and while some of his shipmates feared to go beyond the boundaries of the harbor, he roamed about the strange cities, Los Angeles-Honolulu-Tokyo, his apprehension overcome by his curiosity, talking to workers in the harbors or venders in the marketplaces. It didn't matter that they spoke different languages, they communicated somehow with gestures and smiles. And people responded to the tall boy with flaming, red hair and kind, blue eyes, and he learned that men were basically the same the world over.

He didn't know about the women. He didn't seek them out like some of the men who came back from forays in foreign ports, bragging about, "*deras erovring av kvnor*" (their female conquests). He was basically very shy around women; and had considered himself lucky, and relieved, when Sigrid agreed to be his wife. It meant he no longer had to go through that agonizing ritual of "*uppvaktning*" (courting), which had always left him sweaty and confused. So now he had a wife, and possibly a child, back in Sweden; and he wasn't about to be untrue to them.

Many times he was sorely tempted when his mates urged him to jump ship with them and join the California gold rush. Or, when docked at a South Sea island, they reasoned, "Why go back to Sweden where it's always cold and damp, and life is so hard? Why not stay on these islands where it's warm and life is easy?"

Then he would think, "Maybe I could send for my family when I strike it rich or have a fishing boat in a warm climate." But he carried a picture of *Blekinge* in his mind, with his family, its churches and farms, and he knew Sigrid would never make such a dangerous journey all alone. And so he always replied, "*Jag skal gd hem till min famili* "(I shall go home to my family).

Ma always told that part with pride. Her grandfather was a man who "did the right thing."

And so, when the *Ringaren* arrived back at *Karlskrona* after two years, the crew was elated to be home and anxious to resume their old lives in their homeland; but none more than Gerton who, when he reached *Blekinge*, threw his sea bag on the ground and rushed to embrace Sigrid and his two-year-old daughter Kerstine Matilda. There hadn't been any means of communication during his stint at sea; and although he wrote letters, he was never able to receive any, so didn't know if he had a daughter or son or even if the baby had survived, as many didn't.

Now this little girl peeked shyly from behind her mother's skirt at the deeply tanned man with the flaming, red beard who seemed to want to hug and kiss everyone. His clothes were rough and his boots worn. He wore a bandanna round his neck and his ear lobe was pierced by a gold loop, which happened to catch a sun ray, causing Matilda to squint and turn her face away. She had never seen anything like him and was afraid.

She tried to lose herself in the folds of her mother's voluminous skirt, but eventually was lured by the sight of a shiny, gold coin which her father held out to her. It wasn't until she stepped to reach for it that Gerton saw she walked with the aid of a small, homemade crutch supporting one tiny foot folded back against her ankle. "*Det var vid tillkomsten*" (It was at birth), Sigrid explained as he drew the little body into his arms. Later, Matilda sat on his lap, playing with the gold medal King Oscar I had awarded all who had sailed on the Swedish expedition. Gerton seemed absorbed in examining the lame foot and pressed his fingers into the deep crease between her toe and ankle.

The gold medal went to set up their household on a rented plot of land. Sigrid was especially happy to have her husband back since she had heard about all the men on the trip who had "*jumped ship*" to stay in California and try their hand at the '*gold fields,*' or those who succumbed to the pleasures of the tropical islands. And at first Gerton was content with his lot. Their farm, community and family were like a small microcosm. Sometimes their lives were turned upside-down as if a giant hand had shaken their orb, like when a plague of small pox took the life of their newborn baby, Karin, or the crops failed two summers in a row and they were forced to kill some of their cattle they couldn't feed anyway in order to eat.

Years later Amarantha, Gerton and Sigrid's great granddaughter, would revel in Ma's stories about her sailor grandpa with the gold earring and how the tar on the ship's deck had boiled in the heat when they crossed the equator and of all the men who *"jumped ship"* and were never heard from again. Amarantha was sorry their ship had never encountered pirates, but content enough with the illustrious tales she had. Her favorite story, however, was how Grandpa Gerton, home from the seas, had whittled ever widening blocks of wood, lined them with a soft fabric, intermittently wedged them into the crease between Matilda's foot and ankle, and bandaged all securely. Gradually as she grew, the foot had been pushed down until the sole could lay almost flat against a surface. "And that," Ma would say with her usual triumphant ending, "was why my mother was able to throw away her crutch, even though she walked with a slight limp all her life."

So for the most part life in Sweden was good. But sometimes when Gerton plowed a field on a windy day, he could smell the sea air and imagined he heard the sails flapping against the spar; then a feeling of freedom welled in his chest that sent him striding, with the lurching gait of a sailor, over the newly turned furrows like a giant traveling miles with each step. He was back at sea, and the surrounding forests and fields leveled into a rolling expanse of water and the tug of the horses on the plow became the steady pitch of ocean waves. And it wasn't just that he longed for the sea. He was tired of working another man's land for a meager existence. He wanted more out of life for Sigrid and himself; and sometimes late at night, lying beside his contented, sleeping wife, he'd delve deeply into the inner chambers of his soul and admit that he longed for the adventure of his youth - never aloud, because it wasn't a good enough reason for a man to uproot his family and carry them off to a strange land. "Just one more ocean voyage," he'd pray, "to America where we could make a good life," he'd justify, in case God might think his prayer too selfish.

And so Gerton didn't fear the unknown on the sea, or blanche at the thought of leaving their homeland, as Sigrid did when he would talk about it. As years passed, and he thought more and more about immigrating to America, he tried to influence her and calm her fears by telling her pleasant tales of what he had seen in different lands. He even brought her papers, one telling of 70,000 Swedes who had immigrated to Minnesota. He'd say, "The climate is the same and there'd be plenty of Swedes to talk to *pricis som hemma* (Just like home)."

Then in the 1870s, immigration began to look more acceptable to Sigrid. Failed harvests and cholera had plagued their county for several years. Many of their friends from church had already gone to America and written back glowing accounts of their lives there. Besides that, Matilda was married with three little boys, their parents had passed away, and their young son Andrew could go with them. The time had finally come; and a laughing Gerton, in spite of the gray in his red beard, suddenly looked young again and he whisked an apprehensive Sigrid off her feet and danced her in circles singing, "*Rida, Rida, Ranka! Hasten heter blanka!*" To which Sigrid replied with a dubious look, "*Jag tror du har gott tillbacka till din barndom*" (I think you've returned to that peace of childhood)!

Matilda and John

When they announced their final decision to Matilda and her husband, John Person, their daughter immediately burst into tears. She'd heard her father's tales all her life, and long ago she'd recognized the lightness that entered his voice when he talked of America.

"I think *Far* wants to go back to America," she'd say to her mother; and her mother would reply, "All men think fondly about what they did in their youth."

But the words she imagined time and again over the years lurked in the back of her mind, and now she heard them aloud with her father's dreaded announcement, "Your mother, Andrew and I are going to America!"

Like her parents, Matilda and John worked to raise crops and milk a few cows on their rented farm. They were able to bring in a little more money by working for their landlord in his town house: Matilda as a kitchen maid, John driving their carriage. Matilda was able to take her three little boys, Charlie, Willie, and Otto, to the "*big house*" with her, and John worked long hours to fit his farm chores around the chauffeuring. It was a hard life; but it was what they had expected to do, like most everyone else they knew, and it had grown familiar and comfortable. They didn't know any other way.

That night, after her parents had left and the boys were asleep, Matilda cried into her pillow.

How could she lose her family? The boys would grow up without ever knowing their grandparents! They weren't young and would probably die in that foreign land with no one to comfort them in their old age. Why couldn't her father be content with what he had? Why did he want to leave them?

She didn't give John a chance to answer any of these questions, so he just held her in his arms until the sobs became fewer and were gradually replaced by even breathing, with only an occasional damp catch of the throat to disturb the quiet night.

But he lay awake for a long time after Matilda drifted restlessly into sleep, and with his eyes closed, he looked into the darkness of his mind. His family was gone, parents dead and his brothers scattered. Although he had said nothing to Matilda for fear of alarming her, he had long been dissatisfied with their lot in life. He was often too tired to even notice his boys, except to discipline them; and he'd noticed how sharp and complaining his wife had become and the deep, down-turning lines of exhaustion that had appeared around her mouth and between her eyes. What was there to keep them here, now that her parents were leaving? They didn't own anything but a few cows, and there would never be anything to leave their boys as an inheritance. Maybe they should go to America too! John fell asleep then thinking, "I'll talk to Gerton about it tomorrow."

He decided not to mention anything to Matilda until he'd talked to his father-in-law, so he said nothing at breakfast the next morning. As for Matilda, she acted angry and clattered around the tiny kitchen, slapping handfuls of oatmeal into the boiling water as if she were administering a spanking. Their usually rambunctious boys knew to sit still at times like these, but noted their mother's swollen eyes and looked inquisitively at their father. Waiting until her back was turned, John silently caught their eyes and shook his head. They turned to their breakfasts and kept their heads lowered until they were done.

And so it was decided that the Tulpons would go to America first, then send for the Persons when they could spare enough money to help with the traveling expenses. The two women were delighted with the arrangements and excited at the prospect of this new life. Many hours were spent in deciding what should be taken: the spinning wheels for sure, seeds from favorite plants that they thought might not grow in America, and favorite recipes that would make them feel at home in the new world. The men too were excited and overwhelmed with the prospect of actually owning land and equipment and of being their own bosses.

And so in 1878, Sigrid, Gerton, and Andrew traveled to America, not on a wooden schooner this time but a modern steamship especially rigged to transport the ever growing tide of immigrants bound for the new world. Matilda and John, along with their three sons, joined them in 1881. The two families were among the estimated one and one-half million Swedes who immigrated to America between 1870 and 1914.

They settled on homesteads adjacent to each other in the midst of the great forests of Wisconsin. Their property was heavily timbered with virgin pine, and the first months were spent clearing land and setting up log dwellings. During the winter, they worked in the sawmills which flourished in the area, earning enough money to keep their families and also to purchase stock, equipment, and seed for their farms, which they worked during the summer months. To Matilda and John, four more sons and three daughters would be born and raised on this pioneer farm, one of whom was Amarantha's Ma, Minnie.

For the most part, they were successful. The hard work ethic plus some shrewd timber deals resulted in almost model farms. John and Gerton, by virtue of their having to conduct business with their neighbors and townspeople, became known as leaders and served in a decision making capacity on various community and church boards. Matilda and Sigrid didn't fare as well. Because they stayed at home, they never learned to speak more than a few halting phrases of English, which isolated them more than the miles of wilderness surrounding them. In later years, it was even difficult for them to understand their children whose Swedish, their first language, had became corrupted by the American vernacular.

Life in the new world was extremely difficult; on the homestead sometimes the veneer of civilization wore thin, exposing a human existence not much better than that of the farm animals they tended. Matilda, who in the 'old country' had worked as a maid for rich people, tried to enforce certain standards of hygiene and behavior. But the growing family, the overwhelming work load, and the lack of physical amenities (such as the proximity of water) forced her to abandon many of her "nice" ways and settle for expediency. Still, she didn't succumb to what she considered the low ways of some peasant settlers, who were an embarrassment to their fellow Scandinavians.

Amarantha listened with mixed fascination and revulsion to Grandma's stories (told via Ma) of a low family living adjacent to the Person farm. If Matilda looked up from her work and noticed the matriarch of that family approaching her cabin, she dropped what she was doing and headed her off at the driveway. Much as she must have craved the company of another Swedish speaking woman, she couldn't abide this lady's personal habit of urinating where she was standing, if the urge came upon her, "som en ko pa gron bete (like a cow in the pasture)." This woman was not a time waster. She knitted as she walked, in order to prepare her family for the cold winter, and to her way of thinking, her ankle length garments allowed her enough privacy to relieve herself without taking the time to find a hiding tree. Grandma considered it the height of degradation (as did Amarantha upon hearing) and certainly didn't invite her in for coffee.

Ma laughed when she remembered another story about the same family. The students in their one-room school didn't always maintain the highest standards of hygiene; and in the winter, when the woodstove got hot and the doors were closed, various odors sometimes got bad enough to affect their concentration and interfere with their studies.

"Now you would think the Swansons would have been the worst offenders," she suggested, "but such was not the case. Everyone wanted to sit next to those three kids because they gave off the best smell. It was like fresh bread, all yeasty and buttery, and it was strong enough to make you hungry long before lunch time. Well, one day when the teacher had been working with one of them for some time, she said, pleasantly and by way of a compliment, 'Why is it that you kids always smell like fresh bread?'

"Well, the oldest girl, her name was Ada, looked embarrassed, but she had to answer.

"'Oh, our Ma softens her bread crust in our bed,' she explained.'"

The first time Amarantha heard the story, she didn't know what the girl had meant, but Ma, barely able to talk for laughing over the memory, explained. It seems that one method of ensuring soft crusts on homemade bread was to place a dish towel over the hot loaves, so the contained heat would cause condensation to make the crust moist and soft. Since there weren't many dish towels in the Swanson kitchen, and since it was a one- room cabin, the proximity of the beds gave Mrs. Swanson a time-saving idea. She merely whipped back the covers on the bed, tipped the hot loaves, one at a time, out of the pans, and tucked them in gently. When it was time for bed, the tender-crusted loaves were taken out, and the family climbed in.

"I sure never traded sandwiches with Ada Swanson," Ma would conclude as she wiped the tears of laughter from her eyes.

Ma told many stories of going to school in a one-room schoolhouse. She went to school, sporadically, through the fifth grade. There were frequent and long absences for all the children when they were needed at home for farm work or the birth of a baby. The older boys did not go to school at all. Amarantha wondered at a teacher who tried to cope with all ages, most of whom could not speak English.

"Let's see," Ma would reminisce, "The LaMere boys spoke French, the Schmidts spoke German, and the rest of us spoke either Swede or Norwegian." However, those who were privileged to attend school could at least speak broken English, unlike the older boys and their mother who never did master the language of their new homeland.

Transportation was primitive and distances great. A team of plow horses and a dray wagon took the family to an area church and to the nearest town for supplies. A trip to town was an all-day experience and planned carefully so that it only had to be made once a month at the most. Ma said that her "*Far*" would pull the wagon into an alley when they reached town, so the women could alight without showing their ankles.

Ma was a natural story teller, and many of her childhood remembrances complete with gestures, expressions, and voice dynamics, served as bedtime stories for her little girl. Many would today be considered unsuitable for tender ears, but although violent and sometimes sad, these stories painted a picture of Ma's life "up on the farm;" and even though she knew them all by heart, Amarantha requested them every night and never failed to shudder, thrill, sigh, or laugh as they unfolded.

Amarantha lay under the heavy woolen quilt and heard of a time when wolves howled in hunger around their log house on bitterly cold winter nights; and how, periodically, her grandfather would seize the fire tongs and pull a flaming log from their cast-iron stove, flinging it into the midst of the pack to scatter them for a time. But the beasts always regrouped and returned, haunting the pioneer family's dreams (and eventually, Amarantha's) with their snarling, gray presence.

And woe be to any hapless logger who ventured out of the nearby lumber camps after dark. All that would remain of him was bloody snow and a few tattered rags that had been his clothes. Amarantha hugged her knees close to her chest and didn't dare relax her feet to the bottom of the bed for fear one of those wolves had escaped from the bedtime story and waited on the bedpost. Sometimes the logger (why they always had to be out traveling on such nights, Amarantha couldn't fathom) would climb a tree and escape the circling pack by waiting out the night. Nowadays, many experts insist that wolves will not attack people but prefer to remain in secluded areas, feeding on rabbits and mice. Amarantha always believed Ma. After all, she was there.

Immigrants in America

Of the Person girls, Jennie and Alma married sons from neighboring Scandinavian families; Ma, the only rebel, went to be a domestic in St. Paul, and eventually married Ed Grady, Amarantha's father, an Irish, *fallen-away Catholic.* For many reasons, initially his heritage and religion, he was considered an alien by the Swedish contingent; and, consequently, the Gradys were never truly accepted by the Persons or their offspring.

Of the Person boys, Olaf died in childhood of undetermined causes. Joseph went off to World War I and died of influenza in an army camp in France. The success story, Charlie, married a neighbor girl, and eventually farmed and raised ten children on his grandfather Tulpon's homestead. Four sons remained on the home farm and allowed the isolation, the constant pressure of grueling work and the language barrier to set the stage for what was to be the tragic lives of the four remaining Person men, those Amarantha thought of as, *Her Alien Uncles.*

Ma was forty-four when Amarantha was born, so by the time she was old enough to have any recollections, her grandparents were in their eighties and had retired from the farm, leaving it to the four unmarried uncles. Amarantha kept the family portrait, framed with the curving glass that had been taken before Joseph left for World War II. No one is smiling. The children stand sideways, overlapping like shingles on a roof, and frame the already elderly parents. Her grandfather is bearded and used and her grandmother's eyes show neither pride nor love for this large family, only indifference.

The girls are spare and angular in their high-necked blouses and the men look extremely uncomfortable in their suits and ties. There doesn't appear to be any definite cut to the suits -- The lapels and sleeves are lumpy as if padding had slipped to obscure sharp seams. It was a grim scene, and when Amarantha, as a little girl, looked at it, she hardly recognized her mother or her aunts. They were completely alien to her. So alien that they could easily have landed on a space ship and worked their way to Wisconsin.

By Amarantha's time, the log house had been replaced by a two-story clapboard structure that must have seemed very grand to the family who had shared a twelve by fourteen room with a dirt floor. She, however, remembered it as tall, foreboding and wanting paint.

The log house remained for tool storage in the winter and also served as a summer kitchen. In former years, as soon as the weather turned warm, *the boys*, as her uncles were known, would dismantle the big, black wood range and move it to the summer kitchen; Grandma would cook all the meals there so the house wouldn't be hot and also can all the garden produce. Now, it was solely storage and there was no canning and little cooking done at either location.

The house was built before central heating, so, unlike modern architecture with open spaces and wide arches, it was a series of small rooms each with its own door, eliminating the need to heat particular areas in the winter. The kitchen was the largest room and the only one currently heated. For Amarantha, its main features were the coffee grinder, which was bolted to the wall by the stove and which she turned when they visited, and the pantry, which stored the canning and was especially interesting to a small girl because it had always contained long pans of *rusks*.

Rusks began as tall yeast rolls which, when they were in danger of becoming stale, were cut lengthwise into thick slices and toasted slowly in a low oven. They were golden brown in color and very hard. Sometimes they were sprinkled with cinnamon and sugar. It required intense sucking to render them soft enough to chew, but if you had a cup of strong coffee, made from the freshly ground beans and laced with cream from the dairy herd, you could *dunk* them and prolong the pleasure with slurping and sipping, dipping any broken pieces of rusk off the oily coffee surface with your spoon.

Grandma seldom had cookies, cake or any other familiar bakery. She didn't use icing sugar or baking chocolate. Occasionally there would be a coarse grained, heavily spiced cake to accompany the coffee, and Amarantha would watch in amazement as Grandpa and the *boys* smeared butter or jam on the unfrosted surface.

Grandma wore long dresses, always with an apron, and had white hair gathered in a bun at the nape of her neck. She hadn't a tooth in her head, and *dunked* all her food in her coffee. By the time Amarantha was old enough to have any recollections, her Grandma was in poor health and deep in dementia. Sometimes she didn't know her granddaughter and would peer blankly at her from rheumy eyes. *Minnie* and *flicka* were two words that were recognizable to Amarantha out of the Swedish explanation that followed. She was Minnie's girl. She was always a little afraid of Grandma, Grandpa, and *the Boys*.

In spite of the lack of modern miracle drugs and cures; and not withstanding the hard lives they had endured, Grandma and Grandpa Person lived into their eighties, spending their final years living in town at their daughter's home (Amarantha's Aunt Alma).

With *The Boys* in charge of the farm, the homestead had become a bachelor household and had ceased to possess any refinements that a resident woman might impose. Without plumbing, the rules of hygiene had never been strictly observed; now they were all but abandoned.

Amarantha remembered that the house smelled little better than the barn. The men were no longer careful about their manure covered boots and didn't change or wash clothes often. On visits, Wendel and she used to steal away while the adults were engaged in their undecipherable Swedish conversations and quietly climb the narrow stairway to the sleeping rooms. It seemed as if there were many rooms with iron beds and stained, bare mattresses. The tattered shades were always pulled, so they had to strain to see. Sheets and pillowcases had been discarded long ago, leaving only tangles of heavy quilts made of wool materials that once had possessed colors and designs, but now were just dark. There was no sign of the suits and ties of the family portrait, and only a few pairs of dirty boots and carelessly flung shirts showed that anyone actually lived there. The sour smell of the unwashed coupled with whatever was deposited in the ubiquitous *thunder-jugs* made their breath catch and their eyes burn. They didn't stay long and stumbled and fell down the stairs, tripping over each other and their own feet to escape; somehow they were drawn to view this alien world that they only dared to glimpse briefly lest they be trapped like insects on one of the many fly ribbons that dangled in the corners of the old house and made to sleep in one of the loathsome bedrooms.

"My uncles are dirty and smelly," Amarantha remarked to Ma as they rode home in a cousin's car after a visit to the farm.

"They forget to wash and Grandma isn't there to remind them," she defended.

"How can they live like that?" asked Wendel, who was able to make more philosophical observations by virtue of being six years older than she.

Their much older cousin laughed and said, "They don't even notice how they live. They're *'pickled'* most of the time."

Amarantha's aunt shushed everyone and looked stonily at the road to forestall any further discussion. Amarantha's knowledge of pickling had to do with the large crocks of raw cucumbers immersed in vinegar brine that Ma dealt with each summer. Her imagination soared all the way home as she tried to imagine her uncles suspended in a similar liquid.

One day when Amarantha came home from school, Ma and her Aunt Alma sat by the table. Their faces were grim, and they clutched their coffee cups as if they feared the containers of their favorite drink might fly away if not grounded. They were speaking Swedish, but Amarantha could tell they were arguing, even if she didn't understand what they were saying. She later found out that one of Uncle Charlie's sons had offered to buy the home farm at a ridiculously low price, and that her aunt favored the sale because the land would be kept in the family. Ma, on the other hand, thought they shouldn't sell or, at least, get a fair price.

"Don't give it away," she begged.

But by then the *The Boys* were hopeless alcoholics (for that was how it was viewed in those days), and the farm had fallen into a state of neglect due to their collective, frequent drinking bouts.

"They're off on a spree," Uncle Charlie would announce in his heavy Swedish accent, further advancing the cause of his son. "We've had to do their chores all week. Something's got to be done!"

For their part, *The Boys* favored the sale which would relieve them of their responsibilities along with providing them a sum of money. They had fallen heir to a rich farm which still boasted a stand of virgin timber, but the insidious spread of their disease had rendered them incapable of thinking beyond the next beer at the local pool hall.

Trying to force them to look at the big picture, Ma had argued, "What will you do? Where will you live? You don't know anything but living at home and farming!"

And they would nod sadly, and say, "Ya! Ya!" only to repeat the same when the other side of the family accosted them with the tempting offer. And so, the majority ruled, and Uncle Charlie's son purchased the homestead.

In many ways it was good that the land remained in the family. But Ma always felt that *The Boys* could have somehow been rehabilitated and left to operate their legacy. "As it was," she often recalled, "they were left with no home or work and nothing to live for but the booze. I can't imagine what our Far would have thought!"

To which a defiant Aunt Alma would conclude the conversation with, "Well, that is something we won't know *tills vi trafas ater I himmelen* (until we meet in heaven)."

Amarantha's Great Grandfather Gerton Tulpon lived to be in his eighties also; but, in keeping with his adventurous life, didn't die in his rocking chair contemplating the afterlife. He was walking from town carrying a burlap sack of groceries when a *new fangled* horseless carriage drew up on the road beside him, and a proud and boastful driver offered him a ride. Because it was a hot day and he was an old man (but mostly because he was curious and still ready for new adventure) he accepted and settled himself and his bag on the passenger side.

It was never determined if the driver was showing-off for what he considered an impressionable old rube or if he was merely an inexperienced driver. Whatever the cause, he lost control of the car on the gravel road and crashed into a large oak. And so it was that *Grossfar* Tulpon, who had sailed round the world on a wooden schooner hunting pirates; who had immigrated with his family to the new world and built a successful farm; who had, through patience and ingenuity, enabled his daughter to throw away her crutch; and who had worn a bandana around his neck and a gold loop in his ear lobe, had become the county's first traffic fatality. The driver was unhurt.

To this day when Amarantha visits the old homestead, she sometimes catches a movement out of the corner of her eye—a chimera in human form of the dashing, wind-burned sailor with the red beard. She sees him disappear, more a sense of movement than sight, behind the old summer kitchen or catches him peering down at her from the hayloft of the barn. Then she imagines him striding across the corn field after the plow dreaming of his adventures on the sea. How did he end up land-locked on a Wisconsin farm? Is the chattering of the birds his laughter at the antics of his progeny? Is the moan of the wind in the pines his cry for wasted opportunities or shattered dreams? Maybe his dreams came true. Maybe he was lucky to have had a dream. No one will know, *tills vi trafas ater I himmelen.*

II.
For The Love of A Good Pie

Amarantha loved to bake pies. She liked to work the lard and flour with her hands so that her body heat aided the blending process. She squeezed the mixture together with her fingertips until she felt it to be the desired consistency - like stiff cookie dough.

When she added the liquids, the dough became sloppy at first, but she gradually fondled and patted it into an integrated, if slightly sticky, ball. A chilling half-hour in the refrigerator would leave it in just about the right condition for handling. Rolling the sphere flat to fit the pie pan without tearing the dough was a challenge, but with years of experience behind her, she easily accomplished this with her floured board and rolling pin.

The fillings were usually seasonal fruit mixed with sugar, cornstarch, and appropriate spices. Sometimes she made custards and added nuts, bananas or coconut. But whatever the filling, Amarantha made it plentiful. She hated what she called *measly* pies.

Amarantha's daughter, Wendy, didn't bake pies at all. "It's a waste of time! You can get a frozen pie at the store if you want one." Amarantha thought frozen pies were *measly*, and the crust tasted like cardboard. How could Wendy compare them with her own flaky, lard and butter crusts?

But even her own grandchildren, now teenagers, often refused pie at family dinners. "Too much fat!" or "Too heavy!" they'd complain, and, insult of all insults, her sweet little granddaughter even confided to her Granny that she, "liked those little flat apple pies in a bag that you get at McDonalds."

Amarantha's husband, Frank, used to say, "Amy, your pies are the best in the world." Now that he was gone, no one said that, and she missed it, even though she knew in her heart it probably wasn't true or, at least, hadn't been proven conclusively.

Once when she took an apple pie out of the oven, its browned crust sparkling with cinnamon sugar like a sand beach in the sun, her mind, quite suddenly and unexpectedly, was removed to an afternoon when she was about four years old, going with her mother to clean the offices of their small local power company, The Hydro Electric.

It was 1935, and the depression continued to worry their small, rural town. Ma was grateful for the job and had impressed upon her the importance of, "Being good, being polite, and staying out of the way." It was a lesson which, sometimes to her detriment, stayed with her for life.

As they entered the building that afternoon, Lila Berg, the office manager, was securing the doors at the end of the business day. Amarantha had seen her before and was afraid of her. Her thick glasses magnified her eyes and made her look like an owl. This image was further enhanced by two tufts of tightly permed hair on either side of her forehead that looked for all the world like feathered ears. Her mouth was full and very round, giving the impression of a brightly lipsticked beak; and red, talon-like fingernails completed the likeness.

Amarantha thought she smelled funny too. There was a sweet scent about her that was hard to define, honeysuckle or sweet peas; but her perfume was tainted with a mildewy odor. Maybe it was a chemical reaction of the perfume to her skin. But in Amarantha's mind, it was the smell of disapproval, which seemed to seep from every pore.

The Owl greeted Ma curtly. She had drawn her beak into a tight, round circle; and her smell hung thickly in the air as she fixed her eyes on the small girl with the freckled nose and skinned knees, as if peering at some insignificant and slightly offensive creature. Those luminous pupils remained on Amarantha even though she was giving instructions to Ma.

"We're having an executive meeting tomorrow morning," she said. "Two officers from Northern States Power Company will be meeting with Mr. Lenz, so I want you to pay particular attention to his office. Set up the coffee table with the linens I've laid out."

Amarantha sensed that she was an unwelcome addition to the cleaning crew and stepped shyly behind her mother, partly to convey that she would stay out of the way, but mostly to hide from that unblinking stare.

"Yes, Miss Berg," Ma answered; then, sensing the aura of disapproval, she quickly added, "Sorry about bringing the girl. There wasn't anyone at home to stay with her."

"I guess it'll be okay. But this meeting tomorrow is very important: it's about the sale of The Hydro to Northern States Power, so don't forget what I've told you." She turned to leave, then looked back quickly just as Amarantha peeked from behind her mother's skirt. It almost seemed as if she had swiveled her head on her neck without moving her body, and Amarantha blinked her eyes in amazement as *The Owl* shot back, "Just see that she doesn't touch anything!"

Going to work with Ma was maddeningly boring for an energetic four year old. Once she had spun round and round in an upholstered, swivel chair until she was dizzy; eyes closed, she could almost imagine it was summer, and she was twirling on a breath-catching carnival ride. But suddenly the ride stopped, and Ma pulled her from the chair by one arm. From then on, all she could do was follow from office to office, sometimes carrying a wastebasket or dragging a mop and endlessly waiting, waiting.

Once, while Ma was vacuuming, Amarantha slipped away and began wandering from room to room. It was very quiet. The typewriters were shrouded in heavy, black covers, and machines with numbered keys and long handles crouched menacingly, those handles the curled tails of cats, probably panthers, ready to pounce on intruders like a small girl who, in order to relieve her boredom, stood peering at them through slitted eyes. The smell of furniture polish and floor wax filled her nostrils.

But then, as she walked down a hall, a more pungent, pleasant scent came to her; and she followed her nose into a small kitchen. In later years, she learned that this was a test kitchen for research-ing recipes using the newest in electrical appliances. It was equipped with a shiny, white stove and refrigerator like those she had seen in magazines, not at all like their huge, black woodstove at home. There were enameled, metal counters instead of their wooden table and cupboard, and on one of those counters rested the origin of the smell that had begun to make Amarantha's mouth water -- an apple pie!

Ma didn't make pie. Often there weren't the necessary ingredi-ents; but more often, she was too busy trying to support six chil-dren to do much more in the way of dessert than an occasional pudding or canned fruit which she called *sauce*.

Amarantha's eyes were at counter level, so she pulled a nearby stool over in order to get a better view. At this vantage point, she could see that faintly pink juice had bubbled up through the fork-pricked air vents in the top crust which, in turn, was covered with a liberal coating of cinnamon sugar. She touched the side of the pie tin; it was slightly warm...

The temptation of Adam in the Garden of Eden or the hunger of Esau, ready to trade his birthright for a mess of pottage, paled in comparison to the desire that sparked the moral dilemma rag-ing in that four-year-old breast. She knew she could not legally taste the pie, and she wondered how severe the punishment would be if she were unable to abide *The Owl's* admonition *not to touch anything*. Maybe she could poke her finger into one of the air vents, widening it just a little. At that point, maybe she could extract some filling without noticeably altering the outward appearance.

But desperation often spawns workable solutions, and such was the case with Amarantha and the apple pie. Kneeling on the stool, with her hands pressing the counter on either side of the tin, she carefully leaned over the pie. Slowly lowering her head, she licked the entire top crust with strong strokes, stopping only occa-sionally to gently insinuate the tip of her tongue into the vents to taste the juice. If, in the Garden, Eve had made that apple into a pie, it would have been worth losing Paradise for just such a taste.

And, thus, began Amarantha's love affair with the pie.

The local Hydro Electric was, according to plan, eventually purchased by Northern States Power, and Ma worked there for several more years. Sometimes Amarantha accompanied her, never duplicating her initial adventure in the test kitchen; even a small child instinctively knows not to return to the scene of a crime. And sometimes, now seventy years later, when she takes one of her creations out of the oven, she feels the constriction at the back of her jaw and her mouth begins to water as she mentally experiences that first taste of apple pie. Then a slight smile forms as she remembers *The Owl* and wonders how the Minnesota Power officers had enjoyed their coffee and pie at that long ago executive meeting.

III.
The Aliens Have Landed

Amarantha ran stiffly, trying to hold the cumbersome pumpkin straight so the candle inside wouldn't tip. Wendel was behind her, a ragged, stained sheet over his head. Dark smudges indicated that the cloth had been the recipient of great ministrations, and smears of yellow further indicated that it had been a joint effort with the jack-o-lantern carving. Only two unevenly placed eye-holes suggested any semblance of a human face, and these had to be inwardly adjusted often, since they didn't happen to coincide with Wendel's eyes. The rest of his body seemed to float noiselessly, although she could hear the pounding of his running feet as they hit the ground. She knew her brother was under there; she had seen him pull the sheet over his head and adjust the eye holes. Even so, she felt her heart thump in her chest when she looked at him, and she was a little afraid.

It was a cold Halloween night, black and gelid, without a breath of wind. The smoke from the kitchen woodstove rose in a straight vaporous column from the chimney. *Old Lady Lang*, who lived down the road, used to say, *Ain't nothin prettier than wood smoke from a chimney on a cold night!*

Amarantha remembered the old woman bobbing her head and sucking her lips in around naked gums as she'd make this pronouncement, and often pondered the statement. Maybe it was *pretty* because it meant that people inside the house were warm. Maybe it suggested refuge if you were lost, or food cooking if you were hungry, but *pretty*?

Wendel said *Old Lady Lang* was crazier than a bedbug, to which

Ma would always respond, "Judge not lest ye be judged."

It was an exchange that had taken place more than once.

Ma said when she was a little girl "up on the farm," everybody just called *Old Lady Lang* Edith, and that she was the prettiest girl around and had long, black curls and went to all the dances. "Why, Willie and Emil used to ask her out sometimes."

Amarantha and Wendel always snickered to think of their awkward, immigrant uncles dancing with a pretty girl or, for that matter, to think of *Old Lady Lang* as being a pretty girl. As for the old woman, she never elaborated on her original statement but left it open to interpretation, probably rendering it much weightier than it was meant or deserved to be.

But tonight, to a five-year-old girl who possessed a well-developed imagination and the stirrings of hundreds of years of Irish superstition in at least half her genes, that smoke suggested the unsubstantial emission swarming with simultaneous apprehension and anticipation that arose from Ali Babba's magic lamp; and she half expected to see a genie materialize over the rooftop of their faded old farm house.

"Come on," Wendel yelled back impatiently, "They're all in the kitchen." He grabbed a wooden box by the cellar door and turned it over beneath the kitchen window. Amarantha climbed up with his help while he held her jack-o-lantern. Together they propped the grinning face on the sill and straightened Amarantha's witch's hat, which Ma had helped her make from black paper.

The whole family was in the kitchen, due primarily to the warm stove. Ma was clearing the supper remains from the oilcloth covered table, and Elsie and Jenny did dishes in two large dishpans on the cupboard work space. Harold was leaning against the cupboard, grinning, as he poked the girls in the ribs and ducking as they retaliated with wet slaps. John observed the scene, as usual, and waited for the table to be cleared so he could spread his books and papers.

John was very quiet. He was seventeen years older than Amarantha and acted like a father, although she didn't really know what it was like to have a father. Sometimes he yelled at her angrily and told her to go into the house and sit on a chair until he came in; then he'd talk to her and tell her what she'd done wrong and how she shouldn't do it again. Sometimes he was nice and tickled her and let her ride on the boney haunch of *Bossy* when he brought their sway-backed, wrung-out old cow in from the pasture for her nightly milking.

John had graduated from high school but couldn't find a job, and Amarantha heard him tell her older sister that he couldn't go away and leave Ma when she needed him. So, he worked as a hired hand when area farmers needed help, but mostly he gardened and took care of all the heavy chores on their desperate little farm.

Amarantha was very curious about John. She couldn't understand what she perceived to be his idea of fun. She watched him now as he laid out his notebook and books and the strange instruments: a variety of rulers and something he called a compass. Sometimes she'd sit across from him, absorbed, as he drew circles, divided them into pie shapes and printed numbers in them. If she begged, he'd tear a piece of paper from his notebook and let her use the compass to draw lots of perfect circles, which she later made into faces with round eyes and the long curls which she wished she had.

"Now!" Wendel hissed.

They tapped on the window and began to howl and screech, their breath steaming the glass and framing the flickering candle light. They saw Ma jump and the others turn to stare at the window. The family had all seen them off to go down the road to the neighbors, and they were truly surprised when the apparitions appeared at their own window so quickly. Wendel and Amarantha had seen momentary fear in their startled faces, which meant their trick was a success.

Wendel jumped off the box and fell to his knees laughing. "I knew they wouldn't be expecting us!" he cried. "C'mon! We'll come back later and do it again!"

They ran down the long driveway, Wendel occasionally tripping on his sheet and Amarantha stopping to shift the weight of the pumpkin. The long-awaited evening was just beginning, and Amarantha could feel the excitement in her chest as she strained her eyes in the darkness, hoping she wouldn't encounter some of the spirits that were abroad on this one night of the year.

It was 1936, and the days of store-bought costumes, Halloween parties, and mass *trick or treating* had not even been anticipated. If you were a country kid, you were even less apt to cash in on any organized fun. But the Gradys were used to 'fending for themselves,' as Ma would proudly say, and Wendel had been planning this night for weeks. If he felt any resentment at having to drag his little sister along, he didn't show it and seemed to think that half the fun was setting the stage for Amarantha. Secretly, he took some delight in seeing her eyes widen and her cheeks pale behind the freckles as he read her a ghost story or told her about the evening's activities.

"Let's scare *Old Lady Lang* first," he whispered, as the Lang shack materialized out of the darkness. "I'll bet she gets so scared she pees her pants! Here, I'll boost you up, and you see where she is."

Wendel was eleven, six years older than Amarantha, but skinny and small for his age. Ma said he was the only one of her kids who hadn't gotten the proper food when he was a baby. John said he just took after uncle Emil, also small in stature. Now he held Amarantha's legs to his chest and pushed her up until her chin cleared the window sill. Her weight made him unsteady on his feet, causing her view of the dimly lit room to waver.

"Do you see her?" he whispered.

"No, she's not in there."

Amarantha saw the one room of the shack through a streaked window. It was barely lit by a kerosene lamp on the table. There were few furnishings: a bed with only a folded blanket at the foot, the lack of sheets and pillow case making it look naked; the flimsy table with two wobbly chairs; the round woodstove, which glowed orange and provided solace for two cats that lay at its clawed, iron feet. The bare walls were hung with clumps and garlands of drying herbs. Amarantha had been inside many times, and she found it pleasant: the drying vegetation and the dim light made it seem like a cave to her and she felt cozy and strangely safe.

Just then, they heard dry leaves crackle at the corner of the house and turned to see a witch standing in the shadows. She didn't wear a peeked hat, but her nose did almost touch her pointed chin like the witches in the fairy tale book. An old stocking cap was pulled down over her ears and long wisps of gray hair curled down her back. She had on an old mackinaw with only one button and floppy, four-buckle overshoes.

Had they not been under the spell of the night, they would have recognized the attire they had seen many mornings, as their neighbor plodded determinedly around her tumbling outbuildings carrying wood or feeding her two huge cats. Sometimes Ma sent Amarantha down the road with a syrup pail of Bossy's creamy milk.

"Be sure you tell her the milk's for her," Ma instructed. "I don't want her feeding it to those cats!"

Amarantha couldn't understand this attitude. She had seen the old woman in her yard with one or both cats riding on her shoulders all the while rubbing her cheek-to-cheek and purring loudly.

"What good babies," she'd croon, "Don't you love yer Ma, though!"

Amarantha knew her own mother would never deny her family and couldn't understand why she thought *Old Lady Lang* should deprive her babies; so when she delivered the milk, she didn't include the admonition. Ma would never know; and besides, Pastor said a white lie is okay if it spares someone's feelings.

Now, startled and unable to hold her longer, Wendel dropped Amarantha, then grabbed her hand as she scrambled to gain her footing. They ran out of the yard - Wendel half dragging Amarantha when she tripped - and were well up the driveway to their house before they stopped to catch their breath.

Amarantha recovered long enough to start crying, and Wendel, over his initial fright and feeling braver and not a little embarrassed, resumed his confident, in-charge attitude.

"What's the matter with you, cry baby? It was just *Old Lady Lang*. Come on, let's go down to the Martin's!"

"No, I'm not going by where the witch was!" Amarantha cried, then began wailing louder at a sudden realization: "I lost my jack-o-lantern!"

"Let's go back and get it. It's right on the ground where we left it. I'll go in the yard, cry baby. You can wait in the road."

"No, it's too scary! I'm going home!" Amarantha turned and ran toward the dim glow of light from the house, Wendel following and trying to entice her into staying outside the whole way.

"I'll go by myself! You'll miss all the fun!" he called after her, taking a threatening step back down the dark road, but Amarantha continued to run, and he really didn't have the stomach to continue. He too was scared, and it was no fun alone.

She ran up the back steps and burst into the kitchen, ready to relate the tale and bemoan her loss, but no one took much notice of her. They were all pressing around the radio. Ma shushed her with a wave of her hand, and she quietly stood and listened to the ominous voice of an announcer who sounded alternately excited and foreboding. She didn't understand what was happening but sensed that the Halloween fun was over.

"*Unbelievably tall creatures are coming out of what appears to be some sort of space ship. They are very grim looking and their stride encompasses several city blocks.*" The announcer's voice was backgrounded and sometimes almost drowned out by sirens, shouts, and screams. The Gradys listened.

"What's this?" Wendel said, inclining his head toward the radio.

"It's a newscast. A meteor has landed in New York, and some kinds of aliens from outer space are coming out of it."

"Is this real?"

"It just came on the news. There hasn't been anything else on."

"*Ladies and gentlemen, houses are being smashed with one step of these monsters. All attempts to make contact with them have failed, and it appears that they have come to conquer this planet.*" The announcer sounded as if he were crying. "*Find your loved ones and be with your family and friends. This may be your last chance to be together. We have received word that some of the creatures are crossing Lake Michigan as we speak."*

"That means they'll be here soon," said Harold. The room grew even more silent as the family envisioned the horrible aliens wading Lake Michigan, intent on trekking across Wisconsin to their own shabby dwelling.

Amarantha saw that even John was shaken, which frightened her more than anything.

"Do you suppose this is real?" he repeated. Ma moved decisively, reaching for her coat which hung on the wall behind the stove.

"We'd better go to town and see." They all scrambled for their coats.

"I wonder if they can step over houses," Wendel said as they quickly walked in a tight group up the driveway. Ma ignored the question, and thought out loud.

"We'll go to Ida's," she declared. "They've got a good radio and listen all the time. They ought to know."

"Oh Ma!" Jenny wailed, "Albert and Melvin are really going to make fun of us if it's not true! Can't we find out some other way?"

Ida was Ma's cousin. She had married well and lived in a modern house in town. Her two boys delighted in teasing the Gradys about their clothes, their red hair, their freckles, their poverty - anything that differentiated them from their own well-heeled and pampered selves. John and Harold ignored them. Harold said they were both sissy, mama-boys anyway. But Elsie and Jenny took each insult to heart and nursed grudges that would have terrified the bullies, had they known about them. It was clear that the girls would rather risk being eaten alive by the aliens than provide Albert and Melvin fuel for more gibes.

As they neared *Old Lady Lang's* shack, they saw her standing by her mailbox with Amarantha's jack-o-lantern in her hands. It was still flickering through its triangular eyes and turned-up mouth.

"You kids left this behind. I was just going to bring it down. I knew little Amy'd be missin it."

She flashed a toothless, innocent smile, but there was a glint in her eye which made Amarantha wonder if she had just happened to be outside when they came or had hidden there to scare visiting tricksters.

"You heard about the meteor that landed and aliens are stepping across lakes and smashing people and everything?!" Wendel blurted. The glint in her eyes was suddenly replaced by a piercing gaze as she assessed the strain on the faces before her, accepting it as an indication of the gospel truth with no need for corroboration.

"I knew the end was comin', but I never thought I'd see it!" she said. "Good luck to ya! You've been good neighbors!"

She put the jack-o-lantern on the ground, turned, and shuffled slowly up her driveway. In her life she was used to accepting the inevitable and saw no need to struggle or lament. The overshoes, too large for shrunken, old feet, flopped and made a sound of exhaling air. The jack-o-lantern burned brightly.

Everything seemed normal as they approached town. No sirens blew, the streets were reassuringly empty. In spite of the girls' pleadings, Ma turned into Ida's house and knocked on the door. Ida answered and her face fell visibly when she saw the whole Grady family on her doorstep. She didn't ask anyone in.

"We were just wondering if you'd heard any news on the radio about a meteor landing," Ma said.

By this time, Albert and Melvin had come to stand behind their mother as if to reinforce the barricade against the marauding barbarians.

"There's aliens coming out of it and smashing people and houses and everything!" Wendel added. Elsie jabbed him in the ribs to stop the elaboration.

"Did you find some of your Pa's liquor hid in the barn or somethin'?" Albert smirked as he elbowed Melvin. They both laughed at the witticism.

"You boys shut up!" Ida spoke sharply. She was a church woman and never wanted it said that she didn't do for the lowliest of God's creatures. "Why don't you and the little one come in," she said to Ma, leveling a distasteful look at the rest of the family and raising her nose as if she had smelled something rotten.

Ma and Amarantha stepped inside the door, but stayed on the long rug in the hallway. Keeping her eyes on them, Ida called over her shoulder to her husband in another room. "You hear any news about a meteor and space creatures on the radio, Oscar?"

"Na, I been listening to *Fibber McGee and Molly*," he answered.

"Did you try any other stations. If it happened, it would be on all the stations."

"Our radio's not very good. We don't get but the one station."

"Well, we don't know nothing about it, and if it was true, we'd have at least had a telephone call by now." She indicated the phone on the wall, pleased that she had managed to point out yet another of her advantages to the poor relation. Amarantha watched the two boys as they crowded the hall window and pulled the curtains back to point and laugh exaggeratedly at her brothers and sisters still waiting on the sidewalk.

"Sorry we bothered you," Ma said. "We were coming to town anyway, and we thought we'd just stop and see if you'd heard anything. We really didn't think there was anything to it."

Amarantha knew the last remark was made in the vain hope it would ward off the two simpering goons in the window.

Wendel was just outside the door as it opened, eager to get the latest news. "Did she know anything about the aliens, Ma?" he asked.

"The only aliens around here are you guys," Melvin called after them as they hurried away.

"I told you we shouldn't come here," Elsie moaned.

"Did they know anything?" John asked calmly.

"It wasn't on the other stations, so it can't be true. But I sure didn't hear any announcer say anything about it being a program. He said it was a newscast." Ma paused then and looked around. "Where's Harold?"

"He was here just a minute ago."

Harold came running from the back of Ida's house. A slight grin turned the very corners of his mouth.

"Where you been?"

"Just checking Melvin's and Albert's bikes to make sure nobody did anything to them for Halloween," he said innocently.

Ma looked hard at him, and for a minute Amarantha was afraid she was going to make him go back to Ida's and the grinning goons.

"They were just fine," he added quickly. Finally, she turned without saying anything, and Amarantha noticed that all her brothers and sisters had small, quiet smiles. Wendel gave Harold a congratulatory punch on the arm, and they danced around the road as they walked away from town, sparring good naturedly. Amarantha was too exhausted to care about aliens anymore, and John picked her up and carried her home, with her head on his shoulder, fast asleep.

When Amarantha walked down their road next morning, she saw her jack-o-lantern where they had left it the night before. The weather had turned very cold and the pumpkin was sparkling with frost. When she lifted the lid by the stem handle, she saw that the candle had burned away to a puddle of congealed wax, and the whole face had shriveled and withered until the bottom of the triangular nose had fallen into the drooping mouth.

As she stood, the brittle, yellow sun seemed to warm and seep through her winter coat; she could feel the heat on her shoulder blades. In her mind's eye she saw the pumpkin in the field, embryonic, just a slight bulge on the stem, its withered flower adhering to one end. She had watched it grow and begged John to give it special care. He had instructed her to dig an empty tin can with holes punched in the bottom into the soil next to the plant and to fill the can with water every day. He had supervised the project and turned the growing vegetable periodically to ensure its symmetry. She remembered how excited she had been when the first specks of orange had appeared on its green skin. When it was jack-o-lantern size and a beautiful shade of orange, he had let her cut it, being sure to leave enough vine attached to make a good, strong handle on the top.

She could still feel the smooth, firm surface with its deep ridges expanding from the stem to evenly circle the body and converge again at what John referred to as, *the blossom end.*

Then there was the fun of carving the face. She and Wendel had scooped out the pumpkin guts with their hands, delving almost up to their elbows in the stringy, seedy pulp, and although she wasn't allowed to wield the carving knife, she did instruct her brother as to the design of the face, and delighted in the emergence of each feature. However, nothing could compare with the first sight of the jack-o-lantern with the candle lit; it was a sweet kind of agony to wait until dark for the total effect.

It had lasted such a short time! Now, as she looked at the reduced and wrinkled remains on the ground, she grieved for what it had been; but she also was strangely offended by what it had become and quickly kicked it into the ditch, out of her sight.

That night, her sisters and brothers burst into the kitchen from school with news of the radio program from the night before.

"We weren't the only ones to think it was real," Wendel announced. "My teacher said some people got so scared they even committed suicide."

"I wish Albert and Melvin had committed suicide!"

"*Elsie!*" Ma cried.

"Well, I do! They got the whole class laughing at me!"

"Wasn't anyone else in your class scared?"

"If they were, they sure didn't admit it after those *idjets* started in!"

"Art Pearson down at the feed mill said he thought it was news and called the police," offered John.

"Well, if we weren't the only ones, we got nothing to be ashamed of."

"Tell it to the Halverson boys," said Elsie as she and Jenny ran up to their room to nurse their wounds and feed their grudges.

"What's an alien, Ma?"

"It's just someone who's different." Ma was busy putting raised loaves of bread dough into the black woodstove oven.

"But the radio said they were creatures and monsters. Are we aliens, Ma?"

"We're all the same in the eyes of the Lord."

Amarantha noticed that when Ma didn't want to take the time to answer, she quoted the Bible, and that usually ended the discussion.

That Halloween was the first time Amarantha had heard the word, *alien*; it was also the first time she had thought of herself or her family as different. Once, when she was older, she found *alien* in the dictionary at school. Ma's definition of 'different' was there, but the words *strange, repugnant,* and *outsider* were also used. She was never to hear the word afterward without thinking back to the Orson Welles radio show, *War of the Worlds* or hearing the taunt, "The only aliens around here are you!"

"Ma, are the aliens from the spaceship the same as us in the eyes of the Lord?"

IV.
The One I Love Best

"Skinny! Fly-speck face!"

He circled her like a leering predator, moving in just long enough to poke her ribs, then darting away before she could make contact with her flaying fists. She was too angry to see but lashed out blindly nevertheless, hoping to connect a hard fist to some part of his anatomy.

"Oh, ya!" she shot back. "Well, you're skinny and a fly-speck face *too!*"

She lashed out again to punctuate her words, but he only laughed and continued to outmaneuver her. He was skinny and freckled - more than she - but he didn't react because they were *his* insults, and they couldn't be used by anyone else; it was an unwritten law of childhood.

Desperately, she tried to think of some nasty names of her own, but fury had rendered her incapable of any response but unintelligible blubbering, which spilled from her mouth involuntarily and became confused with the tears that dripped from her nose and chin.

"Amy's an idjet! Amy's an idjet!" he taunted, crouching a couple of feet away and watching her cry.

Then suddenly, Harold was there. She hadn't seen him come around the side of the house, but there he was, behind Wendel, pinning the smaller boy's bony, freckled arms to his sides.

"Leave her alone! What did she do to you?"

He bent one of Wendel's arms behind his back, and the boy's face contorted as he yelled, "Cut it out! We were only playing!"

"Leave her alone!" Harold repeated, releasing their struggling brother. Wendel shot a lethal look in her direction and rubbed his misused arm.

Harold put his hand on her shoulder. "You okay? What started it?"

She ducked away from his touch and ran to peer through the hole in the board foundation of the sagging, old granary. The tears and trauma had left her drawing long, shuddering sighs.

"It's Tilda! He chased her up a tree and she fell on the ground! Here, kitty, kitty..." As she searched the darkness for Tilda's glowing green eyes, she could hear Wendel's defense in the background.

"I just wanted to scare the mangy old thing. I didn't know she'd fall. Besides, she's okay; she ran under there fast enough!"

Amarantha could tell from the sound of his voice, words formed by stretched lips, that he was grinning again; and she whirled and lunged in one motion, catching Wendel full in the stomach with her lowered head. He fell back, surprised, and labored for breath.

In the instant that Harold and Amarantha stood quietly watching Wendel, Ma intervened, her mouth thin with anger and exhaustion. "Can't you kids ever stop fighting?"

"He's teasing her again!"

"He hurt Tilda!"

"She knocked me down! I didn't hurt her!" This was delivered through hiccoughing sobs, as it was now Wendel's turn to cry.

Ma pulled him roughly to his feet and propelled him toward the barn with a hard spank to the backside. "Go get the wagon. You can go with me to get *the relief.*"

Ma worked cleaning houses and some business offices; but those jobs didn't provide enough money to feed her family, and she had to accept government aid with all its accompanying stigma. Because she earned a wage, she wasn't eligible for a cash payment, but that wage was small enough to qualify her to receive surplus commodities, referred to by recipients as *the relief.*

The relief was always one item only and was different each week. Whatever Ma got dominated the menu planning for the household. Sometimes it was corn meal. Then they had mush for breakfast, mixed with a little syrup. Ma always cooked extra mush so she could fry it for lunch. Uncle Emil brought lard from the farm, and she melted it in the big, black cast-iron pan and fried clumps of mush until they were crisp and brown. Supper consisted of corn bread, which she called Johnny Cake, baked thin and hot from the woodstove oven. Corn meal was Amarantha's favorite *relief*. Rice was her least favorite. It was often gluey and wasn't as versatile as corn meal.

Once, Ma came with a whole lug of peaches. Amarantha had never eaten a peach and was wildly excited over the exotic abundance. However, they had been improperly packed for shipping from California to Wisconsin, stored too long and were dark with bruises, showing mold in some areas. Ma tried to save as many as she could by cooking them, but she had to cut away large brown spots and worked a long time for a small kettle of sauce. By the end, the table was piled with rotten peach refuse.

"What a waste!" Ma sighed. "We could have made good use of those."

This statement was repeated often as the depression of the 1930s forced the frantic government to hastily appoint an inept bureaucracy that often allowed warehouses of food to spoil while people went hungry.

Ma finally gave up and set the wooden box containing the remainder of the fruit on the back porch. Wendel and Amarantha sorted through the spongy peaches and salvaged a whole pail full which they took to their secret tree house in the woods. It was a pleasant afternoon, lying amidst the leaves with the breeze altering sun patterns across their faces as they gorged themselves on the fermented fruit. It was not as pleasant later that evening when their stomachs cramped, and they spent most of the night in the outhouse.

Once *the relief* had been eggs, but when they were cracked, they were rotten. Some of the men were so angry and frustrated that they saved them until the next relief day and pelted the local distributor with them. Amarantha hadn't been along to see this drama, but Wendel entertained the family around the kitchen table with descriptions of egg running down various parts of Mr. Petersen's face and body, and supplemented his tale with appropriate sound effects. *'Pow! Smash!'* Amarantha watched spellbound as Wendel played both perpetrator and victim, drawing his thin arm back to throw, and then slapping himself to simulate the eggs hitting their mark and holding both arms up to shield his face. It was a fine story, and everyone laughed, except Ma who looked grim and busied herself starting a fire in the woodstove.

Economic depression didn't mean much to eight-year-old girls who were usually fed; and the isolation of their rural existence didn't allow many unfavorable comparisons with other little girls. Most of the families they knew were, "In the same fix," as Ma said. Amarantha loved to go with Ma to get *the relief.* She almost never went to town, and to her there was a festive, social atmosphere among the crowd as they waited in line for the warehouse to open.

"What do you think it'll be today?"

"I hope it's not corn meal. We're starting to grow tassels!"

"I don't care what it is; I just hope it ain't rotten!"

These were worried people. The desperate look in their eyes betrayed their jokes and laughter. To the children, however, it was like a party; they played tag, threading in and out of the long line of adults, biding time. The older children weren't as thrilled with the duty, but they were compelled to come along to help carry; many of them pulled wagons in various states of deterioration. A plaything which once had meant fun was suddenly the object of their shame and degradation, and they sullenly piled the commodities on, hoping the vehicle would hold together long enough to get away from the eyes of the curious who passed by, or those who had deliberately come to see who was getting *the relief* this week.

Harold lay on his stomach with one arm under the granary. His tongue moved in concentration as his arm swept the darkness under the crumbling building. "There's no cat under here," he announced. "She must have gone out the other side." Amarantha watched, her face swollen and worried.

Wendel appeared at the door of the barn pulling a wooden wagon. It had once been red; small, faded patches of paint still clung to the boards in spots. The wheels seemed to be set on independent trajectories, causing the whole vehicle to wobble and twist as each wheel strained to take the lead. It squeaked and moaned and left a wake of serpentine lines in the dust as if a colony of snakes had crawled through the barnyard.

With the typical attention span of the young, Amarantha immediately forgot the much maligned Tilda when she realized that Ma and Wendel were going to town. "Can I go too?" She tinged her question with the beginning of a whine that promised to get worse. "Pleeese!" she added, as a special enticement, and warning.

"I don't have time to deal with you now; you stay with Harold."

I won't beg for stuff and I'll walk fast."

"You're not going!" The last statement was delivered with a hard shake of her shoulder and a stern look. Amarantha knew that when Ma got that look, it was no use arguing, so she backed away and sullenly watched the preparations. Wendel had the hiccoughs and his thin chest convulsed periodically as he sat on the back porch steps holding the wagon handle. His eyes were red-rimmed from crying and hot with hatred when he looked at his little sister.

"You have to go for relief," she started tauntingly, but then, she abruptly stopped when she saw his eyes change in an instant. Wendel and she played together every day. In spite of the age difference, they were like best friends. They sometimes fought, but usually Wendel was old enough to know that he could coax her into compliance, although sometimes, like today, the little boy in him would surface, and he'd succumb to some good, old *tease your sister until she cries* fun. He thought he could manipulate her, but his insight was as nothing compared to hers. She recognized his every mood, and knew what made him happy or sad. She wasn't aware of loving him so much or wanting to please him: it was that she depended on him to alleviate her loneliness.

Amarantha remembered hot afternoons when John made them work in the garden. He'd show her and Wendel which rows to weed and how to tell the difference between weeds and the tiny corn seedlings. She was to pull and pile the interlopers neatly at intervals. Wendel was to come behind with his hoe and gently loosen the soil along the rows, so the corn could more easily absorb the rain. Amarantha tried to imagine what it would be like in August, when the corn was high and the bulging ears would open their coats and reveal pale yellow faces with greenish-brown corn silk hair. She thought they looked like little men - maybe even like the green leprechaun pictured in her fairy tale book.

She sat in the dirt, changing positions when her folded legs would become cramped and tingly. Small bugs crawled over her arms and legs, skittering first one way then another, trying to escape the giant who had dislodged them from their habitat. She could feel sweat running down her back where the sun was beating. Usually, when she felt as if she could cry, knowing that John wouldn't like it and say she was a poor worker, Wendel would provide a distraction which made her laugh and forget her discomfort.

His favorite skit was to brace himself between the rows and, using his hoe as a machine gun, *mow down* Al Capone and any other ancillary gangsters whose names he could recall. "I'm a G-Man," he'd shout, "Come out with your dirty, yellow hands above your heads. Okay, then! Take that!" Whereupon he'd crouch menacingly and spray the vicinity with bullets. "Ya-ta-ta-ta-tat!" he'd sputter.

Once, he'd used the hoe as a dancing partner and twirled and dipped it in exaggerated movements, all the while singing and keeping time to *Let Me Call Your Sweetheart* and fawningly calling it, "The Duchess of Windsor."

Amarantha's favorite was when he put the hoe between his legs and galloped up and down the rows singing, *I'm an Old Cowhand*, just like Gene Autrey did on the radio.

Then she couldn't help but join in, galloping, whinnying, and slapping her hip as if she were spurring on her imaginary pony.

These antics usually brought John out of the barn or the adjacent field, and it only took one of his stern looks to bring them back to reality and the weeding.

When Wendel wasn't around, the days seemed never ending; and when they fought, as they had today, she worried that he might hold a grudge and refuse to ever play with her again. Now as she looked carefully into his eyes, she felt sorry for him and deeply ashamed of her part in the whole battle. But as he started down the long driveway pulling the rickety wagon, he turned and his eyes said, *'I'm sorry you can't go, Amy!'* And hers said, *'I'm sorry you have to go!'* And they both knew that they had received their just punishment. She watched until they turned the corner and were out of sight.

Harold said, "C'mon Amy, let's go down by the river and catch some minnows."

"I guess I love Harold best," she thought, as she followed him down the rock steps that led to the river. He had a small seine and headed for a deep pool formed where a downed tree protected a patch of shoreline from the current.

Harold was fifteen: too old to play her games, but, also, too old to fight with her. He always took her side, even with the older sisters who, saddled with her care most of the time, tended to be cross and impatient with little Amy. When he hunted, he saved the brightly colored feathers from the ducks for her. If he had any money, which wasn't often, he brought her a treat. She couldn't remember a time when he hadn't been good to her.

Ma worried about her children a lot, but it seemed to Amarantha that she worried mostly about Harold. He didn't like school, even though Ma said he was the smartest of all her kids, and skipped frequently. Once, the principal had come to the house to find him, and Amarantha heard Ma tell him she didn't know what to do with him. Several times she awakened at night to the sound of voices in the kitchen and heard Ma and Harold talking.

"This is a fine time of night to be coming home!"

"Next time I just won't come home at all!"

"You have school tomorrow!"

"I'm not going!"

"You've been drinking, haven't you? You're just like your Pa!"

"I'm a lot of things, but I'm not like him. Don't you say that!"

The exchanges always took the same form: accusations and short, sarcastic answers.

They always ended with his vehement denial of their Pa. Amarantha didn't remember their father and one day asked Wendel why no one had liked him.

"Cause he always had a *snoot* full," he answered.

Now, she knew what a snoot was, but she wasn't sure what filled it. She remembered the phrase, however, and once afterwards, when she had a cold, she told her mother she, *'had a snoot full.'*

"Nice girls don't say things like that!" she had replied. Ma was very concerned with her being a *nice girl*.

The afternoon wore on, as they dipped the seine into the black water and pulled it up dripping and filled with wildly flipping minnows, their iridescent bodies the size and shape of an eyebrow. Harold saved them in the minnow pail for fishing later. "Fishing is best after dark," he confided to Amy. "Sometime I'll take you along, if you can stay awake that late."

Amarantha leaned against the river bank, her eyes half closed from the sun and excitement of the afternoon. "I can stay awake," she murmured.

Harold laughed. "Ya? You're practically asleep now. We'd better go back to the house."

"I don't have to take a nap," she protested.

"Just rest a while. I'll play the guitar for you."

She loved to listen to him play the guitar. Self-taught, he could play some of the tunes they heard on *The National Barn Dance* show from Chicago. It was her favorite radio program.

Harold sat in the rocker picking on the guitar. He was really good at *Wabash Cannonball,* and Amy loudly sang the chorus with him, *Listen to the jingle, the jangle and the roar...*

"I wish I could play."

"You can. Come sit in my lap, and I'll help you." She wriggled between him and the guitar, and he held her fingers down on the proper strings as she strummed with her other hand. It was halting, but she recognized the tune and was amazed and pleased that she was playing. She moved her body with each chord change; she was completely absorbed in her music until she suddenly became aware that Harold had one hand on her hip and was rhythmically moving her body in a circular motion across his lap.

At first, she thought he was keeping time to the music, but it soon became apparent that he was lost in the motion. His eyes were closed and he had forgotten to hold her fingers on the right strings.

"Aren't we going to play any more?"

"Later! I think we need a nap after all."

"No! I'm not tired. Let's play."

He carried her into the bedroom she shared with Ma and lay down beside her on the bed. "Just be quiet. I'll rub your back, and you'll get sleepy."

He pulled her dress up and began to massage her bare back. It felt good, and she really was very tired. *Listen to the jingle, the jangle and the roar*, softly he sang, and eventually her eyes closed and she sank into sleep.

She awoke slightly when he carefully pulled her panties down, but she wasn't conscious enough to know if it was really happening or was just a dream. She did waken when she realized that Harold was lying close behind her, rubbing his private part between her legs. She opened her eyes and turned her head slightly to look at him. His eyes were closed again and she had never seen his face look so pained. He frowned a crease in his forehead and pinched his eyes tightly, breathing as if he were running.

Amarantha lay quiet and confused. She knew what he was doing was wrong. Ma had cautioned her about exposing private parts, and was careful that she didn't run naked, even on bath night. Amarantha remembered a time when she was quite small and her Pa was still alive. She had run into the bedroom and seen him on top of her Ma; she thought he was hurting her, and she beat on his leg with her fists and cried. She didn't remember much about her Pa, but she did remember how mad he was and the only spanking she ever got.

Now she was frightened again. Harold thought she was asleep, and he might get mad if she let on she was awake. She closed her eyes and thought about what to do. Maybe she should scream and cry. Maybe she should get up and say she didn't want to take a nap. Both these courses of action would result in a confrontation she couldn't handle.

Her back was facing him and she realized he couldn't see her face, so she opened her eyes slowly. Maybe he would stop soon. If he didn't, she would pretend she was asleep and wait it out. When she had an earache, Ma would tell her to think of nice things and she wouldn't feel the pain. It had worked a little; maybe this was a good time to practice again.

Her eyes lit on a Christmas card box on the bedside table. The cards had been used for some long-ago Christmas, and now it was Ma's letter writing box. A team of six white horses wearing silvery harnesses pranced along a snowy road, exhaling great clouds of sparkling vapor. They pulled a fancy coach, something like the stagecoach in the cowboy movies, but much grander, and people sat inside holding presents with huge, red bows and waving to Amarantha. The coach was trimmed with wreathes of holly and everyone was smiling or laughing with their heads thrown back.

Suddenly she was in that coach. She felt the rocking motion as the horses sped across the frozen ruts in the dirt road, their labored breathing close to her ear. She felt the cold from the open windows on her cheeks and imagined herself snuggling down into one of the long, gaily-colored scarves they were all wearing. She even felt the tingle of anticipation as she clutched her present tightly and wondered what was inside. She had succeeded in completely losing herself in the picture. Back and forth the coach rocked. Faster and faster the horses ran, and louder and harder became their breathing.

Then, just when she felt she couldn't sustain the *nice* thought any longer and that reality would return with that awful pit-of-the-stomach feeling that came when something was very wrong, the horses slowed, and the coach stopped its rocking, and she no longer heard the horses' breathing. She felt her panties being replaced. Quickly she closed her eyes and feigned a deep sleep. She heard him leave the room, but she lay as still as she could. She couldn't face him.

How long she lay there, she couldn't remember. She didn't dare move for fear he would come back, and she stared at the worn spot in the green window shade which let in thin pinpoints of daylight until she could tell the sun was moving further down in the sky. It must be almost supper time. Finally, she heard Ma and Harold talking in the kitchen, and she expelled her breath in a burst of relief.

"*She's been sleeping for quite a long time. Dreaming too. Making funny noises.*"

"*She usually doesn't sleep during the day any more. I hope she isn't getting sick.*"

"*She was okay before she went to sleep. I'm going downtown.*"

Aren't you going to have supper?"

"*Naw! I'm not hungry.*"

"*Don't you come home here late, now. And no drinking. I wish I knew who was buying that stuff for you, I'd have the law on him.*"

"*Ya, ya, ya! See you later.*" The kitchen door slammed. A moment later, Ma came into the bedroom.

"You okay, honey?" Ma cupped her cheek in the palm of her hand and felt her forehead with the other. Her hands were rough from being in so much water and harsh cleaning powders, but her touch made Amarantha feel comforted and safe.

I'll tell Ma, she thought, *She'll know what to do, and I won't have to think about it any more.* Then she remembered her sisters lecturing her.

'*You've got to be a good girl and not bother being a cry baby or tattle tale to Ma. She's got enough to worry about.*'

She also remembered the minister talking about sin and how everyone should hate it and cast it out. She didn't really know what a sin was, but the Reverend talked about gluttony and coveting. Surely what Harold had done was worse than those words, but she had done it too, and hadn't screamed or run, which meant she had sinned. Hadn't Ma said that only bad girls showed their privates to boys? Maybe Ma would hate her and cast her out. No, it was best to keep quiet and pretend it never happened.

"Come out to the kitchen now. I'm going to make supper. We got cheese today, and I'm going to make hot sandwiches. You like them, don't you?"

The girls had come in from their jobs. They both worked on the Youth Conservation Corp, a government program which paid young people to do certain jobs for local businesses. The pay was minimal, but they bought their own clothes and sometimes gave Ma some of their checks.

Elsie was in high school and worked the summer helping to clean classrooms. Jenny had quit school after eighth grade and worked for the local dime store stocking shelves. The kitchen was alive with their voices, everyone seeming to talk at once. Usually this was Amarantha's favorite time of day, when life returned to the house; but today she was too consumed with shame and guilt to participate in the family interplay.

"What's a matter with you, squirt?"

Ma was standing by the big, wooden table carefully fitting bright orange squares of *relief* cheese between slices of her home-made bread. "Harold said she's been sleeping most of the after-noon."

"How come you don't do that when I'm taking care of you?" Elsie persisted. "When it's me, you have to stay up and whine at me all afternoon."

Amarantha didn't know what to answer, and tried to squeeze back the tears she felt welling up.

"Don't be so mean!" Jenny looked hard at Elsie and came over to put her arm around Amarantha.

"Come on outside, Amy. I've got something to show you." Wendel had saved her from a disgraceful bawling scene, and Amy could have kissed him for it, as she gratefully escaped out the back door. He was smiling widely, showing large, flat front teeth that Ma called, *butter spreaders*. He was very pleased with himself as he opened his hand to reveal the surprise: A piece of cellophane wrapped candy. It was the kind with swirls of tan and white soft caramel called a *Snirkle* and was a particular favorite of Amarantha's.

"Ma gave me a penny. I'll give you the biggest half," he offered magnanimously, and without waiting for a response or thanks, he deftly folded the flat candy in two and proceeded to bite across the indentation, the severed caramel hanging in strings from the remaining side.

They sat on the back stoop and chewed the candy. Amarantha thought she might tell Wendel what had happened that afternoon and then thought better of it. He really was a good guy, especially in light of the treat that she now worried around her mouth, occasionally dislodging the sticky mass from her teeth or the roof of her mouth with her tongue; but he did like to talk, and she was sure he would tell Ma.

Maybe the girls, she considered.

She could go upstairs to their room. She wasn't supposed to ever go in there when they weren't there, but they did let her visit when they were home, and she sat on their bed and listened to them talk, and, sometimes they curled her straw colored hair with their curling iron and declared that she looked just like Shirley Temple with freckles.

But then she imagined how shocked they would be. How their eyes would grow big, and she could almost hear Elsie, "What did you do that for, you stupid little twerp!" And the end result would be the same: they could surely be counted on to tell Ma.

Supper was called, and Amarantha ate and talked very little. The long, summer evening, which was usually reserved for a continuance of the day's play or, in twilight, a spooky game of *Starlight-Moonlight,* was an agony to get through. But at last it was bedtime, and Amarantha was relieved to be alone in her bed without prodding questions and worried looks.

Yet she found herself reliving the afternoon again and again. She averted her eyes from Ma's writing box, hoping that the act would eradicate the memory, then closed them tightly. "I dreamed it!" she repeated to herself over and over again. Now she wasn't really a bad girl, just guilty of bad thoughts. It wasn't nearly the same. Pastor said in your own mind you could overcome bad thoughts, whereas, bad deeds were known to all and might be forgiven but never forgotten. She was so intent on the exorcism of the deed that she didn't hear Ma come into the room until she felt a light pressure on the bed.

"Look who I found," Ma said, laying Tilda beside her on the blanket. The green eyes glowed comfortingly in the dark, and Tilda snuggled close and began to knead Amarantha's shoulder in the way cats do when they are content. Amarantha buried her face in the long black fur and smelled the kitty smell of fresh air and fragrant weeds, and, when Ma had left, she whispered everything that had happened, every detail, into the small, leather-like ear. And although Tilda flicked her ears several times, she didn't move away and she continued to narrow her glowing eyes in contentment and purred loudly. It was plain to see that Tilda didn't consider Amarantha a bad girl. Gradually, with the feel of soft fur on her cheek and the soothing hum of a loving spirit in her ears, Amarantha drifted into the restful sleep that only confession can provide.

The sun shone brightly through the raised shade when Amarantha awoke the next morning. She hardly had time to remember yesterday's puzzling worry because Wendel was jumping on the foot of her bed.

"Get up! You gonna sleep all day?" He was outlining his plan for the day. "We'll follow the river down to the cheese factory and see what they've dumped. Then we'll find the bird's nest and see how big the babies have gotten. Hurry up!"

Quite often they walked along the river, exploring the banks for skipping stones or wading in the water to pick snails or clams. One of their favorite spots was the local cheese factory, strategically located where the current was swiftest, so that any factory refuse the owners cared to dump would be carried away. Wendel had devised a game which involved long poles made out of nearby saplings. They each defended a portion of shoreline and pushed away any floating debris that threatened to lodge itself on their territory. It was a completely absorbing game and demanded a certain amount of dexterity.

Whole large wheels of cheese, rotted beyond even a radical paring of the bad parts, bobbed in the water looking like huge scabby sores floating on the oily skin of the river. Amarantha was repelled by the sight and was doubly intent on keeping them away from shore. Sometimes the factory workers would watch them through the windows and laugh at their efforts. *Free labor! The boss ought to put them on the payroll!*

"There's one coming your way!" Wendel shouted as Amarantha, red-cheeked and sweating, wielded the long pole into the water and pushed with all her strength to direct the cheese back into the current. Maybe this wasn't such a good time to play the game when this week's *relief* was cheese, but it was fun and kept them busy for at least an hour.

On their way back home, they walked away from the river into the trees to find their bird's nest. A couple weeks ago they had spotted the nest before the leaves had gotten so thick. It was wedged in the fork of a sapling, and Wendel had easily climbed the weak trunk and peered into the nest; then he boosted Amarantha high enough to lean against a branch and look in also. The mother was gone, but four tiny, blue eggs lay touching as if for comfort and companionship.

"Don't touch them or the Ma will poke them out of the nest if she smells you on them."

Amarantha drew back to avoid contamination but stared with fascination at the smooth surface and the color as blue as the bachelor buttons on the side of their porch.

"If they're blue, they're robins," said Wendel knowledgeably. And sure enough, as they stood on the ground and watched, a robin flew to the nest and settled herself over the eggs.

From then on, every other day or so, Wendel and Amarantha stopped by the nest to watch the progress of the robins. First they would wait until the mother flew off for food; then they would hoist themselves into the tree. The first sign of change was when the eggs appeared veined with tiny cracks. The next day the ugliest little creatures Amarantha had ever seen squeeled in the nest; their heads, all eyes and beak, strained and wove unsteadily above transparent bodies. You could see their tiny hearts beating beneath yellow skin. How could they have come out of those beautiful eggs? But as the days passed, they grew feathers and were cute as they jostled for position in the shrinking nest.

Amarantha loved them and thought of them as her own; she was eager to see them as she and Wendel neared the tree. But they could immediately tell that something was wrong. There were small, fluffy feathers everywhere on the ground, and the nest was empty.

"Maybe they flew away."

"They couldn't fly yet. They were too little," Amarantha said, her voice shaking with despair. Then a movement in the brush caught their attention, and they stared in horror as Tilda emerged proudly carrying the sole remaining member of the robin family between her teeth, the protruding feathers looking like a mustache. Her black fur was ruffled, and twigs and dry leaves clung to her coat, but her green eyes shone brightly. Although her mouth was obstructed, she gave a muffled meow of recognition, or pleasure, or pride.

Amarantha leaped and wildly threw sticks and rocks and anything at hand as the startled and uncomprehending Tilda scampered for the safety of the brush and disappeared.

Amarantha was inconsolable as they entered their yard, and Elsie, in charge for the morning, rolled her eyes in exasperation as the tale was related.

"I hate that damn cat!"

"Don't you swear, you twerp! Where'd you hear that anyway?"

"I don't care. She's a murderer! That's a worse sin than gluttomy or coverness or swearing."

"She's only a cat. That's what they do. What do you think she's been hunting all this time?"

Amarantha had no stomach for play any more that day and climbed into the tree house where she stayed all afternoon. When she heard Ma home from work, she descended and went quietly to lean against her hip in complete sorrow and a silence close to shock.

"You sure have had a bad couple days, haven't you honey?" Ma said as she patted her back. It was another subject Amarantha couldn't discuss, but at least she didn't feel guilty about this. At least she hadn't participated in this sin.

Later, as she and Ma sat on the back step to get a breathe of cool air, Tilda emerged from under the granary and sat in the waning light of the yard meticulously cleaning her paws and face as contented cats do.

"She's forgotten all about it!" Amarantha turned her body and kept her hands hidden in her lap as Tilda walked towards her purring and rubbing her soft fur against Amarantha's leg. "Maybe you've forgotten, but I *haven't!*"

"She loves you," Ma said, "Look how she tries to get your attention. *You're* her person. You know, Amy, only those you care for can disappoint and even betray you, and then you have to forgive them."

Amarantha lay in bed that night with thoughts of Harold and Tilda and forgiveness and sin swirled like a Snirkle in her brain. She was tired of trying to puzzle it out, and when Tilda jumped onto the bed and curled herself against her to purr and knead, Amarantha nestled her face in the soft fur and fell asleep with the cat in her arms. When Ma came to bed, she smiled at the two sleepers, never guessing the burden of guilt that would burn for life like a tiny ember deep in her little girl's heart.

Amarantha didn't see much of Harold after that. He hardly ever came home, preferring to, *'Hang out with that bad crowd,'* that Ma talked about. Wendel and she had gone with Ma one afternoon to a gas station where Harold had been seen. Several young men and teenage boys lounged around the office area smoking cigarettes they rolled themselves with thin, little papers and drawstring, cloth bags of tobacco. Amarantha watched a boy, not much older than Wendel, as he deftly rolled a neat cylinder and placed it between his lips with exaggerated authority.

"Haven't seen him, Mrs. Grady," responded the owner to Ma's question. But as they walked away, Amarantha turned and saw the boys smiling at each other.

"They know where he is, Ma," Wendel whispered.

"I know!" And Ma's back straightened and her mouth became a line, but she didn't turn to look back.

Pastor said that people were just like onions, and if they're bad on the outside, you can peel away the layers and find the good flesh underneath. Amarantha thought about that; and one day when John had the heavy cellar door propped open to bring up the canning jars, she ventured cautiously down the cold stone steps. She hated the cellar! It was dark, and spider webs brushed her face and arms when she walked. Ma often sent Wendel for potatoes or onions stored in bushel baskets on the shelves, and sometimes he talked her into going along. Even when she was an old woman, she still remembered the moldy smell and the sound of the skittering mice as they approached those baskets. If it was autumn, they'd find fresh, firm vegetables; but toward spring, you might put your hand into a mushy, rotten potato or carrot.

John was up and down the stairs; so she wasn't afraid, and she felt in the onion basket until she touched a spongy one. She got the garden knife from its niche on the back porch and began to peel the brown away. She had removed three layers when, suddenly, the onion fell apart in her hands. She wondered if the same thing sometimes happened to people. When you cut away the bad layers, maybe the goodness just fell apart. The strong fumes made her eyes smart and water, and she ran to the edge of the woods and threw the severed onion as far away as she could.

One day the town's only policeman, Mr. Potter (everyone called him *Potts*) drove into their yard in his old Dodge, which spluttered and backfired to a stop by the porch door. Harold was in the back seat.

"Morning, Mrs. Grady. I'm afraid I'm not here on a very happy deed."

"What's the matter? Is he hurt? You know I can't do nothing with him!"

"No, he ain't hurt, but he got himself into some pretty serious trouble. Him and them Ainsley boys broke into the drugstore and took some money."

Ma sat down hard on the porch step. "How much was it? I'll pay you when I can, you know that."

"I know, but it ain't that simple. Mr. Ogren's pressing charges, and this ain't the first time for the Ainsleys."

"But Harold's never been in trouble before!"

"I know, ma'am, but he's in bad company."

Ma stared at the ground and you could tell she was trying to come up with some solution to the current crisis.

"I can give him a choice, though, that we didn't used to have. Rather than take his chances on going to jail and you having the expense of maybe hiring a lawyer, the Government says we can offer first time offenders the option of going into the army."

"Jail or the army?"

Potts nodded. "You'd have to sign for him, a course."

He opened the car door to dislodge a chastened looking Harold. Ma took his arm, but he shrugged her off and wouldn't look her in the eye. Nevertheless, they walked off, down towards the river together, muttering quietly in conversation to each other. Amarantha started to follow, but Elsie caught her skirt and held her back.

When they returned, there was an air of decision about them. "Harold thinks the army would be better than jail."

Potts smiled. "Well, ma'am, some do say it makes a man out of a boy."

At that time, Ma couldn't have known what Harold would have to endure to become a man. It was 1941, and on December 7th the Japanese would bomb Pearl Harbor, and Harold would not be home again for several years.

Potts got out a sheaf of papers and Ma signed them on the hood of the Dodge. She embraced Harold, telling him to write as soon as he got someplace. He nodded and stopped to scan the old farm, lingering on each building as if seeing it for the first time. Amarantha didn't remember that his eyes had been so blue: she was suddenly reminded of the robin's eggs in the little nest.

Then he was hugging her tightly. "Be a good girl, Amy," he said out loud. Then, "I'm sorry." He whispered so softly in her ear that it was little more than a sigh.

They were gone up the long driveway in a cloud of dust.

"Why did Harold hug me?" Amarantha asked.

Ma took her hand, and Amarantha could see that her eyes were swimming with tears.

"I guess it's because he loves you best."

V.
Becoming a City Girl

After Harold's departure, the family grew smaller as, one by one, the Gradys struck out to improve their lot or merely lurched into different lives. It wasn't as if Harold had started an exodus, it was more that the children were of an age to go out on their own, all, that is, except Amarantha and Wendel.

Being unemployed and eligible, John went into the Civilian Conservation Corps (CCC) and lived in Northern Wisconsin, where he helped build a beautiful park by Lake Superior. He visited home sometimes and told them about this lake that was just like the sea: so big you couldn't see the opposite shore, and so big you couldn't navigate it in a small boat without fear of being caught by one of its sudden and fierce storms. His eyes were alive and darted animatedly when he talked about working on the park, and he proudly revealed that he had been allowed to help the engineer draw up the plans and design various areas. Amarantha could see him with his rulers and compass laboring over pathways and sketching flower gardens. He was tanned and fit: muscles rippled under his rolled-up shirtsleeves.

Besides his books and garden, John loved listening to *old-time* music and baseball games on the radio. When he was home, he still sat in the old rocker and matched its squeaky cadence to the rhythms of Whoopee John and the *Too Fat Polka*, or give rapt attention to a *play-by-play* without ever showing any emotional outbursts, even when the announcer was shouting and excited about a *stolen base* or, *high fly ball* to *left field*. Amarantha had never seen John dance or play baseball; but now, influenced by her sisters' forays into the world of male-female relationships and thinking him almost as handsome as The Duke of Windsor, she imagined him playing ball with the rest of the men in his CCC camp and hitting homeruns that arced high over the great sea/lake and were caught only by the crashing waves, or holding and twirling a mysterious girlfriend to *The Blue Skirt Waltz*, her satin hem almost touching the lapping waves as they danced on the shore of the shining waters.

Her reverie had been shattered by Elsie who, irritated at John's *hogging* the radio, had complained to Ma, "He's one strange *idjet.*"

"Why is John strange?"

"Because our Pa *beat him!*" Elsie drew her face close to Amarantha's and widened her eyes.

"Don't be scaring her, now!" Ma scolded.

"Well, it's the truth," Elsie spat over her shoulder.

Elsie had just graduated from high school and had met her own version of the Duke of Windsor: a handsome, but jobless, boy of nineteen. Amarantha liked him. They all did, but Ma said they, *'needed to get their feet on the ground before they got married.'*

"So, how come you didn't wait a hundred years until you had enough money to get married?" Elsie's voice was hard and taunting, like the neighbor boys when they teased her and sang, *She has freckles on her butt..she is nice..*

"Well, look where it got me too!" was how Ma replied; she didn't seem angry as much as worried, but Elsie, of course, didn't listen, and married and moved away, following her young husband to several neighboring towns seeking, landing, and losing one elusive job after another.

Amarantha loved to have them visit. When they came, they brought life back to the house. Sometimes they'd stay a couple weeks if Jase had used up another in a series of temporary jobs. Evenings were fun again, playing cards around the kitchen table, and sometimes Elsie would make fudge, setting it on the back porch to cool. If it didn't harden; they'd eat it with a spoon, taking turns dipping out rounded globs of syrupy chocolate. Amarantha almost liked it better that way. But sooner or later, they'd hear, *'They're hirin' in Stillwater,'* and off they'd go in the old Ford, the back seat jammed with their belongings, ever hopeful that this would prove to be steady work that would allow them to set up a permanent home and truly begin their married life.

Jenny, who always wanted *nice things* and hated the small town, *their* life and its economic instability, chose to leave school and go to Minneapolis to work as a domestic for rich people. She too came home to visit, less and less as time went by, and seemed to be flourishing in the city. Her bright, red hair was cut fashionably short, and she wore pretty print dresses and white sandals in the summer; once she had worn a slack suit with wide, long trousers and a matching jacket.

"It's the latest thing in *The Cities*," she said defensively when she detected Ma's disapproving look. Amarantha thought she was beautiful and vowed that she too would go to *The Cities* and have pretty clothes and cover her freckles with pancake makeup.

Ma said Jenny was, *'Putting all her money on her back, and should be saving something for a rainy day.'*

Jenny said Ma didn't remember what it was like to be young, if she ever was, and to keep her opinions to herself.

After these inevitable exchanges, Jenny would take the bus back to Minneapolis or, *'go off in a huff,'* as Ma described it, and they wouldn't hear from her for awhile.

Still Amarantha looked forward to the visits from her big-city sister. One Sunday she was playing in the yard when a little cream-yellow car whipped down the driveway, horn blaring. One of Jenny's boyfriends had driven her out to the country on a Sunday jaunt. He was very exuberant and friendly, but it was plain from the beginning that this hadn't been Jenny's idea; and she was visibly ashamed of the remaining Gradys and their lifestyle.

"Don't you ever clean the kid up?" she hissed quietly at Ma as the boyfriend busied himself showing Wendel the rumble seat of his sporty little car. Amarantha felt her chest tighten as her happiness turned sour as curdled milk, and she suddenly noticed her dirty, bare feet and stained dress.

"We didn't know you were coming!"

"If you wore a hat, you wouldn't get so many freckles!" This was said to Amarantha, who only knew about wearing a stocking cap during the winter cold.

The boyfriend heard this last statement and boisterously offered, "Her freckles are cute! She's a regular little country girl!" And with that, he whipped her up in the air until her dress whirled above her panties.

He was fun and called her 'freckles', but in a way that implied the dreaded spots were completely acceptable, even desirable. She wondered if he would be Jenny's husband and asked her when the women were sitting in the shade of the porch.

Jenny laughed and said, "You won't catch me getting married and having a bunch of kids; I've got too many things I want to do. Besides, I'm gonna marry a rich man!"

Afterwards, Amarantha remembered the fun of the afternoon, but also could not help but remember that she had been dirty and much too freckled. After that, she didn't look forward to Jenny's infrequent visits as much.

Two events prompted the remaining Gradys' move to town. The first and most immediate was the loss of the older children to do the chores involved with the makeshift farm. The second was the economic advancement and stability of a permanent full-time job for Ma at the local cheese factory.

Amarantha remembered how proud and happy Ma was when she announced, "I got the job!"

They had celebrated at a supper with roast beef which Ma had bought - splurging for the occasion - at the butcher shop. Amarantha thought roast beef was vastly overrated and chewed the tough meat until it was a stringy cud held in her mouth, waiting for the right moment when she could surreptitiously slip it under her plate to be disposed of later.

But the ensuing changes proved to be not always happy and satisfying. It was with sadness that she saw Bossy herded into Dosches' dray wagon and carted down the driveway. Ma said she was going to a farm with lots of pasture for her. Amarantha saw Wendel wink at Elsie and mouth, *Hamburger.*

All the belongings they weren't going to take with them were piled in the yard, and old *Lady Lang* came to pick and choose what she wanted, moving, with Wendel's help, a varied array of tools and household goods to her shack.

Then they actually moved into their own apartment in New Scandia. Ma kept referring to their new life style as, *light house-keeping* and made decisions as to what was to be taken on that basis. The old woodstove was traded for a four burner kerosene stove, which had a small metal box-oven over two of the burners. They were to struggle for years with this monstrosity, which didn't cook if it was turned too low and gave off black soot and noxious fumes if it was inadvertently turned too high.

One truly modern advantage was the painted wooden icebox which replaced their cellar for storing perishable food. Amarantha loved to chip ice from the large chunk with the sharp pick and suck on the fragments until they melted. She wasn't aware that in the winter, the ice was harvested from one of the lakes surrounding their town and stored (packed in sawdust) in an ice house on the shore to later be sold and delivered. She probably wouldn't have thought of drinking from the lake, but was still young enough to accept many things without question.

The apartment itself was cramped and dirty. A struggling bar/restaurant occupied the bottom floor and a wooden stairway sagged against the outer wall providing access to their three room with bath home. Another advantage was running water and indoor plumbing; but Amarantha hated the greasy smell and noise from the business below and sometimes longed for the cool breezes and open spaces of the farm, especially her favorite haunt, the tree house. The bedroom contained the double bed which Amarantha had shared with Ma for as long as she could remember and a folding metal cot which had become Wendel's.

Life was certainly different for them all. Ma worked from 8 a.m. to 5 p.m. for five days and half days on Saturdays and, during the evenings, was physically exhausted from lifting and moving large cheeses off and on a conveyor belt. It was now her job to cut and shave the *bad* spots from the aged cheeses and ready them for the final marketing process. She wore a white uniform and always had her hair tied up in a white kerchief. She left in the morning crisp and clean and returned at night with her uniform stained by yellow rot and green mold. The smell was the worst thing to Amarantha; it seemed that Ma always stank of decayed or strong cheese.

Without the woodstove, or for that matter any free time for Ma, the homemade breads became a thing of the past. At first, Amarantha relished the soft, doughy store bread, which they referred to as *boughten*, and thought it was just like eating angel food cake; after a while she found herself longing for the crusty, hot loaves from the farm.

But Amarantha did adjust to the town life in time. She could walk anywhere she wanted and frequented the stores of their small town, wandering up and down the aisles in wonder at the glittering array of merchandise. Pennies and even nickels and dimes were easier to come by with Ma's new job, and she and Wendel could even go to the local movie house. One of the first movies she saw was, *The Wizard of Oz*, which would remain a favorite of hers throughout her life.

VI.
The Bedbug

"Ye ugly, creepin', blastit wonner,
Detested, shunned by saunt an' sinner,
How daur ye set your fit upon her-
Sae fine a lady!
Gae somewhere else and seek your dinner
On some poor body."

    - To A Louse
    On Seeing One on a Lady's Bonnet at Church
    Robert Burns

There are far worse things in poverty than hunger pangs or any of the other inherent physical discomforts brought on by the lack of necessitie. Worry and depression erode human dignity and leave self-esteem awash in failure. Many embrace poverty as a way of life and strive for nothing more than society's handouts; others fight to overcome the condition. Whatever path is chosen, there is always a price to be paid, since experiences shape character - for better or for worse.

Ma chose to fight. And it wasn't money she fought to accumulate. Pa's drunkenness, his inability to cope with life, his physical and moral weaknesses that had plunged the family into economic distress lined her face with worry and plagued her existence with an inherent lack of self-respect, or what Ma described as, *having a good name.*

For, sadly, around their small town, the Grady name meant a

series of ramshackle rentals, overdue bills, and standing in *the relief line*. And the family wore that name like a cloak over their dreams and ambitions - a heavy, muffling obstruction that occasionally could be lifted, but never entirely cast aside. Ma spent her life - and, consequently, so did many of her children - worrying about respectability, constantly belaboring what might bring shame to the family and secretly clinging to any possibility of pride.

For some of the children, respectability was something you scorned: *If you've got the name, you might as well play the game,* was their motto. For others it became their duty to seize upon any talent or occasion to wring some degree of accomplishment, not for self-fulfillment, but vindication for the Gradys. That's why Amarantha always remembered one incident when the war for respectability broke out on a Sunday morning right in God's house; and a small girl won a skirmish in that endless battle.

Ma always insisted they attend church. Like a badge of acceptance, it seemed to mean, *we're nice people. We belong to a church.* On this particular Sunday, the minister droned on and on, interpreting an obscure scripture which he felt proved that the Bible was not, as some argued, a collection of folk tales, but a compilation of the true revelations of the Almighty.

Whatever it was, it was a theological concept too advanced to be of interest to a child. Not that Amarantha was always disinterested; she loved the Christmas story and was sometimes moved to tears during the agony of the Good Friday service.

This morning, however, her mind wandered; and she sought points of interest throughout the church which might allow her to escape into her mind and weave a fantasy until the service ended. The stained glass windows were always good for this game. She loved the *Glorious Kingdom of God* window, where rays of golden light radiated from parting clouds and shone on the uplifted faces of kneeling figures. And she'd spent many Sundays concentrating on Mary's mournful look as she beheld the baby, Jesus. Why was she sad? Did she know that fateful Easter was in his future? Was she sad because he didn't have a crib but had to sleep in a manger?

Then the lady next to her interrupted her reverie by clearing her throat into a small square of white lace. Amarantha looked up at her. The church was crowded, and worshippers were packed tightly into the pews. The lady was Mrs. Kremser, whose husband, seated on her other side, was a doctor at the clinic. Amarantha hadn't dared look at them when they sat down but was aware of perfume that smelled of lilacs and a fur scarf made of small animals, one of which trailed a limp foot down to just touch her own shoulder.

Amarantha imagined herself dressed in the elegant blue suit and smelling of flowers; she wouldn't have a fur, though, she decided, as she lifted her eyes enough to see that the scarf was fastened by a tiny head with beady, bulging eyes biting the tale of an equally hapless twin companion, as if the animal considered it his solemn duty and had sacrificed all to keep this somewhat pudgy human warm.

She looked for a while at the dull, gray wool of her winter coat, as it lay next to the blue serge of Mrs. Kremser's suit jacket. And then, it happened! Amarantha detected a small, reddish-brown bedbug as it crawled up her arm. It appeared slightly sluggish, perhaps because it was out of its element or maybe from the warm, golden sun rays that spread across them from *The Glorious Kingdom of God* window.

Amarantha loathed the tiny bugs that shared their lives. Most of the time, she tried not to think of them, especially at bedtime; but when the lights were out and sleep eluded her, she imagined every faint touch of the sheet or twitch of her skin to be one of the tiny, unrelenting vampires. They were especially bothersome on hot summer nights, when the heat seemed to cause greater numbers to forsake the mattress crevices for the relative comfort of their victims' bodies. Then, morning was unbearable when she had to view the small spots of blood dotting the sheets - the night carnage of the greedy vermin that ate too much and fell beneath a sleeping body.

Where they had come from, no one knew. Ma said she thought they *got* them (which always sounded to Amarantha like getting a disease) when they moved to the old Peterson place.

"Probably in the walls and woodwork and we didn't know it until it was too late."

Periodically the edges of the mattresses were doused with kerosene, the residual fumes alone making sleep difficult, and a small, fiery torch made from twisted newspaper was passed over the metal springs. The family hoped, but, inevitably, a night would come when someone discovered a small survivor and soon they would be back in full force.

"Throw those old mattresses out," Jenny would say when she visited, but Ma didn't have the money to replace them and was so used to just putting up with squalor that it didn't seem to bother her.

"What if one gets in my suitcase and I give them to Mrs. McGuiness?" Jenny would ask hotly.

Jenny worked in Minneapolis for the McGuiness family and had her own, clean room with matching curtains and bedspread. The very thought of a repulsive, egg-laden insect stowing away to start a new colony frightened Amarantha. She actually wondered if the McGuinnesses would fire Jenny and have the police come to throw out Ma's mattresses.

Amarantha tried never to touch a bedbug. If she saw one, she brushed it away furiously with a shudder. Now, she debated as it crawled laboriously up her arm. If she picked it up, she would have to hold the loathsome thing in her fingers until church was over; but, if she let it crawl on, Mrs. Kremser might notice it and think poorly of them or, worse yet, the bug might crawl up that dangling fur foot and they'd end up giving it to the Kremser household. What would be the consequences of defiling the doctor's beautiful home on the hill? Surely they would know where the plague had originated! Maybe the Gradys wouldn't be able to be in the church any more!

As if she were scratching her arm, Amarantha put her hand to her sleeve and pinched the slow creature between thumb and forefinger.

The service was endless, as she felt tiny, squirming sensations, and the sun beat through *The Glorious Kingdom of God* to drench her body under her winter coat and blur her vision. Ma squeezed her knee as a signal to quit fidgeting, and Amarantha tried to concentrate through The Doxology - *til we meet at Jesus' feet. God be with you 'til we meet again!*

As the last strains faded, she br1ushed past Ma and ran to fling the tiny symbol of depravity over the railing of the church steps.

"Are you sick?" Ma put a hand to her sweating forehead. She leaned against the railing.

"*The Glorious Kingdom of God* made it too hot in there," she replied as they walked in the cold December morning.

When they got home from church, the radio announced the bombing of Pearl Harbor, and the wrinkle, like a pleat between Ma's eyes, deepened as she talked to Elsie about war and the two brothers who were already in the army.

"I guess they won't be getting home for Christmas leave now," she concluded, as if concentrating on this trivial disappointment would eliminate other possibilities too horrible to voice.

After the initial shock of Pearl Harbor, Amarantha sometimes almost forgot about the war. There was school and her growing addiction to the movies. Of course there were war films, but they depicted the romance and excitement of it all.

She saw the straight line of Ma's mouth relax and her eyes get shiny when she saw the contents of the stiff, manila envelopes that arrived with postmarks from large, important cities. Photographers were always plentiful around the military bases, ready to claim a portion of the enlisted man's pay with their urgings to, 'Show your family how you look in uniform,' or, the more blatantly ghoulish, 'This may be your family's last picture of you.'

The sight of her sons, barely more than adolescents, but clean-cut and serious in their crisp uniforms and jaunty hats, granted Ma a sense of pride she had barely known.

The Gradys were good people. They served their country!

But eventually the horror of the war did visit them and took a heavy toll on their family. Amarantha watched Ma's face when each of the two telegrams arrived. Harold had been badly wounded during the landing in Italy. There was the intake of breath, like a sob, and the exhale of relief.

"He's only wounded."

She couldn't know he would be physically and emotionally crippled for life.

And dear, funny Wendel was killed in Okinawa. Amarantha cried for her playmate--her wonderful brother who teased her and played cowboys and Indians with her and always shared his treats. Ma just sat in the chair and stared at the wall, even after it got dark outside.

When World War II was over, Amarantha, now a teenager, and Ma moved to yet another shabby apartment. They were alone now, the older Gradys grown and gone. On moving day, the two women struggled to lay the old, iron bedsteads and stained mattresses on a small patch of grass outside the door of their new home. Ma had bought a can of insecticide developed during the war to use on tropical insects that irritated the GIs. She doused the frames and headboards and rubbed a soaking rag over all the mattress crevices.

Nothing was ever the same again in the Grady family; but, at last, thanks to the DDT and much to Amarantha's relief, the bedbugs never returned.

"O wad some Power the giftie gie us
To see oursels as ithers see us!
It wad frae monie a blunder free us,
An' foolish notion;
What airs in dress an' gait wad lea'e us,
An' ev'n devotion!"

To A Louse - Robert Burns

VII.
Just As I Am
(As Long as Hollywood Comes Along)

To truly understand the daily dynamics for a child growing up in rural Wisconsin in the 30s and 40s, you would have to remember, or imagine, a time before television, with all its ancillary (if doubtful) enhancements such as video games, MTV, and Psychic Network.

You would have to project back to a time before the personal computer, when no one even conceived of going on-line to do homework or enter chat rooms. It was a time before sex education in the schools (or, more truthfully, taught by the media), when knowledge of anatomy was clandestinely acquired from the underwear section of the Sears Roebuck catalog.

It was a time when the Church was strong, and loomed large in almost everyone's life, for better or worse. The family was strong and also loomed large in almost everyone's life by virtue of the fact that the *Working Mother* hadn't made the scene yet, so most moms were home to check on comings and goings. Also, fast-food restaurants hadn't made the scene yet, so families had to go home to eat...for better or worse.

In this pre-technology era, movies were king of the entertainment world, particularly in the small towns where live theater existed in the high school class plays, and lack of transportation and money prevented people from traveling to city productions.

But you didn't have to go to the city. Thirty-five cents (a dime for those under twelve) provided two hours of escape to other worlds, sometimes with *Short Subjects* or a cartoon thrown in.

Amarantha saved her earned and begged dimes to attend every time the local theater marquee announced the latest change of shows.

On Friday night, she might watch a western thriller with Roy Rogers and his horse Trigger galloping across the prairie after the black-hatted bad guys. She laughed at the comic relief of the side-kick, Gabby Hayes, and recognized the origin of that ploy years later in college, when she encountered *Macbeth's* drunken messenger, knocking at the gate. It was as if she'd met an old friend, although Shakespeare, evidently confident enough in his ability to write dialogue and set scenes, allowed his characters to keep their teeth; while poor Gabby acted on *sans teeth, sans lines, sans everything.*

Or maybe it was Barry Fitzgerald who was typecast as the kindly Irish priest dispensing his syrupy, homilies or lamenting, *'Byes, ya haven't lived 'til yar awfter look'in down from the Ring o' Kerry at the farty shades o' green o' the Oirish valleys.'*

At the movies, Amarantha was transported from the dingy apartment she shared with Ma; from the boredom of childhood where all activities were determined by adults with their arbitrary *yeses* and *noes*; from the wrangling and teasing of schoolmates and, mostly, from that disappointing, freckled image that looked at her from her mirror to a world of beauty and excitement...of romantic, unconditional love.

In the movies, married couples slept in twin beds. Pregnancies were greeted with joy but surprise and puzzlement, as if the happy couple hadn't known how such a miracle had occurred, just as Amarantha hadn't. In the movies, both awards and retribution were swift and deserved, and moral shades of gray nonexistent. Moviemakers of the day labeled their products as having, *'redeeming social value,'* and they probably did.

But whatever the subliminal messages, Amarantha lived each plot and emerged from the darkened theater in a trance of unreality, not wholly attributable to the shock of being thrust into the light and bustle of the exiting crowd. She fell in love with the heroes; she cried with the heroines, she was righteously indignant over injustice. She danced with Fred Astaire, skated with Sonja Heinie, and sang like Kathryn Grayson. She found herself spending long periods of time in school or alone at home fantasizing over her most recent viewing and embroidering the plot in her mind, inserting herself as the star, of course. In short, movies had become her life! That's why one particular, hot, summer night left her feeling like the Biblical Jacob after his all-night battle with those tricky angels.

Amarantha and her friend, Lynn, were walking along the lakeshore, trying to catch any stray breeze from the water. The upstairs apartment had been stifling and sour smelling, and when Lynn had called from the bottom of the stairs, "Let's find something to do," she had gratefully escaped.

Both the girls had seen the current movie and didn't have a dime for a repeat performance, but were content, for the time being, to wander aimlessly in the humid night air. It was almost like slowly swimming in a warm pool.

As they rounded the corner from the lake, they noticed that lights were ablaze in the high school, and cars were parked up and down both sides of the streets for several blocks.

"What's going on at school?" Amarantha asked.

"I don't know exactly, but Mom said it was some kind of singing group or something."

"You wanna go in? Are they charging?"

"We could see. We can always go if they are. There's nothing else to do!"

The girls approached the door where two men stood dispensing blue mimeographed sheets of paper. Their painfully red ears and the sunburned napes of their necks branded them as fair, Scandinavian farmers who, after a day of hard labor in the fields, were perspiring in wool suits in order to hand out what must be an important message.

"How much? Lynn asked premptorily.

"No charge tonight."

He blew his nose, then mopped his brow with a bandanna handkerchief, having forgotten to tuck a white linen into the pocket of his Sunday suit. They entered a filled gymnasium, clutching their faintly-purple, lettered missals and searched for vacant chairs. Overly cheerful teenagers worked the crowd, joking with those in aisle seats and calling pleasantries to those stuck in the middle of the packed rows.

"Down here, ladies," called a boy not much older than they. "You're in luck! I've got two left right here in front."

The girls sank gratefully onto the metal, folding chairs and only then unfurled their papers to look for some clue as to what they would be witnessing.

"It's a revival," Lynn hissed in surprise. "Let's get out of here!"

"What can it hurt? Your Mom said it was singing, didn't she? Besides, I'm not getting up now and walking back down that aisle in front of all these people."

"Something wrong?" The young usher had evidently detected their whispered quandary.

"Well," Lynn stammered, then squared her shoulders and asserted, "It's just that I'm Swedish Lutheran!"

The room quieted and the lights dimmed as two men carrying guitars, a woman with an accordion, and a woman who headed for the piano bench took the stage.

The usher crouched down beside their chairs and made a placating gesture with his hands as he whispered confidentially, "That's all right; I think they'll take you no matter what you are."

"What do you mean, *take* me?" Lynn started, but the boy put his finger to his lips and pointed to the stage.

As if on cue, the woman pounded out an intricate, many trilled introduction on the piano and the other instruments joined as a red-robed, jauntily marching choir of eight men and women entered from both sides of the stage harmoniously questioning, *Are you washed in the blood of the lamb?*

They were good! They sounded to Amarantha like the choir in *Cabin in the Sky,* a movie she'd seen a couple weeks ago.

The singers spread their arms wide to the audience and seemed to be making eye contact with everyone. They marched in a military drill as they launched into *Onward Christian Soldiers,* their expressions determined and grim - *marching as to war*. Then, as they slowed to deliver the inspiring conclusion - *with the cross of Jesus, going on before* - they dissolved into an informal group, their faces turning soft and sweet. *Softly and tenderly Jesus is calling*, they crooned, *calling for you and for me*.

Completely vulnerable to the world of the stage and players, Amarantha mouthed the lyrics and assimilated the rhythms into her body as if they were food. She had sung these hymns before in church, but, led by a tone-deaf minister and a plaintively bleating choir, they'd never had this effect on her before.

As the choir hushed to a background hum, a man in a white, satin robe walked from the wings and raised his arms over the audience.

"See by the portal, he's watching and waiting!" he spoke loudly, "waiting for you and for me. Is Christ waiting for you friends? How long has he been waiting and watching? Months? Years? Your whole life?"

Amarantha hated this type of inquisition, where adults didn't give you a chance to answer before bombarding you with the next question. But just as the glow of the music began to fade for her, the white-robed player lowered his arms and walked to the edge of the stage in an almost conspiratorial manner. "I'm so glad you've all come here tonight, because that tells me you're looking for something! And friends, I'm going to help you find it!"

He turned to the front row and looked directly at Amarantha and Lynn. "I'm especially happy to see the children here tonight, because we're going to have some fun. Do you kids want to have some fun?"

It was a trick question...You had to say yes. Didn't all kids want to have fun? Only stupid kids would reject fun when given a choice. Inwardly squirming in the limelight and ready to agree to almost anything to divert the audience attention, Amarantha and Lynn both nodded, dumbly.

The choir had broken into a swinging, *Dem bones, dem bones, dem dry bones....*

"Good! Because I want all you kids to come up here and sing

with our choir. You all know this song. Come on up here!"

His voluminous white robe rocked back and forth like a peeling bell as he shouted and paced and beckoned. The cheerful ushers once again appeared amongst the audience and urged the
younger crowd toward the stage.

The girls' cheerleader stepped between their chairs, raised
them by their elbows, and personally marched them to the stage.
Not wanting to make a scene, they submitted. Thankfully, the
embarrassed and stumbling aggregation, desperately trying to
hide behind each other, numbered quite a few, providing the
proverbial safety.

At first, they were stiff and mumbling; but each choir member
singled out several desperate *fun seekers* and took their hands.
They seemed almost to dance with them as they pointed to the
appropriate bone and slapped them, good-humoredly, on their
backs. They danced in a circle holding hands; while on the side
lines, the minister, as Amarantha thought of him, laughed and
clapped his hands.

Next came *Ainta That Good News*, which hardly anyone knew;
but the choir's enthusiasm and joy was so infectious that they all
cavorted around the stage, mumbling the verses until they could
shout the easily discerned chorus, *A ainta that good news? Good
news? Good newwwws?*

Several other rollicking and familiar tunes followed until the
whole gymnasium was swaying and clapping, some occasionally
shouting out agreement or encouragement to those on stage. All
inhibitions vanished. Caution was thrown to the winds! It *was* fun!

At the conclusion of one hymn, the musicians all seemed suddenly tired and out of breath. They laughed and shook their heads,
holding their sides.

"What? You can't go on? Boys and girls, maybe we'd better give
our choir a little rest here. You may take your seats. Thank you!"

The choir members filed to the back of the stage and filled a
row of empty chairs. The instrumentalists relaxed back in their
seats and rested their instruments in their laps or on the floor.
Lynn and Amarantha, having considerable experience in church,

knew what this meant. It was time for the sermon.

Now their Congregational and Lutheran sermons were generally scholarly treatises on obscure religious theory such as, the distinction between the *Father*, the *Son*, and *The Holy Ghost*. And these would be delivered by the minister standing straight and unmoving behind a podium, his voice revealing little expression, his face none whatsoever. That's why the girls who, along with the heavily perspiring audience, were trying to bridle their frivolity after all the fun, started in surprise when they heard the thundering shout, "*You are all sinners!*"

The minister stood center stage. Clearly, the fun was over. His expression was angry and fierce. With one arm extended, he pointed his index finger toward the crowd and moved slowly to encompass the entire gymnasium. "Some sitting here tonight partook of the evils of alcohol before they came!"

Silence reigned, except for an almost inaudible shifting sound.

"Some lied to their wives or husbands or mothers before they came! Some of you cheated your boss or a friend!"

The litany of audience sins proceeded, and it was plain to Amarantha that this guy wasn't going for the big punishable transgressions, like killing or stealing, but was hitting them where it hurt. It was interesting and clever. As she surreptitiously turned to look at her neighbors, she almost enjoyed their obvious discomfort as the minister explored the evils of alcohol or *the web of deceit*. Then, like a thunderbolt from the blue, he hit her where she lived!

"How many of you children spend your spare time in darkened rooms watching flickering, graven images made by people whose sinful lifestyles you support with your dimes?!"

His eyes bored into Amarantha as if he knew all about her passion.

"You admire and idolize these movie actors more than you admire and idolize our Lord, Jesus, or any of the Apostles? You'd rather go to the movies than to church any day?"

So far, he was batting a thousand!

"I say to you, you have taken a step down the road to the same sins your idols are committing. Soon you will be drinking, lying, cheating, stealing, or committing adultery because you admire those things, don't you? *You must!* You admire the people who commit them!"

He paced from one end of the stage to another. He modulated his voice from almost a whisper to a shout. He curled his upper lip in disgust or shook his fist in the air. He folded his hands and closed his eyes. His performance was unlike any Amarantha had seen in that "darkened room with the flickering images."

Now Amarantha wasn't too worried about becoming addicted to any of the sins he mentioned (except adultery, and she didn't know what that was, although it sounded pretty bad from the way he sneered when he said the word), so she remained unconvinced that going to the movies was sinful.

He was crouching by the edge of the stage, one elbow resting on his knee and talking confidentially. "You want to know what's gonna happen? I'll tell you what's gonna happen. One of these nights, when you're sitting in that dark movie theater, Jesus is going to come back to earth to call us home to heaven, and you're not going to hear him because you'll be locked away behind those doors watching those sinners on that screen. And once you miss that invitation to heaven, there's only one other place to go." He turned his thumb down, and the audience sighed with one voice. If Amarantha wasn't convinced with argument, she did respond to threat. After that, the evening began to go from bad to worse.

The choir stood, the instrumentalists sat forward, and the strains of a familiar hymn provided background music for the minister. *Just as I am without one plea...But that thy blood was shed for me...*

"Now ladies and gentlemen, children, no matter what you've done in the past you can come forward and repent of your sins and be saved here tonight!"

The ushers were once again among them, urging quietly while the minister continued in a seductive voice, "It doesn't matter what your sin, once you're saved, the burden will be lifted and you'll walk with God."

The room was filled with rustling as crying people passed

down the rows and into the aisle making their way to the stage. The minister had shed his robe and knelt in his white shirt to receive the penitent. Amarantha saw the young, sunburned farmer who had been at the door, now coatless also, kneel before the minister, his shirt clinging to his back in large, wet spots.

They prayed together with their eyes tightly closed. Amarantha wondered what his particular sin was...maybe adultery. She felt an unexplainable sympathy for him and hoped he'd only cheated, or danced, or (horrors) gone to a movie.

The girls were fascinated with watching those who trooped down to be saved and failed to notice the cheerleader until he was again upon them. "Are you girls ready to be saved?"

Lynn stuck to her guns. "I'm a Swedish Lutheran. We don't have to be saved!"

"Are you saying you have never sinned?"

"No, but we don't believe in being saved."

"You can never be forgiven for your sins?"

"I'm not saying that."

It was clear that she was getting nowhere, and when he again took their elbows to escort them to the stage, they submitted as the line of least resistance. They knelt on the stage. Fortunately, they were grouped with several other young people. Amarantha kept her eyes on the floor: it was grimy and hard on her bony, bare knees.

"Do you all admit that you have sinned and come short of the glory of God?"

Amarantha thought hard about her sins. She knew what he would consider her greatest sin, but frantically searched her mind for substitutes so she could keep her beloved pastime. She thought she remembered from Sunday school that pride was a sin, and she was proud of her good grades. But if she hadn't gotten good grades, Ma would have been unhappy, and she also remembered that you were supposed to, 'Honor thy father and mother.'

This was a real dilemma which clearly warranted serious thinking. But the minister wasn't allowing for any definitions or clarifications, and, as sudden thunder rattled the gym windows,

he decided to speed things up and opted for a group absolution
without listening to their individual confessions. She was sunk! In
her heart of hearts, she knew her movies were sloshing around in
that slimy pool of collectively absolved sins.

When they were thankfully back in their seats, they sat wood-
enly within a dim, crying, rustling, microcosm of sin and shame,
listening over and over to the softly murmuring choir singing the
same hymn....*Just as I am, without one plea, But that thy blood was shed
for me, And that thou bidd'st me come to thee O lamb of God, I come. I
come.* They were vaguely aware of a collection plate being passed
but stared ahead without touching it.

Then the lights were on and, as if startled from a dream, normalcy seemed to have returned. People greeted each other and
asked about the crops. They joked and made arrangements to meet
somewhere for coffee. Amarantha saw the young, *saved* farmer put
his arm around a girl and whisper something, followed by laughter. She even saw the minister, not two minutes before on his knees
in a deep religious trance, now explode with laughter over a passing remark by a choir member.

Amarantha was always amazed at the way adults could switch
from one scenario to another. She had seen them cry inconsolably
at a funeral, only to fill their plates with food and crack jokes afterwards in the church basement. Maybe she'd be able to do that
when she got older, but at this moment she moved slowly in the
heat of the gymnasium, the voices around her, the scraping of
chairs on the wooden floor, the rustle of feet as they all slowly filed
to the open doors seemed muted as if heard from under water. She
struggled within herself to surface. She felt as if she could barely
breathe.

Outside the sky was afire with lightning. People called to one
another and ran for their cars, anticipating the arrival of the storm.
There wasn't time to talk to Lynn about the evening's outcome.
They started to run , but as they parted in their separate directions,
she heard Lynn call, "Do you wanna go to the show tomorrow
night? It's a new one."

Now there was constant thunder, and when the sky was alight

you could see the rolling clouds as the wind rose, bending almost double the tall elms around the high school. Amarantha ran, forgetting her breathlessness, and reached the outside stairs to her apartment just as the rain started. Large, warm drops splashed and spread on her face as she climbed.

"Well, thank heavens you got home before the storm. Where you been? I was just getting ready to go look for you."

Ma was in the doorway with an old shirt around her shoulders. Often when she had lost track of time and stayed late at Lynn's or Karen's, she would meet Ma on her way home. With no phone, it was the only way to check on her daughter. Years later, Amarantha would wonder at Ma's patience, because she wouldn't scold or threaten, just show concern. Somehow it made more of an impression on Amarantha than punishment.

"Just walking around."

"Well, you better get to bed."

A sudden crack of thunder, a gust of wind and rain drenched them as they stood in the doorway. Ma leaned on the door to close it against the gale. Amarantha stood inside but didn't move. Ma ran to close open windows that admitted the deluge, the limp curtains billowing in the wind. She returned to see Amarantha in the same spot.

"What's the matter? Did something happen tonight?"

Amarantha threw herself into Ma's arms as her personal storm broke into a torrent of tears. "I was saved," she gulped.

"At the revival?" Amarantha managed a nod. "Well, why are you crying? That's not a bad thing is it?"

"But they said going to the show is a sin, and now I won't ever be able to go again." A fresh series of sobs ensued at the revelation of the expunged transgression.

Ma patted her back. "Our church doesn't say going to the show is a sin," she reasoned.

"But I promised before God, and I know I'm guilty."

"I think God is just happy you promised to try to be a good girl. People sin everyday, big or small. One night at a revival isn't going to stop that."

"Do you sin, Ma?"

"Of course, but I try to keep them small."

"You think going to the show might be a small sin?"

"I'm sure of it." The corners of Ma's mouth twitched a little, but she didn't smile. "Why don't we have a fried egg and bacon sandwich before we go to bed?," she offered. Ma lit the kerosene stove in the kitchen and laid the bacon out in the old, black frying pan.

It was nice. They sat with their sandwiches, Amarantha's favorite, and shared a bottle of strawberry pop at the table by the window. The storm was over, and a cool breeze stirred the damp curtains. The lingering smell of smoky bacon mingled with the smell of the rain and ozone. Sometimes the apartment wasn't so bad. She could be herself here. Somehow, she couldn't imagine Lynn's or Karen's mom making bacon and eggs at eleven o'clock at night.

Amarantha slept late the next morning. The heat wave had broken, and the day was fair and cool. She saw Lynn at the drug store and they arranged to meet that night for the show. Neither of them mentioned their night at the revival. She knew Lynn hadn't been bothered by it, and she envied her strong convictions: If her *saving* hadn't occurred at the behest of the Swedish Lutheran Church, it didn't count.

As for Amarantha, she decided it was best not to think about it too much. Ma had given her a legitimate out, and she was going to take it.

Honor thy Mother.

Later at the movies, although Amarantha was completely engaged with the night's showing (it was *Road to Morocco* with Crosby, Hope, and Lamour), she did look back up the aisle toward the door several times to see if, by chance, a phantom figure stood beckoning; but the only appearance was by an usher with her flashlight. Then, with a sigh of relief, Amarantha would return again to where she lived, in her world.

VIII.
The Alien Uncles

Amarantha learned, of course, that not all aliens are from outer space, but that the word applies to anyone or anything different, foreign, unfamiliar, or strange. In the case of humans, an alien most likely would have trouble communicating effectively, might have a strange appearance, and most probably, would have definite cultural differences.

It was with this broader definition in mind that she remembered Ma's immigrant family, who drifted in and out of the shadowy land of her childhood like unthreatening wraiths, never essential to the recollection but always clinging to the borders and emanating a damp sadness, which evoked certain guilty feelings she would rather have forgotten. These feelings centered mostly around her four unmarried uncles, Willie and Otto, who had been born in Sweden and were next in age to the successful Uncle Charlie; Emil, who was Ma's favorite and her childhood playmate; and John, the baby of the family. Ma always defended them and hinted darkly at their being treated unfairly, although even Ma couldn't condone their wild intemperance.

With the sale of the home farm, it seemed that all of Ma's dire predictions came true, and rather rapidly at that. It turned out *The Uncles* hadn't thought about where they would live or what they would do when they had divested themselves of their inheritance.

At first, they didn't appear to have a problem. Their nephew and his wife had plans for a massive cleaning and refurbishing of the old, neglected farm house, a project that had to be completed before they would even consider moving in. This meant that the house remained unoccupied; so *The Uncles*, seeming incapable of thinking beyond one day at a time, returned from drinking bouts to sleep off the liquor in their old rooms, oblivious to the changes occurring around them. When they were sober, they worked on the farm helping their nephew repair the out buildings and move in his stock and farm machinery. They earned a few dollars and, after all, they had their sale money—a sum which they considered, having always had their father or brother handle the money, an inexhaustible well from which to drink.

Then came a day when the young Mrs. Person, touring the house in preparation for the next renovation, found John lying on a urine stained mattress on the floor of an upstairs room. Bile and anger rose in her throat simultaneously, and she marched to confront her husband working in a nearby field.

"They've got to get out and stay out! They've been paid and it's my place now!"

Uncle Charlie listened to his son's complaint, nodding much as his brothers did when someone tried to reason with them, always trying to avoid confrontation in the *Svensk* (Swedish) way. "Ya, Ya, I know," he'd agree.

Uncle Charlie was tall with a rigid, dour face. He walked ram-rod straight and maintained that posture even when sitting: he never slumped. He had inherited Grandpa Tulpan's red hair and beard, but lacked the lively blue eyes with the mischievous glint. One would never imagine him with a gold hoop in his ear.

He knew that some in his family, mainly Amarantha's Ma, thought he had duped his brothers into selling, but he had thought the whole transaction through thoroughly; and could sit in his pew at Our Redeemer Swedish Lutheran Church every Sunday with a clear conscience.

The land had to be kept in the family and his eldest son was hard-working and ambitious, what was needed to restore the farm to the way it was when *Far* had been in charge. After all, he had maintained and improved *Grosfar Tulpan's* farm and remained en *nykter man* (a sober man) without succumbing to drink and dereliction. His brothers had their chance, and now they must live with their choices. If they had gotten more money from the sale, it would just have gone to waste. And Uncle Charlie further didn't consider that his sisters had a voice in the matter. He subscribed to the old fashioned view that property was divided among the sons. Let the daughters' husbands take care of them. Once again, they had made their choices.

Amarantha would remember that even when Ma was in dire straits, she would not ask her brother for help. She had crossed a line with him in opposing the sale; so perhaps she knew what the answer would be, and perhaps these feelings initiated the bad blood between the Gradys and the Persons.

Uncle Charlie was, however, not without a certain amount of regard for his siblings and pity for the men his brothers had become. So he went to another son, who owned a *forty* nearby and asked him to let *The Uncles* live on a small, abandoned farm on that land. He agreed, and he and his wife were kindly landlords, not to the point of investing any money in the disintegrating buildings; but they hired *The Uncles* for farm work when they could, and generally kept an eye on them. The wife brought food down to their living shack once in a while and saw that they had a supply of milk, salt pork and a chunk of fresh meat at butchering time.

Amarantha visited their shack with Ma and Aunt Alma, and though her own living conditions left a great deal to be desired, she never ceased to be shocked at the dark, tiny room lit only by kerosene lamps. Four bunks took up most of the floor space, and a small wood-burning cook stove doubled as their heat source in winter.

Once a year, usually before Christmas, the two sisters would persuade a motorized relative to take them to the shack, hauling an incredible amount of supplies which *The Uncles* seemed to regard as unnecessary frills but, in the spirit of being good hosts, tried to appreciate. All year Aunt Alma, who cleaned and ironed for people in town, collected cast-off bedding or clothing, which she washed, mended, and adapted. The result was a collection of pieced together sheets and blankets and patched shirts and pants. As *The Uncles* looked on uncomfortably, the sisters dutifully stripped off the filthy bedding they had installed the Christmas before and made up the bunks afresh. Ma had knit mittens and socks and had always managed to set aside a small sum to buy something new: underwear or a warm cap. Sometimes she included a bit of tobacco for their pipes, although Aunt Alma disapproved. They made coffee then and everyone dipped rusks, store-bought now but still a favorite with the Scandinavian community and a reminder, for *The Uncles*, of a *varmt hem* (a warm home) and better days.

But they didn't seem to mind how they lived. They had no means of transportation, but hitched rides to town ostensibly to get supplies but really to drink at the Pool Hall. When no ride was available they walked on the highway, and like their *Grosfar* before them, carried a burlap sack for the supplies, if there was enough money left after the Pool Hall to get any. Amarantha saw them occasionally on the street, where she tried to avoid them, or when they stopped to have coffee with Ma, when she found better things to do and left the room. Their appearance, their thick accents, their extreme poverty offended her; and although it never occurred to her, she tended to treat them in somewhat the same way the Person cousins treated her family.

Amarantha rarely saw them between Christmases, and even stopped making that visit when she got older. They didn't figure in her world any more. Then one day, when she was in high school, they suddenly emerged, like skeletons from her closet, forcing her to recognize and own them. It was a serious assault on the façade she had built for her personal protection, and resulted in a close examination of *The Uncles* as well as painful soul-searching on her part.

It began on a perfectly normal day after school. Amarantha collected her homework from the green metal locker outside her homeroom.

"Are you going to the drugstore?" Lynn asked as she too contemplated the innards of an open locker which spilled crumpled papers, dog-eared notebooks, and mismatched mittens onto the hall floor.

"Yeah! I've got fifty cents. Want to split a malt?"

"Sure! What flavor are we on?" Their current gastronomical project was to sample every flavor of malted milk offered by Erickson's Drugstore. Their favorite so far was pineapple, but who knew what flavor would pique their taste buds to the supreme level and be proclaimed the ultimate best.

Lynn scooped the detritus of high school life off the floor and pressed it into the locker, closing the door quickly before the very pressure of its contents caused another explosion.

Lynn and Amarantha had been friends since kindergarten. The relationship hadn't always been friendly. Once the tomboy, Lynn, had smeared mud on Amarantha's only good dress, worn to school for some forgotten special occasion. Once Amarantha had summoned her courage and called Lynn a *rich, little brat.* Similar cases of injury, verbal abuse, and bouts of hurt feelings marked the passage of elementary school, but somehow there were always apologies, sometimes tears and the inevitable exchange of loyalty vows.

With high school and their burgeoning maturity, came a comfortable, if competitive, friendship, the kind that nurtures secret dreams and ambitions and provides a confidante in times of happiness or sadness.

It was an odd alliance to the casual observer. Lynn, the only child of comfortable parents, was indulged and sometimes painfully outspoken, but good-hearted, fun-loving, and fiercely loyal. Her mother had a college degree, and their house reflected her exposure to the liberal arts curriculum of classical music, art, and languages. Framed prints of the Degas ballerinas decorated Lynn's pink and white room; recordings of operas were filed in upright positions in the volume filled bookcase, next to the Seth Thomas clock.

But Lynn was a throwback to earlier ancestors: a rebel who shunned the soft cashmere sweaters of her mother's Minneapolis shopping trips for her father's flannel shirts and pouted and sulked her way through her dancing lessons, slapping her feet awkwardly to the beat of the music. Amarantha accompanied

Lynn to many of these bouts of enrichment and watched, jealousy forming a sickening knot in her stomach, as her friend pounded a piano as if she were driving nails or extracted torturous squawks from her clarinet.

Amarantha's jealousy acted as her motivation, however, and she responded to this exposure by vowing to herself that she too would go to college and, someday, live in this cultured environment she so admired.

She, of course, had only Ma, who struggled daily to keep them afloat on the turbulent sea of economic instability. The brothers and sisters had gone their separate ways, leaving the two of them in a hot and depressing little apartment above a local tavern. Ma worked at the cheese factory now and was happy to have a steady job and ensured paycheck. But the hard work and long hours left her too tired to think about anything domestic, and the three, beer-reeking rooms they called home became increasingly filthy, as they carried on their daily schedules around stored boxes and bundles filled with the remnants of their lives in other places, at different times, with other people.

Amarantha tried to clean sometimes, but the coal stove, their winter heat source, daily left a thin coating of black coal dust on all flat surfaces, and the boxes, almost heaped to the ceiling in some areas, made sweeping and mopping futile. And so, mother and daughter surrendered to the inevitable march of neglect, only occasionally attempting to push back the invading squalor with a broom or scrub brush.

Amarantha was ashamed and never asked anyone to her house but Lynn, because she didn't seem to mind or even notice the condition of the apartment. They'd spread the Monopoly game out on the oil clothed surface of the rickety, old table and eat hamburgers from The Coffee Cup restaurant across the street, not having to worry that their strawberry pop bottles might leave rings on the table. Sometimes they'd open the air vent from the tavern downstairs and sit with their ears pressed to the screen, listening to the patron's conversations and alternately suppressing giggles or staring at each other in wide-eyed shock at the swearing.

Several times, while Lynn was there, *The Uncles* came to visit Ma. They rested their burlap sacks on the floor by the door and sat around the table to have coffee. They spoke mostly Swedish, and the sing-song lilt of their native tongue floated softly from one to the other. Since they couldn't understand a word of the conversation, the girls usually stayed until one of *the Uncles* would hand them each a quarter and they'd adjourn to the drugstore for a malt.

"I love coming to your house," Lynn would say as they left, "My place is so boring. Nothing ever happens there."

But Amarantha loved especially to spend the night with Lynn in her ruffle bedecked bedroom, listening to records and planning their lives after high school. She loved that the family sat together around the table and used cloth napkins rolled in little carved rings. She admired the healthy, green house plants and noted the arrangement of the mother and father overstuffed chairs around the console radio. And she would repeat her mantra to herself:

This is the way my house is going to be when I go to college and get a good job.

Now the two friends walked, absorbed in their own conversation until they neared the main street. They could hear singing and laughing. People had gathered in a semi-circle on the sidewalk, and Lynn and Amarantha couldn't see through the crowd to the entertainment. The action was taking place outside the local pool hall and saloon.

Ma had cautioned Amarantha many times to walk on the street opposite this popular all-male establishment. A metal railing ran in front of the building, and, in good weather, the customers stood outside, leaning on the railing and hailing or conversing with passersby. Ma considered attention from and proximity to these nere-do-wells tantamount to, 'tainting your reputation.'

But today, when everyone else was stopping, the girls stepped into the gutter at the fringes of the crowd to see what was happening. When Amarantha saw the burlap bags on the sidewalk, she wanted to turn and run; but Lynn was standing on tiptoe and jostling for position. She wouldn't be willing to turn away now.

The railing was lined with clapping, guffawing men who shouted cheerful encouragement to two obviously drunk dancers who staggered and twisted grotesquely in an alcoholic inspired reel.

One sang in Swedish as he danced, the words sometimes lost in coughs and belches, to the added amusement of the onlookers. *Rida, Rida, Ranka, Hasten heter blancha*, he sang; and with a sinking heart, Amarantha recognized a song Ma sang when she told stories of the games she and her brothers and sisters played up on the farm when she was a little girl. The dancers staggered to the edge of the crowd and held out their hands to the onlookers. *Ringdans*, they offered , but no one came forward.

"It's your uncles," Lynn shouted over her shoulder as she laughed and joined in the clapping. Several people turned and looked at Amarantha.

A boy from one of her classes said, "Are those drunken, old bums really your uncles?"

Amarantha's face burned with shame; and she managed to blurt out as she ran away, "No, Lynn just thinks she's being cute again!"

The persistent boy stopped Lynn as she walked away from the crowd looking for Amarantha. "Are they really her uncles?"

"No! I was just kidding her. I guess she didn't think it was funny!"

Amarantha ran through the growing crowd, everyone wanted to see the show, and she arrived out of breath and sweating at the steps to her apartment. As she waited for Ma to get home from work, she nursed her shame and attempted to assign some blame for the incident, which is always a comfort in times of embarrassment. She was the victim. It wasn't Lynn's fault: she had innocently happened upon them, as Amarantha had. She shouldn't have labeled them so loudly, but Amarantha had to admit that it was blurted out on impulse and not meant to be hurtful.

No, it was *The Uncles'* fault. Why did they have to be the way they were? If they couldn't be decent, why didn't they just stay in their shack? And, even more viciously, why didn't they just die and put an end to their miserable existence? She hurtled the same questions at Ma when she came home, as if it were *her* fault.

"Don't talk like that! They're my brothers and I love them, just like you love yours. They weren't always like this, and I remember them before they let the booze take them. There are many reasons that you don't know or understand for them being the way they are and we're not in their shoes, so we can't judge. *Let he who is without sin cast the first stone!*"

Amarantha remained silent. Ma concluded by saying, "They've been good to me, and maybe you should try to think back to all the times they've been good to you in the past."

Amarantha stalked off to fling herself on her bed, her face turned to the wall in case Ma came to continue the conversation. But Ma busied herself with supper, having decided not to attempt to justify her brothers. She knew her daughter, however. Much as the teenager often wailed, *You don't understand how it is,* Ma knew that she had given her food for thought, and Amarantha wouldn't fail to look at every angle of the situation. So in the time it took for the potatoes to boil and the pork chops to fry, Amarantha was able to remember several instances which showed the good side of *The Uncles.*

The earliest she recalled was when she was very little. They were all at the farm one early spring Sunday. A plot of virgin pine forest still stood on a back forty, and Wendel and Amarantha decided to explore it. They had to stretch their heads back as far as they'd go to see the tops of those trees, and although it was a bright, sunny day, it was shadowy and gloomy among the pines. And so quiet; not even a bird sang.

As they ran from trunk to trunk, their heads thrown back, Amarantha slipped into a newly thawed patch of mud and sank in over her rubber boot tops. Wendel tried to pull her out, but he started sinking and barely jumped to solid ground before he was mired as well. He tried to extend a branch to her, but he wasn't strong enough to overcome the suction of the mud.

Finally he convinced her that the best course of action was for him to go for help. She was afraid to stay alone, but he was gone before she could protest, his thin body like a deer leaping downed trees and skirting bushes. They were both under the impression that Grandpa's farm harbored quick-sand similar to the quick-sand they had seen in their beloved Tarzan movies, and that she would completely disappear under the slimy ooze if not rescued in a timely fashion.

Abandoned and frantic with fear, Amarantha imagined it had gotten darker. The wind moaning in the tall pines sounded like ghosts, and she thought every shadow might be one of the legendary wolves come to finish her at last. She cried, she screamed, and she shook with cold.

She didn't see him approach, but suddenly Uncle Emil was beside her. "Shhhh! Shhh! *Lille flicka,*" he soothed.

She clung to him as the suction broke and the mud finally yielded her up into his arms. He pulled the open flap of his coat around her and carried her across the field to the farm house. Strangely, his clothes didn't smell bad or seem dirty then, only warm and comforting, the rough material chaffing her chin.

"Shhh! Shhh! Shhh!" he crooned.

She remembered other times when the uncles would visit and give her a whole dime if she sang *Wabash Cannon Ball* for them. Then they'd smile at Ma and talk softly in Swedish about the *Lille Flicka.*

Sometimes they'd come to visit a little *pickled.* Then they seemed like different men and would dance drunkenly and try to get Ma to circle with them, as they had today at the pool hall. But Ma only shook her head and made her mouth a straight line. Amarantha watched and longed to join hands with them and dance around the kitchen; but she was reluctant to touch them and even more reluctant to express such outward emotion in front of others, that Scandinavian trait *The Uncles* were able to shed when possessed by alcohol.

Was alcohol fun? Why were adults so against it when its influence seemed to provide instant relief from isolation, loneliness, and the silent world of the chronically reticent?

"What does it mean, *Rida, Rida, Ranka*?" she asked Ma.

"Ride a cock horse, the horse named Blanka...Little knight so sweet still has no spurs. When you have won them, the peace of childhood will be gone."

"But what does that *mean?*"

"It's just a children's game about a boy growing up. First the peace of childhood goes, then the peace of youth and, finally, the peace of manhood. I remember one day when we played *Rida, Rida, Ranka* all day. It was one of those fall days when it's warm as summer but the air is full of falling leaves. There were two big maples on either side of our driveway, one red and one yellow, and their leaves were blowing around us as we held hands and circled under them. They were almost dancing with us."

Ma's eyes had that far away look when she told stories about the farm, and a slight smile twitched at the corners of her mouth. "We played so hard that day that when we went to say our prayers at bedtime, instead of *Now I lay me down to sleep* I said, *Rida, Rida, Ranka* and got a slap on the head from my Ma who thought I was being smart."

"Had you been drinking moonshine?"

"Of course not! What would ever give you that idea?"

"Cause it's the only time *The Uncles* sing is when they've been drinking."

"We were just kids. It's a children's game!"

She looked as if she might give Amarantha a slap on the head for her question, but then she got the far-away look again and said, "It turned real cold that night, and when we got up the next morning, there was snow on the ground and the trees were all bare. No leaves danced in the air."

"Was the peace of childhood gone?"

"I guess you might say that." She patted Amarantha's head, then visibly returned from her reverie with a shake of her head.

Amarantha thought about the food from 'up on the farm.' Her mouth watered when strangely, the thought of *Kalvdans* suddenly popped into her mind. The Uncles used to bring the Gradys dairy and produce from the farm. Sometimes, when *the relief* was sparse, it was all they had to eat. Milk and eggs were a given, but sometimes the tightly-lidded ex-syrup pail held a special milk that Ma mixed with the fresh eggs, a little sugar, pinch of salt, a generous portion of *Watkins* vanilla, and sprinkling of nutmeg for their favorite dessert. At supper time, it would come out of the oven with a golden-brown, sugar-crisp topping. Her mind was alive with memories of the kitchen with its big black woodstove and the whole family around the table.

That special milk was a cow's first milk after calving or, as they said on the farm, 'coming fresh.' Although the calves needed that thick, colostrums rich liquid for a good start, a few cups were always put aside for a pan of what Ma called 'Feastings,' and what Amarantha preferred to call by the Swedish name *Kalvdans*, which means Calves Dance.

Part of the enjoyment of the dish was picturing in her mind's eye those velvety infants on their hind legs, front hooves entwined, doing a sprightly circle jig around the mother cow. Sometimes she and Wendel performed their own rendition, which definitely added a dimension to the experience.

There was the January birthday when particularly cold and bleak weather had left the Gradys scouring railroad tracks near their house for any lumps of coal that had fallen from the open storage bin of the train's engine just to keep their kitchen warm. It was a desperate time. Ma had warned her that there wouldn't be toys; but Jenny had scraped together enough ingredients to make a plain white cake (warning that there wasn't anything for frosting) and there was a lumpy package on the table that elicited excitement even though Amarantha knew it was probably mittens and cap knit by Ma.

As they prepared to begin the meager party, an old Model T pulled into the yard and Uncle Willie was at the door with a large box. Amarantha didn't remember all that was in it, but she did remember thick cream and strawberry jam, which Jenny quickly whipped and combined into a beautiful fluffy, pink topping, making her cake look like the fancy confections she had seen in pictures.

But, best of all, Uncle Willie got a gleam in his eye as he carefully took out an old shoebox and offered it to Amarantha, mumbling something about *flicka* (girl) and *den glada festen* (the happy celebration) and *lille katten* (little cat). She lifted the lid and looking up at her with big blue eyes was a black kitten. It was trembling with fear and cold, and smelled strongly of barn, but she petted it and held it close to her chest until it started to purr.

"Its name is Tilda," Uncle Willie offered, "but you can call it whatever you want."

He looked pleased with himself as he accepted a plate of birthday cake, sitting to fork the pink frosting into his mouth with relish.

"Tilda sounds good to me," Amarantha answered. Tilda slept on the pillow next to her that night, and Amarantha whispered into her tiny, leather-like ear the first of many shared dreams, fears, and confessions. "You're the best present I ever got," and the *lille katten* purred and kneaded and closed her eyes in contentment.

Amarantha remembered that many of Ma's bedtime stories centered on her brothers and the adventures they had on the farm. She grimaced inwardly when Ma told of the time when she and Emil were chopping pumpkins to feed the pigs, and an overly energetic whack of Emil's knife had cut off the first joint of his index finger. They didn't dare tell their parents, so they wrapped his hand in an old glove, and climbed to the hay loft where they deposited the severed digit high on one of the roof's beams.

"I don't remember how long it took Ma and Pa to notice Emil's hand. I do remember that in the spring, we climbed up in the loft and found a little skeleton right where we had put the finger."

Uncle Emil was quoted more often than the other brothers, maybe because he and Ma talked and shared more than the others. Ma was fond of the story of Pearl Buckmand and it was a favorite of Amarantha's too.

Pearl Buckmand was a young girl who lived near them 'up on the farm.' She went to school with Ma and Emil but was not a particular friend of theirs or of anyone's. She just showed up for school one fall, she named one of the local Swedish women as her grandma, and became part of that eclectic gathering that made up the student body of their one room schoolhouse. She seemed to carry the curse of the Scandinavian reticence to new levels, sitting alone and removed at recesses or lunch times. She rarely offered anything during school discussion but if called upon, she did answer the teacher. Ma said she wasn't aware that there was anything particularly different about her, although she stood out amongst all the tow-headed, blue-eyed Scandinavians with her brown eyes and black, curly hair. Ma said she envied that curly hair and those dark, liquid eyes but couldn't be Pearl's friend because she refused to get close to anyone.

After a rebuff from Pearl one day, Ma brought up the subject with Emil as they walked home from school. "Pearl Buckmand is so stuck-up," she complained. "She's too good to talk to any of us and just walks away. She thinks she's better than us."

"She doesn't think she's better, she doesn't think she's as good. She's afraid of us." This from Emil, who almost sounded defensive and angry.

"But why should she be afraid of us?"

"Gill Swanson told me her Dad is a Negro from St. Paul, and that her folks sent her up here to school because the Negro kids down there teased her about being half white."

Ma said she didn't know much about Negroes, since she'd never seen one; the only ones she'd ever seen were in pictures in *Uncle Tom's Cabin* that the teacher read to them in school. But she said she felt terrible to think that Pearl belonged nowhere.

"After that I tried even harder to be her friend, but not as hard as Emil. Oh, the fights he got into if anyone even looked like they were going to tease her; and the fights he got into because the boys taunted him, asking if they should organize a *svensexa* (a bachelor meal for the bridegroom).

"Then one day Pearl's Grandma came to visit my Mother, and I sat in the background to listen to their talk over coffee. Even though my Mother tilted her head towards me and said, *Sma grytor ha ocksa oron* (Little pitchers have big ears), they let me stay. Most of their talk, conducted exclusively in Swedish, was of no interest to me, but my ears perked up when they brought up

Pearl's Mother and Dad."

Pearl's Grandma related her daughter's meeting with the mysterious Negro man in what Ma said, in her childish mind, she considered most romantic. The Grandma said, "When first he saw her on this earth, he liked her and she liked him." Then she concluded with what would not seem a lavish compliment to her different son-in-law, but nevertheless meant to say it was a good match, "And oh, they have it nice." This last line delivered with extended arms to indicate they shared the riches of the world and not a shack somewhere.

"Whatever happened to Pearl? Did she become Uncle Emil's girlfriend?" Amarantha asked Ma the first time she heard the story.

"No, It couldn't be in those days. She never married and neither did he. She quit school when she was old enough and lived on her Grandma's farm. You'd see her in town sometimes, getting supplies, but she kept to herself. She never married and, when her Grandma died, rented out the farm fields, just keeping enough land around the house for a garden and a cow. She was a recluse, just like your Uncle Emil." Ma would look sad and wistful. "Maybe if they'd married, he'd have made something of himself, and even kept the home farm." Then would come the inevitable shake of the head, as if clearing her mind of futile *might-have-beens*.

Amarantha would recall those words many times in her life and hear again the sing-song Swedish, "he liked her and she liked him, and oh they have it nice!" She thought of it again now, in terms of her recently despised and drunken Uncle Emil. How different both their lives would have been if her Uncle had been as strong as Pearl's Mother and leaped the race barrier. Then she remembered how outcast her family was just because Ma had married outside the Scandinavian community, much less into another race altogether. Maybe that was why her uncles drank so much, because they were aliens. Her cousins had once called her and her family aliens too. Is everyone an alien to someone else? Is it bad or good? How do you stop being an alien?

Amarantha felt a little sheepish. Feelings of guilt welled in her throat when she joined Ma at the table for supper. She wished she had gone forward when her Uncles offered their hands to *Ringdans* and circled with them right there on the sidewalk. But that would have taken more courage than she had. How could she expect her uncles to stand up to the whole community when she couldn't even acknowledge that they were her relatives? And would they even have recognized her or realized what a sacrifice it was for her to know them?

"I'm sorry, Ma," she said, feeling it was the least, and the best, she could do. She picked up her fork and began to mash the boiled potatoes into a shape flat enough to hold butter and salt. They ate in silence, and she vowed she would be nicer to her uncles the next time she saw them.

But deep in her heart she knew that, should she encounter them on the street again, she would probably cross to the other side, as if mere close proximity might taint her reputation.

VIX.
A Killing Frost

It was the winter of 1943. The snow storms had begun to arrive shortly after Halloween and were unrelenting throughout the months of the long winter. The only time it didn't snow was when the temperature hovered near or below zero. Then the cold sun would rise on a landscape glittering with ice and sparkling with snow crystals. Hoar frost coated every surface and the trees rubbed their branches together in the wind, making a sound like whimpering animals.

If the temperature moderated, it would snow. Amarantha knew what to expect weather-wise before she got out of bed in the morning. If it had snowed, the plows, housed at a gas station across the street from the apartment would roar to life about four a.m., their headlights making ricocheting patterns on the walls as they pulled out of the parking lot. Cold or snow: either way, life was difficult.

It was a lonely winter. Wendel had been drafted into the Navy as soon as he'd turned eighteen that October. He'd graduated from high school the previous May and spent the summer partying with his friends, sleeping late in the mornings. Ma didn't approve, but she hesitated to reprimand.

"There isn't much point in his getting a job, and I guess he deserves a little time to have fun before he has to go," she'd defend, when Aunt Alma inquired about him through pursed lips.

Ma loved all her children, but there was something in Wendel that she found herself responding to more than the others. He was unfailingly cheerful, often teasing everyone into a good mood, and he had inherited her story telling abilities, which further endeared him to her. He asked her for very little and seemed happy with what he had. That made him aces in Ma's book, since *very little* was what she had to give him.

Maybe it was guilt; she'd always said that she felt he hadn't gotten the proper food when he was a baby. Ma told of how Dr. Cornwell had called her into his office one day with a proposition. He said he knew how strapped the family was and that maybe having one less child would ease the situation. He continued that he knew a family who wanted a little boy and would be willing to adopt Wendel and give him a good home.

"What did you *say?*"an aghast Amarantha had asked the first time she heard the story.

Ma laughed and said, "I told him I couldn't do without my sunshine."

"Did anyone ever want to take me away?" Suddenly Amarantha was a little jealous, and although she would never want to leave Ma, it would have been nice to know she'd been desirable.

"Maybe they did, and they brought you back when they saw what they'd gotten," a grinning Wendel would tease.

So when he left, it seemed the last of the life had gone out of the house. His athletic prowess had been a source of pride for Amarantha and Ma. His slight build and quickness had made him a valuable player in most sports, and they'd gone to all his basketball and football games. It was the height of fun when the cheerleaders chanted, 'GRADY! GRADY!' as he stood at the free throw line, or ran down the field with the football.

Now it was a silent house, and Ma didn't go to the games any more. It didn't hold the interest for Amarantha either and simply wasn't the same when she did go with her friends.

With only the two of them left, the household routine was the same: Amarantha would come home from school and begin to fill saved, brown grocery bags with briquettes of coal, which were stored under the steps leading to their apartment. She needed about six bags to get them through the night. These were carried up the stairs and stacked beside the old furnace. If she was lucky, there would still be a few embers in the stove from the morning, and she could put a bag in and it would catch fire. Most of the time she was unsuccessful in this endeavor and would have to wait in the cold until Ma came home and worked her alchemy with the kindling and matches.

Her next duties were peeling potatoes, immersing them in cold water until it was closer to supper time, and organizing the rest of the meal. There was wartime rationing, and they had a book of stamps which were counted out with the money at the grocery store. Since it was only the two of them, they weren't allotted many red points for fresh meat. Consequently, Ma and Amarantha ate a lot of Spam, Polish sausages, tuna, and tinned meats of many varieties. Because of these days, Amarantha would forever carry an aversion to processed or canned meats.

One frigid morning they woke to a freezing cold apartment. The undependable coal stove had gone out in the night. As Ma struggled to get a fire going, Amarantha ran to the bathroom, where she discovered that all the pipes were frozen: first, when she tried to flush the toilet and again, when she turned on a faucet. "You'll have to run across the street to the gas station toilet," Ma said. Amarantha dressed in her coat and boots over her pajamas and took a soap and towel. She got the key from a man in the station office and opened the tiny bathroom. Heat poured out of a vent in the wall, and it was pleasingly warm when she closed the door and brushed her teeth and washed in hot water right out of the faucet. Their apartment had only cold water, making bathing and dishes time consuming chores requiring the heating of pans of water on the kerosene stove.

Amarantha assumed that Ma would report the frozen pipes and water would be restored by the time she got home after school; but that night when she turned on the faucet for the potatoes, she heard clanking noise, but no water. "They didn't thaw the pipes," she reported as soon as Ma came from work.

"I didn't have time to tell them. Here, take the tea kettle. I'll take a couple pans and we'll get some water from the gas station."

Ten minutes later, they struggled up the stairs, the water lapping over the edges of the pans as they climbed.

And so the routine continued all that winter. Magically the gas station bathroom remained unlocked and warm. Had Ma arranged it with the owner, somehow? If she had time to do that, why didn't she report the frozen pipes to the landlord and have them thawed? Amarantha questioned Ma at first, but then it became a sore point and she didn't want to bring it up. Carrying water became another after school chore. Did Ma think the landlord would blame her and make her pay for something? Was she so used to putting up with adversity that it didn't occur to her to complain?

The subject was never brought up again.

Then it happened, on a bitterly cold night. They had just finished supper and were waiting for the dishpan of water to heat on the stove when they heard footsteps on the stairs. They thought it was Aunt Alma, as she was practically their only visitor. Ma said, "What on earth is she doing out on a night like this?" and went to open the door before she was even at the top of the stairs.

It wasn't Aunt Alma. The local telegraph agent stood in the open door, looking devastated and desperate with this new wartime duty of his.

"Sorry, Mrs. Grady," he said, as he handed Ma the familiar yellow telegram and fled down the stairs. Ma had gotten a telegram before when Harold was wounded, and she ripped at this one savagely, hoping that the news would be the same. *Wounded* meant away from the fighting and coming home. Two more sons remained in harms way: John and Wendel. Which one was it?

Amarantha stood rooted as the paper fell from Ma's hand and she collapsed into a chair. Her face had turned chalky and her mouth was slack. Her eyes registered the fever of extreme pain. "He's dead," she said quietly, "My *lille poike* is dead."

When Amarantha heard that Swedish phrase, she knew it was Wendel, because that was how Ma often referred to him, *lille poike*, my little boy.

There were things to be done. Arrangements to be made.

Comings and goings in the house. Wendel's name was in the New Scandia paper, which every week listed the local wounded and dead. They even did a story and the headline read, "Local Athlete Killed in Action!"

Many people remembered Wendel from the high school sports, some from various jobs he had held throughout his school years. People brought scarce cuts of meat, which neither Amarantha nor Ma could eat, as if sacrificing something precious would convey how sorry they were.

And then, everyone went away. The war continued to go badly, and Wendel was forgotten when other local boys were wounded or killed. Amarantha found tears coming to her eyes at odd times. Sometimes when she watched a basketball game, she heard again in her mind the chanting, *'Grady! Grady'* and she'd stoop to tie her shoe until she could recover. Often at night she'd awake to the sound of Ma's squeaky rocker.

Once, she'd gone to her, and when Ma saw her in the doorway, she said, "I was never able to give him what I wanted to." Amarantha had shared her grief by returning to bed and silently crying into her pillow.

Above all, we must not show emotion, she'd think, *because that would bring embarrassment to the family.*

Gradually the weather improved, along with the war news. The sun was higher in the sky, the days lengthened, and melted snow dripped from the roofs to form overnight, long dagger-like icicles.

Miraculously, John was sent back to the States and was able to get leave. His homecoming seemed to do wonders for Ma. Amarantha could hear their soft voices after she'd gone to bed, talking....*talking.* Ma was letting out her grief to another adult who had also loved Wendel. Amarantha was sorry she couldn't be that relief for Ma, but understood that she, herself, needed more comfort than she could give.

Amarantha's spirits rose one day after school when she came outside to find a strong sun shining on rivers of melting snow. The sound of water dripping, running, splashing, was everywhere, and she ran out of joy, mindless of the puddles and mud. When she went to get the pans for carrying water, she noticed that the abandoned sink faucet was dripping brown drops of liquid into the sink. Slowly she turned the tap, as if any sudden movement might discourage the flow, and was rewarded with hissing, spouting pipes that eventually yielded a steady stream of water.

She waited impatiently for Ma to get home from work. The potatoes were boiling and there were hamburger patties. She met her at the door with the greeting, "The water pipes thawed, It's running again."

Then, as a sign that the long, difficult winter was at last over, Ma and Amarantha celebrated the return of spring with a long, unaccustomed hug.

"Maybe the sunshine has come back," Amarantha ventured. But Ma just smiled and shook her head.

X.
A Time To Forgive

Harold did eventually return from the war, wounded in body and broken in spirit. He was thin and nervous and walked with a pronounced limp, even with the aid of a cane. Shrapnel had lodged in his spine in places that proved to be too risky for removal. An army doctor told him he was lucky.

"If you hadn't been a growing boy" (age 19 when he was wounded) "you wouldn't be walking at all."

And so he was discharged with promises of life-long pain whenever the shrapnel shifted and a small monthly stipend *'For his sacrifice on behalf of his country.'* His psychological wounds, which proved to be more serious than the physical, went unnoticed and untreated, maybe because, like all the Gradys, he was adept at hiding any emotion and taught not to complain.

He was the first service man to be wounded from their small town, and many considered him a war hero. He enjoyed a certain celebrity in the local bars where he was rewarded with drinks and congratulatory slaps on the back. Only Ma and an older and wiser Amarantha saw how fragile he was and heard the outpouring of his war experiences when he would leave the bar a jovial drunk and lurch up the apartment stairs, unable to contain the tears and the horror that poured out, as if a safety valve had been suddenly opened. And so he took up his civilian life where he had left it: drinking and, in Ma's opinion, *'hanging out with a bad crowd.'*

It was now 1944, and the war was, at last, favoring the Allies. Harold spent a good deal of his time listening to the news on the radio and commenting on the troops' progress (or lack of) with bitterness and profanity, almost as if he wished he were there.

"*Sure, liberate, liberate! March into Paris! Those sons-a-bitches did-*
n't have to spend weeks layin' in the mud for nothin'! Shit!"

He'd prop his bad leg on a chair and open beer after beer, his
tirade becoming more vehement, but less coherent, as the empty
bottles accumulated.

One late afternoon, Mr. Peterson, the same Mr. Peterson who
used to distribute *the relief,* knocked on the door. With the economic prosperity of the war his job with the welfare department
had become redundant; but he had managed to land a real position with the Northern States Power Company when some of their
men had been drafted into the services. Because of his ingratiating
ways, and being an opportunist, he had risen in whatever ranks
the small town office afforded, and was now a vice president.

His face was flushed from the exertion of climbing the steep
stairs to their apartment, and he carefully cleaned his forehead
with a large, white handkerchief. Momentarily, Amarantha's mind
returned to their farmhouse kitchen where, years ago, Wendel
mimicked him wiping his face after the rotten egg pelting.

"I've come to see the war hero!" he boomed jovially. "Actually,
I've got some business with him!" He talked with exclamation
points, and his loud voice reverberated off the walls of the low
ceilinged room. He was obviously proud of having made the trip
personally instead of sending a subordinate or phoning; or maybe
he tried to phone and found they didn't have one. He advanced
toward Harold's chair with his hand extended. "I'm happy to make
your acquaintance, son! Let me congratulate you on the effort
you've put forth on our behalf!"

Amarantha noticed eight or nine bottles littering the floor
where Harold sat; his eyes didn't focus, and she could tell he had
a *snootful.*

"Oh, I've met you before."

Harold's voice had taken on a nasty edge that had become all
too familiar to them since his return.

"Is that so? I don't remember!" Mr. Peterson was unsuspecting
and vulnerable. Why *would* he expect an attack when he was on a

good will mission? Amarantha wanted to warn him, to quietly tell him to leave. He was nothing to her. She had seen him on the street, at church, or through the tinted windows of The Power Company, but the local caste system didn't allow him to actually speak to her or Ma:; it was what she understood and accepted.

But now she saw him as a great, bumbling animal about to be ambushed by another who possessed the cunning and passion of the damaged and impaired, and she viewed the anticipated cruelty of the confrontation as something that must be avoided at all costs.

Ma was evidently of the same opinion, as she suddenly stepped in front of Harold and clasped the outstretched hand, visibly embarrassed at her own audacity. "Harold's not having too good a day, Mr. Peterson.."

"What d'ya mean? I'm havin' a *great* day! We're whippin' ass in Europe, and Mr. Peterson is kissin' ass here! What more could I ask?"

Mr. Peterson looked confused, but was determined to continue with his original errand. "Yes, yes! Great news these days. God willing it will soon all be over, which is what I came to talk to you about, son."

"You came to talk about God? Is he a personal friend of yours? 'Cause if he is, I got a few questions I want you to ask him. Like, where he was when I watched the guy next to me get his head blown off? Or, why have I got a back and leg full of shrapnel that they can't take out?" Harold had lurched from his chair and stumbled, only partially because of his bad leg, toward Mr. Peterson.

"No, actually, in the spirit of rewarding and thanking our returning servicemen for their sacrifices, I came to offer you a chance of employment within the family of the Northern States Power Company."

The exclamations had gone out of his voice, and the whole statement was delivered tentatively, as if he were a small boy, uncertain of the words, reading a passage from a book. He had paled and stared, not afraid...more in awe of what he saw and heard.

"You slimy bastard! How come we never got any rewards or thanks when you were handin' out the wormy cornmeal or rotten eggs? That's where I met you before! I had to take your handouts then, but I sure as hell don't have to take them now, so take your *chance of employment* and shove it up your fat ass!"

For an instant, everyone froze. It seemed to Amarantha that even the clock stopped ticking. Then Mr. Peterson, a seasoned survivor, turned and in two steps was out the door. As for Harold, the outburst had expended his alcohol depleted energy, and he sank back into the chair, tears of self-pity falling on his cheeks and a steady stream of vitriolic obscenities slurring from his lips.

Amarantha had never seen Ma as angry. Her hand whipped through the air and landed with a sharp clap on Harold's face.

"How dare you embarrass me and our name by acting like that? Haven't you grown-up or learned anything? I've been letting you be because I know you've been through a lot, but the babying stops here and now. If you aren't going to take his job, you better find another one, because you're not lying around here drinking!" Ma's face was scalded red with fury.

"You don't have to say it," Harold spat, "you wish I'd been killed instead of Wendel!" It was an accusation he'd made drunkenly many times before and, eventually, no one bothered to argue with him. He dragged himself to his makeshift bed in the only other room in the apartment where they all slept. They soon heard his loud, wet snoring, and Amarantha felt as if she had been holding her breathe since the episode had begun, and could now exhale loudly and gratefully. Ma trembled as she poured a cup of coffee from the pot on the kerosene stove.

Neither of them felt strong enough to discuss what had happened but quietly went about their evening's business, stepping politely aside for each other when their paths crossed and speaking in hushed voices when it was absolutely necessary to communicate. It was as if there had been a death in the house; a point of no return had been crossed; an ultimatum had been issued. Ma's dignity, preserved through years with a drunken husband, had been dealt yet another blow.

Appearances were everything to her, and now Harold had peeled back the façade she so carefully layered over years of personal example and dutiful acceptance of her role in society and exposed the Gradys as coarse, embittered, and vengeful. They were trash! Just like so many others!

Amarantha awoke later that night to the squeak of Ma's rocker. She could see her through a crack in the curtain which served as a door from the bedroom. Her face was expressionless and empty, and she kept muttering, *'What's the use?'* over and over. Harold turned and belched loudly in his sleep.

"I hate you," she thought, surprised to hear that she had whispered it out loud. She closed her eyes and tried to fall back to sleep. *I wonder if that relief cornmeal was really wormy like Harold said,* she mused, half asleep but remembering (a bit uneasily) how much she had enjoyed that hot *johnny cake* at those long ago suppers.

Harold got a job tending bar at a local night club and was home very little. Amarantha was often awakened late at night when he'd come home from work. Sober, he was quiet; drunk, he was noisy and inconsiderate. He slept late in the morning, so Amarantha went off to school before he was up and didn't come home until he'd gone to work again. He spent his free time elsewhere; but it was generally known around town that he was a hard drinking, good-natured party boy. He was polite, but didn't talk much to either of them, and although Ma tried to talk to him about going to school on the GI Bill, he put her off and avoided them both as much as he could, which suited Amarantha just fine.

One Sunday afternoon, Ma and Amarantha were getting ready to go to the matinee at the local movie theater when they heard footsteps on the stairs. Harold hadn't been home for several nights, but they didn't think it was he, because he always came home alone.

However, it was Harold, accompanied by a slightly chubby girl who looked to be about eighteen years old. She wore brilliant fuchsia-colored lipstick and nail polish and revealed an ample bosom over the top of a see-through blouse. She smiled, confidently flashing large white teeth, and guffawed loudly over some remarks made as they opened the door.

"This is Amy and Ma," Harold said when he saw them standing in the middle of the room. "This is my wife, Elinor."

They were speechless and immobile, but Elinor immediately
rushed to embrace each of them in turn, crushing them to the soft
pillows of her breasts and filling their nostrils with strong, but not
unpleasant, perfume. Elinor couldn't have known their family reticence at touching or outwardly expressing emotion; only in
extreme instances did they hug. But her smile only widened and
she announced, "Nice to meet you, Ma, Amy!"

Automatically, Ma rushed to do the one thing she knew in
times of crisis: she filled the coffee pot and positioned it over the
flame on the kerosene stove. Amarantha remembered that they all
smiled and said little until the brew was at last done and they
could sit together, their cups clutched tightly as lifelines, making
small talk.

They talked about where the two had met (at the tavern where
Harold worked); where her family lived (on a farm outside of
town); who her relations were (several Ma knew vaguely); and
other such superficial sharings of strangers.

"We're goin' out to her folk's farm to tell them now," Harold
finally offered, "so we'll probably spend the night there. But I was
wonderin' if we could stay here with you until we can get on our
feet? It's easier, bein' closer to work and all."

"We don't have it very nice here," Ma started.

Elinor interrupted any further excuses with, "Don't worry
about that. I'm not used to fancy, and it won't be for long."

Looking shell-shocked, Ma said, "I guess it would be okay if
you don't expect much." Before she could utter another word,
Elinor was upon her with another hug, this time accompanied by
a loud kiss to the cheek.

"You're the best, Ma!" she called over her shoulder as she
turned to the door. Ma took Harold's arm as he started to follow
and attempted to engage him in a whispered conversation as he
edged away.

"If you have a wife, you're gonna have to straighten up, quit drinkin', and get a decent job."

But the belated wedding advice fell on deaf ears, as he put up his hands in mock defense and whispered back, "Ya, Ya, I know. Now quit your preachin'!"

As the footsteps faded down the stairs, Ma and Amarantha looked at each other in dismay.

"Where will they sleep?" Amarantha asked. The bedroom housed a double bed, where Ma and Amarantha slept and a rickety, metal daybed where Wendel had slept before he went into the service and where Harold had slept since he came home.

"They'll have to have the double bed. I'll open up the daybed, and you and I'll sleep there." She started pulling boxes out from their storage places, finding sheets and blankets Amarantha didn't even know they had. "Clear out that dresser. She'll have to have some place to put her things."

And so the movie was forgotten as the rest of the afternoon and evening was spent moving everything aside to make room for the newest family member, or whom Ma referred to as, *'Harold's latest folly.'*

Amarantha was happy that it was summer and she didn't have to go to school the next day. She wouldn't have missed the moving in for anything in the world. She was up early waiting for them to show up, and was just about to give up around noon when she heard slow and heavy footsteps on the stairs. Harold entered first, limping and dragging a belted suitcase with one hand and carrying a six pack of beer in the other. "What the hell you got in here, anyways?" He sounded cross, and Amarantha wondered if he'd been drinking already.

"Now, honey, I've gotta have my things." Elinor was smiling broadly (a common expression for her, although Amarantha would come to know that it was all-purpose and didn't necessarily reflect any emotion at all). "Hi, Kiddo! How's tricks? Wanna help me find a place for all this junk?"

She deposited a couple garment bags on the now expanded daybed and plunked an oversized makeup case on top of the dresser. Harold headed for the ice box where he stored his beer, then came to lean against the door frame, watching her as he opened a bottle. Soon both beds were covered with sweaters, underwear, magazines, and oddly shaped containers of makeup.

"You gonna leave any place to sleep," Harold asked, grinning lazily.

"Oh, I'm not gonna forget that," she cooed, and she threw her arms around his neck and gave him a long, hard kiss - the kind you saw in the movies. Amarantha didn't know where to look and felt her cheeks redden in a blush.

"Oh, hey! We're embarrassing your little sister. You got a boyfriend, honey? Do you kiss him like that?" She laughed and tickled Amarantha until she smiled and moved away.

I think you meant to embarrass me, Amarantha thought, but she looked at her shoes and kept silent.

And so began the era of living with newlyweds.

Elinor kept pretty much the same schedule as her husband, even though she didn't have a job. They both slept late, then drank a lot of coffee, listened to Elinor's portable radio, and read magazines until it was time for Harold to get ready for his bartending job. While he shaved and put on a fresh, white shirt (laundered by Ma), she washed her hair, selected the evening's costume, and applied her makeup. She left with him everyday; and sat at the bar with him until he closed at 1 a.m. Sometimes they were both drunk and silly when they came home. Sometimes only Harold was drunk, then they would argue in exaggerated whispers as if they were really trying to keep from waking their roommates. The worst for Amarantha was when they felt amorous and made love loudly (for Elinor was not one to hold back), causing the old double bed to creak rhythmically.

It was the forties, and Amarantha was thirteen. She wasn't sure she had all the right information about sex because what she knew had been surreptitiously scraped together from chance remarks, learned at slumber parties, or by eavesdropping on adults. She knew that Ma was under the impression that she knew the facts of life, and it had been easier to let her think that somehow, through osmosis, heavenly revelation, or whatever, her daughter possessed the knowledge of a woman.

The truth was, Amarantha did know what she considered the animalistic and seamy side of sex but preferred to think of it in terms of Betty Grable kissing (the way Elinor kissed Harold) Jimmy Stewart and shyly informing him that they were going to have a baby, to which he would react jubilantly, swinging her off her feet, then setting her down gently with a worried look. Whereupon, he would be assured that she was perfectly healthy and, after a quick hug, go off to war looking handsome and determined to make the world a better place for his son (would his first child even dare to be a girl?).

But night after night of the long, cold winter, that happy image was pretty much shattered as she lay stiffly beside Ma on their wobbly daybed and listened to the moaning and grunting not four feet away. In retrospect, Amarantha thought that maybe it had been good for her to abandon her unrealistic ideas; but shock treatment has a way of leaving burns, and even though she would come to know better, deep in her heart she always thought of lovemaking as toppling from a higher plane or giving in to baser instincts.

Worst of all, after successfully suppressing it for years, she was again reminded of the first sexual encounter of her life, and it had been with the same man who was now uttering soft, cajoling tones in the next bed. Could she be jealous? The thought revolted her.

After all, it had only been a series of touching, and she had been so young. And try as she may, she couldn't hate Harold. No one could deny that he was prone to bad behavior, but sober, he was a friendly, easy-going brother who had always been kind and generous, never attempting to repeat the *coach ride*. Amarantha was fairly certain he had forgotten it, or at least thought she didn't remember it. But she remembered every detail vividly, and sometimes she wondered, in her sexual ignorance, if she were still a virgin. At a slumber party her friend Bonnie had said a man could tell if a woman was a virgin, and that all men wanted to marry virgins. Maybe she would never be able to get married. And what would Ma, or the slumber party girls, think of her if they knew?

All of this swirled in her brain as she lay unmoving, so as to make Ma, whom she knew also lay awake and listening, think she was asleep. Sometimes it was hard to get back to sleep even when the lovers lay sated and snoring. The result was a dull student in school the next day.

"What's wrong, Amarantha?" her eighth grade teacher asked. "Your grades are down. It's not like you."

"It's nothing, Mrs. Lien. It's just that I'm up all night witnessing the mating ritual of a resident Homo Sapiens." That was what was on her mind, but of course, Amarantha quit talking after the first sentence and dutifully added, "I'll try to do better."

It was uncertain as to whether it could be attributed to the lack of sleep, the bitter winter, or just an errant virus (pretty much unheard of in those days); but Amarantha got very sick in March. A bad kidney infection kept her in bed for weeks until the doctor finally tried a new miracle drug on her, and sulpha (developed during the war to use on the troops) produced a cure. It was during that time, however, that Amarantha saw another side of her brother and his wife.

During the first days of her illness, Amarantha was too miserable to be aware of much more than the iciness of the cold cloths administered to bring down the fever and the occasional spooning of broth into her mouth. But Ma had to go to work, and to Amarantha's surprise, Elinor started appearing beside her daybed with the cold compresses, cool water, and later the tiny wonder pills. There would be that big smile and the teasing voice, "You better take this medicine, honey. You don't look so good, and your boyfriend's not gonna like that."

"I don't have a boyfriend," Amarantha croaked, "I'm too ugly!"

"Now you ain't ugly! Get that right out of your mind. You just need a little help. All us girls do. When you're feelin' better, I'm gonna show you how to put on some makeup and fix your hair. You just wait. Now swallow this pill and I'll peel you an orange."

And she was true to her word. She stopped going to the bar with Harold and stayed home until Ma came from work. Some afternoons they spent working together on Amarantha's makeover. They applied brilliant blue eye shadow to her lids, drew new black and shapely eyebrows over her own white, wispy ones, brushed her eyelashes with a black brush until they looked like two spiders crouching on her lids, and contoured her lips with an orangish lipstick, *because that goes good with your reddish hair.*

The first time Ma saw the finished product, she got a pinched look and went for a soapy washcloth.

"Oh, Oh," Elinor whispered with her big smile, "from now on we'll wash it off before she comes home." And she giggled and hugged Amarantha to that bosom which strained at a tight, red sweater: a gesture that grew more and more comforting as time passed.

Some afternoons she'd just play the radio and gyrate crazily around the sickbed. *Goodman and Kaiser and Miller – They make things all right! Juke Box Saturday Night!*

"I'm gonna teach you to jitterbug as soon as you're better," she'd promise, as she twirled and kicked, her bosom flopping in time to the music.

Even Harold seemed different. He spent hours playing Monopoly with Amarantha and brought ice cream home - a real treat since their apartment had only an icebox. All in all, Amarantha remembered that illness as a fun time in her life.

Money we really don't need that, we'll make out all right - Lettin' the other guy feed that - Juke Box Saturday Night!

But all good things must come to an end, and soon Amarantha was well again, and the young couple resumed their usual schedule of spending most of their time at the bar. But Amarantha always would remember how they had cared for her, and that in itself helped to erase the bad feelings of the past and made future transgressions easier to forgive.

Elinor would always have a place in her heart. She was outgoing and friendly, completely uninhibited. In short, everything the Gradys weren't. Her skirts were short, her heels were high, and her general flamboyance was captivating. Amarantha admired her lack of reserve which, in the Gradys was often labeled as *cold.*

That's why her indiscretion came as a blow, and Amarantha bristled instantly at Ma's reaction.

"I knew this would happen. She's too young and irresponsible, and you're not much better!"

This accusation was flung at Harold who sat in the living room, tears slowly brimming from his eyes. He was sober, and he usually didn't cry unless he was drunk.

"I just didn't see it comin'," he said, "she started leavin' the bar, but I thought she was goin' home or gettin' a burger with her girl-friends. Then I saw her goin' out the back door with him one night just before I closed. She says she wants a divorce."

At this point, his tears became sobs. The news was devastating, but Amarantha was absolutely flabbergasted to see Ma cross the room and cradle Harold's head in her arms, her hands smoothing his hair and her fingertips collecting his tears to wipe on the bib of her apron. As unlikely as it seemed, maybe they had all learned a little about expressing love from the hapless Elinor.

He left town and never returned, nor did Amarantha ever see him again. He hugged her before he left and whispered, "I'm sorry," into her ear.

Amarantha cried then and Ma comforted her.

"I guess he still loves you best," she assured.

Ma made several trips to various places throughout the country over the years to see Harold, and always had pictures of his family. But she also alluded darkly to his drinking and abusing or abandoning his family at various intervals, always adding quietly and regretfully, "He's just like Pa."

The telephone rang one evening in Amarantha's sixtieth year, and Elsie told her of their brother Harold's death in an obscure southern town. When she'd replaced the receiver, she felt again the familiar burning in her chest, now much duller with time and experience.

She waited by the phone, thinking, for a few minutes, then went to rummage in a storage closet. She sat under the hanging light fixture at the dining room table with a box of old pictures. Holding a pile of yellowing photographs in one hand, she looked at each in turn, flipping them back into the box when she had fin-ished. The last in the pile was a picture of Harold taken on some army post. He wore a uniform and overseas cap, but looked like a little boy dressed as G.I. Joe for Halloween.

His eyes were large and guileless, set in an open, freckled face with a high forehead - many of the same features she saw reflect-ed in her mirror - but she looked a second longer into those blue eyes. Knowing the disappointments and disasters of his life, at that moment it seemed as though she could see into his soul and read his darkest thoughts.

"I cannot cope with life. I refuse to control it, but rather, act on impulse without thinking of the consequences of my actions to myself or those I love. I have no will power, so I do what I want and can never be blamed for poor choices because none of my actions are ever premeditat-ed. I blame the war, my injury, Elinor, my never getting a break, and my abusive Pa for all my woes. I lived my life without ever intentionally harming anyone (except for the war), was known as a good guy to casu-al acquaintances, and didn't complain. My conscience is therefore clear."

Amarantha turned the face in the picture against her breast. *Who knows what makes us the way we are,* she thought. Sometimes, she'd wondered why she'd harbored and belabored the *coach ride* for so many years. Was it really so awful? Why couldn't she let it go? Why couldn't an older, educated Amarantha realize that young boys sometimes can't control their urges when hormones surge through their adolescent bodies? But her eldest brother had never given in to any of those urges with her, nor had her beloved Wendel.

If Ma hadn't stressed the good/bad girl morality, it might never have been more than a bad dream to me, she pondered. But betrayal and shame can never be forgotten.

Then she remembered her Ma's words to her. "Only those we care about can betray us, and if we love them, we have to forgive them."

Then, whether in grief for her dear Ma or the remembrance of the young brother who, *'Loved her the best,'* she sat back and cried.

"I forgive you," she whispered to the picture.

XI.
Becoming Amy

Woodland College

Small, private colleges are like large, rowdy families; and the different departments within the confines of the hallowed halls are the children: competitive, greedy, argumentative, ruthless, sweet, manipulative, altruistic, dissatisfied - what you would expect to see in any large group where it is necessary to vie for attention, recognition, and rewards. Add a shortage of funds and the competition becomes intense indeed. To their credit, however, colleges (like families) *circle the wagons* when attacked from the outside. It is to everyone's advantage, not to mention necessary for survival.

With this picture of a typical private college in mind, we examine Woodland College, located among the pines of Wisconsin near the Canadian border. It was founded in the 1890s by a group of well-meaning protestant clergy. Its original mission was to provide spiritual inspiration and higher education to the young people in the northern tier of states who chose (out of personal lifestyle preference, lack of funds, or fear of leaving) to eliminate or postpone the move to larger colleges in the big cities.

In the beginning, its students sang hymns while they cleared land and conjugated Latin verbs in makeshift classrooms. And miraculously Woodland grew, thanks to the missionary zeal of those same enterprising ministers. Eventually churches of like denomination throughout the country found it more rewarding to send money and missionary barrels of outdated textbooks and clothing to their *'children in the northern wilderness'* than to ship the same to villages in 'heathen countries.' They didn't realize that the college students' perplexity and then laughter that followed the removal of celluloid collars and high button shoes from these barrels was surprisingly akin to that displayed by their counterparts in Darkest Africa.

The biggest and best result of the church affiliation, however, was the unexpected creation of a truly unique student body. Originally, eastern churches embraced their brothers in the hinterlands, and what started as a mission for these erudite and often condescending institutions evolved into a student feeder for Woodland. When the mission barrels stopped arriving, a gradually increasing flow of eastern hopefuls, flush with the prospect of pioneering in the wilderness, began matriculating with the local scholars.

As is the case with most mixed marriages, both entities assimilated many of the other's traits, resulting in a group that possessed the survival instincts of both an urban dweller, who fought for space and a voice in the crowds, and a north woods dweller, who endured the elements and isolation for the sake of nature's beauty and a simple lifestyle.

After World War II and the advent of The GI Bill, many colleges, largely inhabited by women during the war years, were once again becoming co-ed. With unlimited federal funds and lofty career goals in mind, many prospective students chose to attend prestigious colleges in locations that offered greater cultural opportunities than the north land. A few local GIs did choose Woodland, but, for the most part, it remained a small outpost (fewer than 1000 students) struggling to maintain the practices and standards of large universities.

Now, in 1950, the spiritual inspiration had become minimal, although the college still operated under an umbra of the founding fathers' legacy, which added the burden of factoring morality into the in-fighting and academic back-stabbing. Woodland had done well in the rationalization department, however, and many ill-conceived deeds with far-reaching consequences were dismissed as, 'For the good of the college and the Glory of God.'

Into this heady atmosphere (seemingly reserved and focused but inwardly teeming with personal agendas) came the innocent Amarantha, under the sponsorship of the New Scandia Congregational Church Ladies Aid Society. The minister and his wife drove her the 150 miles to the campus, the furthest she'd ever been from home. For some reason, Ma hadn't been invited to ride along, but stood waving at the bottom of the apartment stairs, her chin trembling from the effort of keeping her tears back. It certainly wouldn't be acceptable to cry, and Amarantha as well struggled in her own way to keep from displaying outward emotion.

As they drove north, she began to have reservations about her decision. The landscape grew wilder and more devoid of habitation. She thought of Ma, now all alone in their rooms over the tavern, and wished she had chosen the state college closer to home that most of the New Scandia High School graduates attended.

But she'd been determined to start a new life in a place where no one knew her. If she could escape the caste system of the small town, the shabby reputation of her family (in spite of Ma's struggling protection), and the fetters of past relationships, mistakes, and choices, she knew she could become the person she wanted to be and enjoy success and recognition.

She'd taken the first step by signing all official papers 'Amy.' *Amarantha* was in her past, along with the Person relatives and her former existence. But now, as she stood in her empty dormitory room, she felt sick deep in the pit of her stomach and longed for all the familiar *disadvantages* of home.

She was woefully early for check-in and hoped Rev. Wilson and his wife would suggest a tour of the town or a bite to eat; but they had seemed anxious to leave, glancing at their watches and making comments about the long ride home. And when she urged them not to worry about her, they finally left, to her mixture of relief and apprehension, and she was left alone in what seemed like a huge room, sitting on the bare mattress of a narrow metal bed. Every movement (and sometimes when there was no movement at all) produced an echoing sound that resounded from floor to floor along the empty halls.

The dormitory was a grand, old, three-storied brick building of Gothic style with dormered windows and multi-paned glass. Amarantha would come to love it and remember it all her life as one of the places where she was the happiest. But now that *pit of the stomach* feeling that she would endure intermittently for weeks threatened to overcome her and send her running after the Reverend in order to hitch a ride home. But that would be too embarrassing to endure, so she took a deep breath, snapped open the old trunk that Ma had lined with a calico print, took out her new sheets, and began to make up her bed.

She had worked all summer at the local canning factory to buy *things* for college: sheets, towels, a decent bathrobe, a few items of clothing. She looked at them now, piled carefully, folded and stiff, waiting for her to begin her new life. She worked slowly, smoothing each wrinkle and executing precise hospital corners.

She had just finished when she heard voices in the hall arguing loudly about the room numbers and a woman's voice cautioning against dropping anything. A girl and what Amarantha assumed were her parents stumbled into the room, satchels hanging from their elbows and suitcases in hand. The man deposited his load and left breathlessly, announcing he was making another trip to the car.

The room was suddenly much smaller. The college had sent each girl the name and address of her roommate, so they had written over the summer, but not met until now. Tina was dark-complexioned, tan, and looked good in her khaki shorts and red blouse. Amarantha unconsciously smoothed the skirt of her Sunday dress, feeling overdressed and awkward.

"Hi, I'm Tina," came the greeting, a tan, outstretched hand gripping her's strongly.

Amarantha tried to exude as much confidence, and was fascinated momentarily by the contrast of Tina's hand to her own, pale and freckled. She knew that her handshake was weak, and her greeting came out a mumbled, "Hi, I'm Amarantha," forgetting in her flustered state that she was now *Amy*.

"What an unusual name," the mother smiled. "Is it a family

name? Or an ethnic name?"

"Not really...I mean, yes...Well, it's sort of a flower...It was my Mother's idea...I don't know--"

"Ah, yes! Mothers will have their ideas about daughters, won't they?"

Tina smiled at her mother, but her eyes rolled and her head shook in mock frustration.

"Now don't start, Tina!" Her mother almost whispered this in a tight voice and her face had turned hard and combative. "Can't we get through one day, your last day?"

"Sure, Ma."

"And don't call me 'Ma'!

Amarantha made a mental note not to refer to her Ma that way; evidently it wasn't proper.

"All right, Mother dear, now will you quit the inquisition of my roommate and give her a chance to talk? So, you got a nickname? I'm good at nicknames if you want one."

"I like to be called Amy," Amarantha managed to assert.

"Great, I like it! Amy it is and ever shall be!"

She pretended to dub Amarantha with an imaginary sword, and *Amy* breathed a sigh of relief with the first hurdle of her new life cleared. From then until the parents took their leave, Tina's mother stayed in the background, folding and refolding stacks of underwear and reminding her returned husband that they had a long ride home. It seemed almost like a conspiracy, this concerted fixation by parents/ministers, et cetera, to suddenly put miles between them and their charges.

Tina presented an entirely different face to her father, who was quiet and kindly mannered. It became apparent that he and his daughter were the best of friends, as she lovingly teased him and asked his advice about her check book and other financial matters, calling him *Daddy*.

When the girls were alone, they began to unpack their belongings. Tina hoisted the first of her set of matched *Samsonite* luggage onto the bed and released the clasp. It was so tightly packed that it literally exploded, scattering clothes over the bare mattress, when she opened it. Amy with one swipe, lifted her clothes onto her bed from the cardboard (colored to look like leather) suitcase that Ma had given her as a graduation present, and pushed it with her foot under the bed before Tina saw it. She had told Ma she wanted luggage, but realized she should have been more specific when a beaming Ma presented her with the gift.

"Wow! That's a neat old trunk!"

Amy stepped in front of the trunk, but Tina walked around her and fingered the ornate trim and weathered wooden panels. "It's just an old thing my Mom had," she explained. "I'll keep it in the closet."

"It's beautiful! Let's use it as a coffee table. I saw that in a magazine. Let's go find some more furniture, there's gotta be more than this somewhere."

They wandered down the hall, opening doors as they went, and eventually found a room crowded with chests of drawers, tables and chairs. The next couple hours were spent moving two of everything they could find into their room. Tina talked constantly about high school, her friends, who had cute nicknames, and with whom she'd had fabulous, outrageous times together, all her dates and dances.

Amy had high school friends, but had never been one of the pretty, popular girls boys dated and took to dances. Her experience was a platonic matter. The boys on the debate team thought she was a good partner and even some of the athletes valued her friendship because she was always willing to share class notes or help with assignments. Occasionally, they even asked her advice as to what Christmas gift or what corsage for the prom they should get their *girls*. She did her best to be *just one of the boys*, without ever revealing that these encounters were humiliating for her. Oh, she went to prom - with her debate partner. They doubled with her friend Lynn and another debater and really had a wonderful time. They were comfortable with each other and laughed and joked the night away.

But when they danced, stiff and halting as they struggled with the steps, she would watch the girls with real dates holding each other closely and swaying to the music or kissing in the shadows, and she envied the romance. That's the way proms were supposed to be. That's the way they were in the movies and in *Seventeen* magazine.

She had read somewhere, however, that college men were more mature and valued a woman for many more attributes than popularity or looks, and it was her fervent wish that this would prove to be true here in the piney woods of northern Wisconsin. As a sign of her faith in this theory, she had devoted a portion of the carefully spent college money to a silky, navy blue dress with white polka dots that, in her mind, became her *date dress,* deemed truly essential on the 'College Wardrobe List' that was published in the 1950 August issue of *Seventeen.*

Amy and Tina worked on their room and settled for duplicate furniture arrangement: beds side-by-side, drawers on the opposite wall, desks and chairs bedside. The trunk held a place of honor between their beds, and Amy felt flattered when Tina arranged some of her knickknacks and magazines on it. For Amy, this would be the first time she had not shared a bed and chest of drawers with Ma, and she marveled at the luxury of a personal closet and shower stalls with running hot water. These were perks she brought to mind in the weeks to come, when she found herself in the throes of homesickness.

The next few weeks were hectic but painful for a shy girl because of the newness of everything. She had been recognized in high school for certain skills: grades, various extra-curricular activities, and the simple fact that she knew her classmates well, since she'd been with them from kindergarten.

Now the very thing she'd wanted, to start anew, threatened to relegate her to the loser ranks before anyone even got to know her. And that surely would have happened if it hadn't been for the irrepressible Tina. It didn't matter where they were or who was there, she was offering that tan, firm handshake, rattling off a brief personal vita, and pulling Amy forward.

"And this is Amy."

They didn't slink into the back row of the daily general assemblies (labeled *Chapel* as a bow to the founding fathers) as Amy probably would have, but marched past the eyes of countless students to the front row. They frequented the Student Center, squeezing into crowded tables in order to drink cokes and absorb the gems of wisdom carelessly dropped by the upper classmen. Amy learned to laugh when they did, even though she frequently didn't get the jokes. They referred to the college as 'Old Woody' and that always produced a snicker, which an intuitive Amy decided not to discuss, even with Tina.

In her mind, Amy began to compare Tina to her ex sister-in-law, Elinor, who in many ways, for better or for worse, had given her a glimpse into a life less restricted. Of course, Tina was smarter and more ambitious than Elinor. She used correct grammar and had definite goals, which she shared often and widely. But she too played her radio loudly and pulled Amy to her feet to jitter bug crazily around the room. Fortunately, she remembered Elinor's tutelage and was able to perform a more inhibited rendition to Tina's surprise and delight.

"Whoeee! Let's hear it for Amy!"

Living with someone so charismatic was tiring and invigorating at the same time. When Amy tried to analyze it at night in the quiet and privacy of her bed, she couldn't decide exactly what the attraction was. Tina had pretty brown eyes, but sharp features and a rather prominent nose. Her smile was large and ready, however, and it must have telegraphed to others - as it had to her - friendliness and love of life. But most of all, she liked herself and believed in herself. Amy vowed to like herself also.

Tina couldn't drag her everywhere, however, because Amy also knew the danger of being classified as someone's *faithful companion*. She'd occupied that spot in high school and was determined to not put herself again into the role of advisor to the stars. Thus, Tina's social life expanded rapidly beyond her roommate's. She'd come squealing into the room, execute a little pirouette, plop onto her bed and announce, "I've got a date!" Then she'd immediately go to her desk to write her best friend at home, relating her fabulous social life.

Once, when she had left for the bathroom, Amy peeked at a letter left open on the desk and was amazed at the description of her date, who *'looked just like Tyrone Power'* (Amy thought him quite ordinary, and even kind of a *'drip'*) and all the malts and dancing and movies that had gone on, which in reality were the Freshman Mixer and coffee in the Student Center.

In light of these revelations, Amy began to question her roommate's previously much-envied high school antics a little. But whatever her motives and however she achieved them, you couldn't argue with the strategy, and Amy remained happy and grateful to be included in Tina's exaggerated view of life: if things were less than perfect, she made them so in her mind. It was what Ma used to call, *'Making a silk purse out of a sow's ear,'* and was certainly better than agonizing over negatives.

One afternoon Tina sat on her bed and said, "Please, please, please, sweet roommate, could I borrow that polka dot dress in your closet for my date? You can borrow anything of mine, anytime."

And so it was that *Seventeen* and Amy had been right: *the date dress* was to fulfill its destiny, except that its *maiden voyage* would not be to adorn its owner on the romantic, exciting encounter of her dreams.

Gradually, Amarantha began to fit into college life on her own. She worked in the cafeteria and made friends with students there. She had decided on a major in English/Religion and sat through Ethics and Religion classes taught by an ancient, prune-faced, retired minister who droned on about the importance of the born again life. At home, she had enjoyed some success in leading services for the church Youth Group and, in lieu of having anything better in mind, had hit upon training for the ministry, not an easy road for a woman in the '50s. Ma had been over *the moon.*

Learning the Ropes

Her English classes were her meat, however. The professor was new and had been born and raised in Boston, where he attended the prestigious Trinity College, eventually returning there to teach before coming to Woodland. He was very short, extremely thin, and almost gnome like. He seemed to have a deformity in his midsection which Amy couldn't quite identify; but in spite of his imperfect stature, he was always dressed in suits and ties, his shirts starched and dazzling white, his shoes polished to high brilliance. He had an open, approachable face and, she would soon learn, an incredible mind. They read plays, poetry, essays, and novels which he would not only analyze, coming up with incredible insights that made the literature live; but he would relate stories of the authors' lives that had influenced their writing and compare their thoughts to those of contemporary philosophers and current events.

It was everything Amy had envisioned college classes to be.

But while she was heady with excitement about Dr. Savin's lectures, some of her classmates were less than enthused. There were several football players who congregated in the back of the room and provoked Dr. Savin no end. Amarantha had seen them behave similarly in other classes, but those professors ignored their rudeness and immaturity. Dr. Savin was different. He valued his time and respected his duty to share knowledge. Unfortunately, he chose to confront the offenders with ridicule, hoping to shame them into being adults.

"If you don't care to learn, kindly be quiet so others can," he'd emphasize meaningfully, if unoriginally.

One day he came into the assembled group in flannel shirt and jeans, which he held up with wide red suspenders. He had a baseball cap on his head and sat on top the desk, chewing gum loudly.

Amy cringed inwardly. She knew he wouldn't win this one, and found it totally illogical that someone so brilliant should know so little about human nature. Evidently he'd never had to deal with difficult, unmotivated students at Trinity.

At first, the room erupted in laughter, then the back row hecklers began their mumbled comments, vaguely concealed references, and rude noises. When Dr. Savin protested, they answered, "Hey, we're just acting like north woods hicks."

His jibe had hit its mark, but there was strength in numbers. He ordered them to leave, which they did amidst loud epithets and chairs *accidentally on purpose* overturned. They weren't in class the next day, but arrived late to the next session carrying excuse slips from the Dean's office. They filed by the desk making a neat pile of their entry tickets and sullenly took their places in back. From then on, they offered nothing during discussion and, if called on, would sarcastically reply, *I don't know, Sir!*

"Don't they know they're all going to flunk?" Amy asked Tina one night.

"Oh naive little girl," she teased, "they're not going to flunk, at least not until football season is over and then they won't care. The Dean'll see to that. Who do you think got them back into class?"

Tina's response marked Amy's first disappointment in *Old Woody.* It was like high school all over again.

Amy knew a little about Dean Herregan, since one of her work study jobs was in the secretarial pool outside his office. Currently, he held two positions, Dean and Acting President, since the new president wouldn't assume his duties until spring.

Dean Herregan, like Dr. Savin, was from the East, a Harvard graduate, who in spite of having been in Wisconsin for 25 years, still spoke with a heavy *Hawvahd* lilt. He dressed in tweeds and often wore knickers with long stockings. He played the role of college eccentric and had reached the status of *beloved,* especially with the football team, since he was absolutely mad for the game and even madder for winning. Amarantha often heard the team members refer to him as *Old Woody Himself,* but they were always respectful when he was within ear shot.

Dean Herregan had an assistant, Chester Rilke, a slight, meek fellow with a receding hairline. No one knew exactly what his duties were, least of all Chester, but he followed the Dean around with a clipboard and pencil, always walking a respectful two paces behind and never lifting his eyes from his frantic note taking. They would circle the campus as if on a military inspection, and the interchange sounded like:

"The grounds look a might neglected. *Shedule* a meeting with maintenance next week."

"Would Friday suit you?"

"Good *Gawd* man, no! That's the stawt of the the *hah* school Bible Study Weekend. I'll have *fahrty* little souls waiting to be settled into *hawf* as many rooms. When more little souls are made than saved, eh Chester? Good Gawd man, don't write that down!'

Chester erased frantically, then poised his pencil in anticipation. "Thursday, then?"

"That's the inauguration committee meeting. It will take *hawf* the day, especially if that pompous *ahss*, Baumgahten gets the floor. Good *Gawd* man, don't write that down!"

"Next week?"

"On second thought, it's too late to do anything this yeaw. File it away for next spring." Chester remained poised. "Good *Gawd* man, write that down!"

Always lurking on the outskirts of the inspection tour was another decidedly odd character who followed the Dean whenever he walked about on campus. Amy had seen this man going in and out a basement door of Old Main. His gray hair was shoulder length, wild and matted. He always carried a long walking stick, almost like a staff, although he didn't seem lame, as he was fond of striding along behind Dean Herregen, careful to stop and assume an innocent demeanor if the Dean halted for any reason and looked around. He had also taken to dressing like the Dean in knickers and tweed jacket, his being ragged and filthy but recognizable as an attempt to copy (whether in true admiration or derision, it was impossible to tell).

Amy's concern was the way his eyes were wild and darted constantly, giving him a frantic and frightened air. After a hallway encounter with him one day, she asked Mrs. Simon, the Dean's Secretary and Office Manager, who he was and what he did at the college.

"Oh that's Stewart; he's harmless really," she laughed. "He tends the coal furnace in Old Main. It's a sad story really. I've heard he was a brilliant student from a fine family who was studying to be a doctor when he just went *round the bend*." Mrs. Simon made a circle around her ear with a forefinger and wrinkled her nose for emphasis. "The Dean arranged the job for him out of the goodness of his heart, and now I'm afraid it sort of back fired, really." She came close to Amy's ear and whispered, "I'm afraid he has sort of a crush on the Dean. It's awkward, you know, really."

None of the students were outwardly mean to Stewart, mostly they ignored him. Amy had heard some of the girls allowing as how they were so desperate for a date they'd even go out with *Old Stewart*, but no one teased him or baited him in any way. Once she had seen him standing under a tree on campus talking loudly to himself. When she got closer and heard, *Tell me not in mournful numbers, Life is but an empty dream...* she recognized the classical poem and could have wept for that lost genius that still surfaced occasionally, taunting his tortured brain and mocking his current condition.

Stewart was one of Woodland's eccentrics that generations of graduates would remember when they reminisced about their *alma mater* and the colorful Dean, including him as a member of Herregen's personal entourage, whether or not the Dean would have approved.

Amy hadn't been working in the secretarial pool more than a few weeks before she realized that the two events uppermost in the Dean's mind were the Homecoming football game that fall with arch rival River Jordan Baptist College and the inauguration ceremony for the new president slated as part of the graduation exercises. In fact, one of her first duties was to help in the typing of letters to hundreds of colleges throughout the United States and Canada, asking them to send a representative to the festivities.

"This is going to be a *grawnd gawla*! It's going to put Woodland on the map, as well as constitute a fine welcome to *ah* new president." The Dean spoke to the group of girls waiting at their typewriters as if he were their coach delivering the half-time pep talk. "*Awnd* you all, right *heah* in this room, will be playing a pivotal role in the success of this event! So I *wahnt* you to jump into the game and give it *awhl* you've got, the *old college try*, as it *wehre*, Heh! Heh! Heh!"

Mrs. Simon stood at his side, nodding after each vocal punctuation. Chester held his usual position behind, scribbling furiously. And when Dean Herregen and Chester entered his office and closed the door, Mrs. Simon raised her arm as they held their hands in position over their typewriters, and lowered it in a quick, chopping motion. The absence of a red flag and starter's gun were the only things lacking for this race. The collective *rat-a-tat* of those old, manual typewriter keys exploded with a sound like machine guns, and the next hour was feverish with the tapping, now unsynchronized, the carriage return bells, and the frustrated sighs of the typists, as they sought to erase mistakes through bulky carbon packs.

Mrs. Simon patrolled the room, often pulling the paper from a machine and advising the typist to start over. Amy had excelled at typing in high school, so her letters remained intact making her eligible, in the future, to be entrusted with some of Dean Herregen's personal correspondence.

And so, she began to build her new reputation one small success at a time. With the hecklers silenced, Dr. Savin's English Class became her favorite once again, and she religiously read the materials and took detailed notes in class, to the point where sometimes she'd realize that she'd taken down almost his whole lecture verbatim. Then it was time for the first test, and the night before, she reread and, in some instances memorized, the material they'd covered.

But when she opened her test blue book and saw the first question written on the chalk board, her heart sank and panic gripped her. Somehow she managed to fill the pages and worked until the end of the period. The hecklers closed their books within the first seconds and marched silently out, throwing their tests on the desk as they left. Others made an attempt, but sighed and shrugged as they left. Amy was almost in tears and hurried back to her room before disgracing herself in public.

Dr. Savin handed back the test books with a grim face a scolding for the poor showing. Amy, who had never gotten a grade lower than an A in an English class, opened her book to a large, red

C-minus. She barely heard the lecture for the day, and waited after class to try and find out what had happened. She knew the material backwards and forwards. Was she just incapable of handling college? It took all the strength she could muster to confront Dr. Savin, but she was desperate. Maybe she'd have to go back home in disgrace, living with Ma in the tiny apartment and working at one of the local stores for the rest of her life.

"I'm wondering how I can get better grades."

"You're not satisfied with a C minus? It was the highest grade in the class." He spoke sarcastically.

"Well, no. I guess I'm used to better grades. I've read all the literature."

"The fact that you want a better grade is a good start, and it's good that you've read your assignments, so few do. But I want you to do more than read and regurgitate themes and plots and my analyses. Authors write to reach all their readers, not just teachers who then tell you what you've read. I want to know how a story affected you. How did you feel when you'd finished reading? Were there certain elements that related to your own life or the life of someone you know or love? Did you laugh or cry or both? How does a certain poem compare to another on a similar subject by a different poet? What criteria do you use to determine if the writing is good or bad?

His questions were fired at her, his delivery very passionate. Amy wasn't even sure he knew she was still in the room. When she thought about it later, she realized he had been venting his frustration with all his classes at Woodland and wasn't singling her out for her stupidity. She managed to keep from crying, but knew she was crimson faced and shiny eyed Of course everything he said made sense upon reflection. Then suddenly Dr. Savin seemed to see her again and his face softened.

"Look, you're doing well and working hard. I just want you to *think* too." He touched her shoulder, then brightened with an idea. "Why don't you come over to my house for dinner this Friday. Friday is special for my Mother and me, and she always makes a chicken dinner. It's only a few blocks from the campus. We can discuss this more then. You'll like my Mother."

"His Mother! Now there's a new angle! You'd better watch yourself, Little Girl!" Tina had taken to calling her *Little Girl* a lot, even though she wasn't physically bigger. It just denoted superior experience, and Amy couldn't argue with that and even kind of liked the idea of being looked after.

"It's nothing like that," Amy replied. "He just wants to discuss the class and how I can do better."

There came Tiny's trademark eye roll and exaggerated nod. Amy grabbed her towel, attempted to snap her friend with it, and left to take a shower.

As the weeks had gone by, Amy's self confidence had blossomed, partly due to Tina, but also due to the group of girls on her floor. They loved nothing better than to get the *freshies* together in one room or another and advise them, shock them, tease them, and generally act like traditional big sisters. A pretty girl named Kathy was the self-appointed leader of this college level pillow talk and had come up with the idea of a slate of 'Rules For The Behavior and Advancement of College Coeds.'

This unwritten decree became oral history only and began with an honest-to-God rule that a past Dorm Mother had imposed (probably during the ultra-Christian days): *If a young lady expects that she will be accepting a ride during which she will be required to sit on a gentleman's lap, she must first lay down a catalog.*

This rule had been handed down from dorm dweller to dorm dweller, and some artistic coed had cross-stitched a brightly colored plaque of it, which occupied an honored place beside the bulletin board over a small shelf holding a thick Sears Catalog and a smaller caption, *'For your use.'*

Kathy sought to add new rules for modern times which, of needs, remained unposted. "Wear your tin pants if you get a date with a Baptist. They can't dance, drink, or go to movies. They can only do one thing!"

Amy reasoned that if they were that religious, they probably couldn't do 'that one thing' either.

"One more reason not to date them," Kathy would answer,

with an exaggerated wink. "JoAnne and Carol on the first floor are *fairies*, so don't let them ask you in for a back rub, or anything."

Amy knew about homosexuals, but had neither encountered any in New Scandia, nor thought much about them and reasoned that if they had each other, they probably wouldn't need to ask anyone in for a back rub.

"You ever heard of a ménage a toi?"

Amy hadn't, but just laughed with the others.

"Stay away from Baumgarten's history class if you can help it. He's used the same notes since the college was founded."

Amy reasoned that history doesn't change, but the indisputable answer was always, *Ya, but times do.*

Mostly the girls talked about their boyfriends, parties, clothes, and which male classmates were *cute.* Sometimes they had serious discussions about what they'd do if they got pregnant. Sometimes they talked about their families or what they hated or liked about themselves.

Amarantha said little, but learned a lot about human nature. She learned that they all had many of the same fears, some more terrifying than the fear of meeting new people or getting tongue-tied when talking to boys. They talked about 'going all the way' and many implied they had; others said they were contemplating. Girls sometimes made confessions that brought tears, and the whole group would comfort them and everyone hugged, a thing that Amy had to learn the way she learned to jitterbug, by relaxing and letting herself go.

No simple task when you came from New Scandia.

Some of the more useful behaviors she learned were not to cringe under constructive criticism (*Quit being so quiet, people will think you're a dummy!*), not to be so self conscious (*Everyone's not always looking at you!*), and endure teasing without personalizing it.

The latter was to prove very important to Amy's future. She learned that if she called attention to her perceived shortcomings (anything potentially teasable) first and made fun of herself, people laughed *with* her and not *at* her, usually vehemently denying her perceptions. In fact, the girls in the dorm began to find her innocence and self deprecating manner appealing. One night for some odd reason and in some related context, she shared the *Date Dress* story with the assembled pajama-clad group.

"Oh my God, Little Girl," said Tina. "Why didn't you tell me you hadn't worn that dress before?"

Then laughter threatened to asphyxiate everyone in the room and a surprised Amy, who had considered the dress a symbol of everything that was supposed to be different at college but wasn't, suddenly saw the humor and joined in.

"So how did that *date dress* work, Tina? Did it get you any results?"

"Oh, I *always* get results!" This remark was followed by another burst of laughter, although nobody was willing to believe what she said.

"Hey, I've got a date on Friday. Can I borrow the *Date Dress* Amy?"

"I want to try it too!"

"Me too," came the calls from several parts of the room.

From then on, in their dorm, *The date dress* became the barometer for co-ed, social interaction. Few actually borrowed it, but the term was used to describe good dates: *that date dress was really working tonight;* bad dates: *too bad I didn't have the datedress tonight;* blind dates: *even the date dress couldn't have salvaged this night.*

As for Amy, she gave up on Woodland men being different from high school boys and started wearing the *date dress* to church.

Making a Friend

Her first Friday night with Dr. Savin and his mother had proven to be very enjoyable, but also made her homesick for Ma. Mrs. Savin was about Ma's age and was *old country* in the same way. Her grey hair was in a bun, and she wore oxfords and an apron over a house dress. She had an accent which Amy couldn't place. Her chicken dinner was a boiled bird, which was rather stringy and tough, and the boiling broth was served as soup before dinner. There was a ritual involving a candelabra, and Dr. Savin explained that they were Jewish and Friday was the beginning of their Sabbath. It was all very exotic and exciting for Amy, and she enjoyed Mrs. Savin's fussing over her and referring to her as, *Maynard's prize student*, even though she knew she wasn't.

Dr. Savin treated both her and his mother like queens, pulling out their chairs and serving them first, referring to his mother, in Shakespearian tones, as *the author of the feast*.

After dinner, he even hugged a flustered Mrs. Savin and told her what a good cook she was. Then they moved into comfortable chairs and had a sweet, grape wine and discussed literature, while Mother sat silently knitting. Amy hadn't had wine before and felt herself relax, even to the point of expressing her opinions, as the fruity liquid warmed its way down her throat. Dr. Savin asked her what she liked to read in her leisure time, why she liked certain authors, had she ever thought of writing herself? And as they talked, what he wanted from her in class discussion and on her papers became obvious, and she was ashamed it hadn't occurred to her before.

There were many Friday nights with Dr. Savin and his mother during Amy's first year at Woodland. She felt honored at being included in their religious celebrations; and although they remained *Dr.* and *Mrs.* to her, she thought of them as friends and even dared to share some of her personal problems or triumphs, valuing their advice or congratulations. For this, she was rewarded when Dr. Savin shared with her his life at Trinity College and, in glowing terms and to Amy's surprise, talked about a fiancé back in Boston.

One story especially touched her when he looked into space with a tender smile on his face and told about his elation at walking with his intended into Tiffany's in New York City to buy an engagement ring. Mrs. Savin mumbled an excuse and went to her room. Tears shone on her cheeks, and Amy thought it was sweet of her to be so overcome by romance.

"Why did you ever leave all that made you happy to come here?" Dr. Savin seemed to physically pull himself back from his reverie by sitting straighter in his chair.

"Maybe it was too perfect, Amy. Maybe I felt the need to step back and experience another life to make sure that what I had was real and not just me projecting my hopes and dreams onto places and people. Sometimes it's good to be humbled, and to realize that things are never perfect. He leaned back again and began to recite in a soft voice:

> *"May she be granted beauty and yet not*
> *Beauty to make a stranger's eye distraught,*
> *Or hers before a looking-glass, for such,*
> *Being made beautiful overmuch,*
> *Consider beauty a sufficient end,*
> *Lose natural kindness and maybe*
> *The heart-revealing intimacy*
> *That chooses right, and never find a friend."*

"That's Yeats." He shrugged and smiled jovially, "Besides, if I hadn't come to Woodland, I would have missed having you for a friend."

It was a beautiful thought, but any way she looked at it he was back to Ma's adage about, *making a silk purse out of a sow's ear.* Or maybe that was *exactly* what Dr. Savin was talking about. Maybe he was afraid he'd made that *silk purse* out of his life back East and was going to wake up one morning to find it was only a *sow's ear.*

Homecoming Mania

So Amarantha managed to get through the first weeks of college by studying and working her jobs. Towards the end of September, the whole college became obsessed with Homecoming preparations, egged on by the head cheerleader, Dean Herregen. For weeks from her spot in the secretarial pool, she had watched different groups meet behind the closed doors of the Dean's office: the coaching staff, many times; certain staff from the business office; the varsity football team itself. And there seemed to be great secrecy involved and much clandestine whispering in the hall before a group departed, and once she even heard the Dean say emphatically, "I'm calling in some favors, but this must not go *bey-ohnd* this room."

One day she was working alone in the office, Mrs. Simon had a hair appointment, when two huge men approached her desk. Both were well over six-feet tall and had abnormally broad shoulders from which hung well-developed arms that terminated in baseball mitt hands. Their necks were so thick, she could hardly tell where they ended and faces began.

"We'd like to see Dean Herregen," one said.

Amarantha went to Mrs. Simon's desk, snapped on the intercom, and informed the Dean he had visitors. She wished she'd asked who they were, she knew that was proper procedure, but she was too startled by their appearance to remember. Even though they were polite and smiling, maybe the Dean should have been warned.

But when he opened the door, his face lit up with a broad smile of recognition and he grasped their hands, cupping their elbows with the other, as men do when they really are glad to see another man.

"So good to see you, men, come in! come in! Amy, scare us up some *cahfee* or a Coke. Would you *rahther* have a Coke?"

Both said they would and closed the door, leaving Amy at a loss as to how she was going to get three Cokes out of the machine in the hall without any money. She rummaged in her purse and finally came up with the requisite thirty cents. She all but ran with the cold bottles to the coffee room where she found glasses and a small tray. She felt as if she had a part in a B movie as she balanced the tray and tapped on the door.

"Aw, *hehr* we are men. Help *youhrselves*. Amy, Tom and Anthony *hehr* are two new students, so you'll be seeing a *laht* of them *arohnd cahmpus*."

There were *thank yous* and *how-do-you-dos* all around, and then Amy backed out of the door, closing it softly behind her. New students? They looked much too old. Maybe they were veterans. And since when did the Dean greet new students with a private audience and soft drinks?

Mrs. Simon came in then, removing her hat and using two fingers like scissors to pinch and fluff the flattened waves of her fresh hairdo.

"Any calls, Amy? Did the Dean need anything while I was gone?"

"No calls, but the Dean has some visitors. New students, I believe." She pointed to the closed door.

"New students? But what...?" Her voice trailed off as something occurred to her. "What did you do, really?" She seemed nervous now, almost accusatory.

"They just asked for Cokes, so I got them out of the machine." She hoped Mrs. Simon would offer to reimburse her, but she was far too distracted, pacing in front of the closed door and staring at it as if she had the x-ray vision and enhanced hearing of Superman. The class bell sounded, and Amy packed up her books and headed toward the hall, but Mrs. Simon stepped in front of her and put a hand on her shoulder.

"Forget you saw those students today, really."

It was like something out of *North by Northwest,* with Cary Grant, and it wasn't likely now that Amy could forget them even if she tried. In fact, she saw them again that very night when she went to work in the cafeteria and was assigned the duty of waiting on the Training Table.

While all the other students formed a line and picked up their food, the football team sat at one long table and were served a special menu, usually steak. Her job was to refill pitchers of milk and bread baskets, which usually kept her running throughout the meal. They were voracious, taking three or four pieces of bread on their plates at a time and drinking glasses of milk in one gulp.

Tom and Anthony sat among them tonight, eating and laughing with the others. They recognized her and said, "Hello, Amy," causing a semi-flurry among the regulars who usually ignored her except to point, mouth stuffed, at the milk pitcher or bread basket. Amy was pleased, but couldn't control the blush that revealed the greetings to be more important than they were meant to be.

Aside from Training Table, she didn't see Tom and Anthony around campus. They weren't in any of her classes, although when she was given their student folders to file, she noticed they were signed-up for her *World Lit* class. That Friday night she asked Dr. Savin if he had either of the new students in any of his classes, to which he laughed sarcastically.

"Not likely! They don't need to attend classes. They're ringers for the big football game coming up. They'll disappear after football season, like most of the team."

"But that's not legal, is it? What's in it for them? Where do they come from? "

"Rumor has it, they're second string Green Bay Packers, and they're on work study, like you, only they get paid considerably more per hour. It's common in many colleges, and the Dean is always bragging about how he institutes many of the practices of the larger universities here at Woodland."

A Glory in it All

When Homecoming weekend finally arrived, it dawned on perfect autumn weather. In spite of what Amy knew about the game, she found herself excited and eager to join in. She attended the huge pep rally/bonfire, helped with the dorm float, and decorated the student center for the dance. Of course Tina had a date for every event and rushed off to the game sporting a huge, gold mum on her chest, repeating, 'We just *have* to win or everyone will be too depressed at the dance!'

Amy hadn't told her what she had learned. She didn't want to spoil her roommate's fun, but also preferred to forget so it wouldn't spoil her own fun, or any more of her illusions about what she was beginning to fondly think of as the *Dear Old Woodland* of the College Hymn, sung every morning at Chapel.

So what if they bent the truth to beat River Jordan Baptist? *The River Rats*, as everyone at Woodland called them, were so pompous and condescending when they'd played them earlier in the season, praying before each quarter as if they were on a holy crusade and doing battle with the heathens. Then too, the local contingent of Baptists turned out for the games and had the effrontery to sit on *The Rat* side of the field and cheer for them. Everyone wanted *badly* to take them down a peg, if not downright humiliate them.

Amy had made arrangements to go to the game and dance with the cafeteria gang and, once again, even without the romantic connotations of a real date, found herself anticipating both. She'd had to cancel her Friday night dinner with Dr. Savin and felt a little guilty about that.

Not that he'd made her feel guilty. "Go with your friends and have fun," he'd urged. She felt a twinge of disloyalty when she thought about how the team had treated him, not to mention the Dean's duplicity.

All was forgotten on game day, though. It was a warm afternoon and the bleachers were packed with people of all ages: parents and grandparents sitting on cushions clutching thermoses; the college students surrounding the pep band, with short-skirted cheerleaders directing their exuberance like choir masters; little boys playing endless games of touch football on the sidelines, shouting and screaming and paying no attention whatsoever to action on the field.

The maples that lined the football field were ablaze with color framed by a background of dark evergreens. Dry leaves didn't just fall from the branches, but drifted and then soared with passing gusts of wind to take, unattached, one last graceful dance to the treetops. The air seemed to hold all the smells of things full and ripe. The excitement of the crowd and the beauty of the day were overwhelming, and Amy wouldn't have missed it, even at the risk of being disloyal to a friend or acting on principles. Sometimes, she even guiltily thought that having principles was limiting and boring.

Across the field sat the Baptists, the quiet *fat-cats*. No garish display of cheerleaders or brass band was needed to show their support, rather they viewed it as a chance to exhibit their faith by smiling complacently, as if having a secret communication with the Almighty allowed them to see in advance the outcome of the day's competition. Little did they suspect that Satan himself, striding the field opposite them in tweed knickers and sport coat, was even among them, ready to wreak havoc with their heaven-sanctioned plan.

Dean Herregen and Chester paced in front of the Woodland bench, the Dean conferring with the coaches and beating lustily on players' backs. Tom and Anthony were easy to pick out of the line-up, both being a foot taller, fifty pounds heavier, and inches broader of shoulders than any of the other players.

Amy was suddenly worried that some of *The Rats* might notice what she considered a glaring, obvious physical disparity, and start to smell a real rat. But what could they do? She herself had filed their student folders, complete with transcripts, class schedules, and notices of scholarships and work-study jobs. She sat back and prepared to enjoy the mortification of the Baptists.

And mortification it was. Tom and Anthony were everywhere. Sometimes they could have played the game alone when they darted from tackling to receiving and running. *The Rats* were demoralized by half-time, and when play resumed, Amy noticed that many from their bleachers now stood on the sidelines, their faces distorted with anger and disappointment, shaking their fists and shouting, *Take 'em Down!* or more passionately, *Kill 'em!* No one remembered to call for a prayer before either the third or fourth quarters. As for Woodland, after the third quarter, the coach took Tom and Anthony out for a much deserved rest, and let the original varsity *take it on home.*

Needless to say, no one at the dance was depressed, and Dean Herregen made a *grahnd* entrance, regaled in dress kilt and tam, the ubiquitous Chester replaced by his dour, little wife who bore a striking resemblance to Queen Victoria. He held court as well-wishers congratulated him on the win as if he himself had played.

Amy spotted Stewart standing against a wall muttering to himself, "for the soul is dead that slumbers and things are not as they seem."

She watched and wondered how many people had helped

plan the deception and how many had just turned a blind eye. She guessed she was one of them, for better or for worse.

> *Long have I known a glory in it all*
> *But never knew I this,*
> *Here such a passion is*
> *As stretcheth me apart. Lord, I do*
>   *fear*
> *Thou'st made the world too beautiful*
>   *this year.*
> *My soul is all but out of me — let fall*
> *No burning leaf; prithee, let no bird call.*

Losing the Faith, But Finding Love

Amy took the Greyhound bus home for Thanksgiving. She sat impatiently, waiting to catch the first glimpse of the New Scandia sign on the outskirts of town, and then they were at the depot and Ma was waiting and hugged her so tightly that even with her newly learned ability to hug, she was a little embarrassed by its intensity.

John and Elsie and her family were there for the dinner, and they were all eager to hear about her adventures at college. She felt quite sophisticated as she told them about the classes and her jobs, but a little sad as she realized that already, because of her new life, new experiences, she had grown apart from them. It was a wonderful, long weekend, but on Sunday when she stood waiting for the bus to take her north to Woodland, she felt almost as eager to get back as she had to get home.

And this time, coming into the dorm was a joyous occasion. There was much hugging and screeching, as if they'd been away from each other for weeks, and the promise of a meeting of the Rules Committee in Kathy's room later.

Amy stood under the shower for a long time, enjoying the endless supply of hot water which didn't have to be heated on Ma's kerosene stove, so many of these simple things were still luxuries to her.

It was early, so she dressed in jeans and shirt and opened her notebook to see what work was due in what classes on Monday. Tina wasn't in the room. In fact, not a soul seemed to be around. Then suddenly, they were upon her, holding her down and tying her arms with one scarf and using another to blindfold her.

"You're being kidnapped, so don't resist," came the warning, and she didn't, giving herself up to the gayety and the heady and pleasant sense of inclusion.

They threw her coat around her shoulders and plopped her hat on her head, and after a treacherous descent of the stairs, Amy could feel the cold outside and then the maneuvering to get into a car.

"Where are we going?" she'd asked several times.

"Time will reveal all!" came the reply. And it wasn't hard to guess when she was extracted from the car and heard loud music and many voices as she stumbled along frozen ground. They whipped off the scarf, and she was in the middle of a barroom complete with juke box blaring and pool balls colliding.

She started to protest, "I don't go to bars," but they led her on and somebody put a glass of beer in her hand. They crowded into a couple booths in the back room. It was very dark, lit only by the garish colors of the juke box, and couples were dancing, whereas the front room held the bar and pool table and was the site of intense pool playing and vigorous beer consumption.

Jukebox Saturday Night began to play and Tina screamed and pulled Amy to her feet, almost causing her to turn over her beer. Then she was again performing the dance Elinor had taught her, and really enjoying it partly because of the dimness of the room and the admiration of other dancers.

And so she drank the bitter beer. And even a second. Her friends assured her that the more she had, the better it tasted. She didn't really find that to be true, but by now she was having so much uninhibited fun, she would have drunk swamp water in order to prolong this new experience.

She recognized lots of kids besides her dorm buddies. The

cafeteria crew was there and many girls from the secretarial pool. They'd all asked her to come with them many times, but she had remembered Ma's aversion to alcohol and the places that served it.

"It's the ruination of families," she'd caution. And who knew more about that than Ma?

Then the music went from jitterbug to a lilting ballad with a mesmerizing beat, '*The wheel of fortune keeps spinning around, will it ever smile on me,*' sang Kay Starr, and couples held each other close and swayed on the crowded floor. Someone draped a coat over the jukebox, so it was even darker. Amy was happy to sit down and regain her breath from the fast dancing, when suddenly Frank, one of the cafeteria crew, was at their booth beckoning her to the floor.

For the first time, she was held in a tight embrace and moving slowly to the music, as in her romantic dreams. But it wasn't exactly right; she was in old jeans and shirt, and she wasn't in love with her partner.

It was nice, though, and she felt grateful to Frank for asking and melted into the feeling of the moment and rested her head (now also *spinning around*) on his shoulder......

'*...as the wheel keeps turning, turning, turning, I'll be ever yearning for love's precious flame.*'

Breaking her trance was the start of a new song which was evidently the favorite barroom anthem. Everyone stood, beer glasses aloft, and shouted the lyrics.

"Detour! There's a muddy road ahead
Detour! Paid no mind to what it said
Detour! All these bitter things I find
Should have read that detour sign!"

And even though her thoughts were a bit fuzzy in their beer-soaked condition, she fervently hoped the song wasn't a prophecy of things to come in this exciting new life.

November wore on and she became happier every day with Woodland. She still studied and kept her jobs, but now she had a busy social life. Going to *Woody's Bar* became at least a once a week thing, and she sometimes saw herself as a debutante whose *coming out* party had been her initial appearance there.

Now people knew her and talked to her, even asked her to join sororities and clubs. She continued her Friday nights with the Savins, but, more and more, had to be excused for other events.

Frank from the kitchen crew became very friendly after their dance, and even in her inexperience, she knew he was setting the stage to ask her out. But she didn't want that. She wanted him to go back to being her friend again without the sexual tension. She held no romantic feelings for him.

"If you wait until you're in love to go out on a date that polka dot dress is gonna be worn out from going to church!" Tina advised.

But Amarantha became more and more confused and apprehensive as far as her male-female interaction was concerned. She postponed any embarrassing confrontations with Frank by being careful not to be alone with him and rushing away with a hurried, *"Gotta Go!"* if he got too close.

What was wrong with her! Wasn't this what she'd wanted?

One day when she was working the lunch serving line, one of the few football players who had remained in college after the season asked, "What kind of soup is it?"

Without thinking, she had replied, "Yellow pea."

"Sounds appetizing. Think I'll pass."

She felt herself turning red, and attempted a half apology/half explanation as the rest of the servers and those in line behind him started laughing and making comments like, *'she's probably right'* or *'Atta girl, Amy!'*

She didn't think much more of the incident until that evening when she was called to the telephone in the lobby.

"Hi! This is Jack, from the lunch line today, you know?"

"Oh, hi! Oh, you know I wasn't trying to be smart or anything, I sometimes do that, I speak before I think how it sounds."

"No, hey! I called to apologize. I shouldn't have embarrassed you like that."

They proceeded to talk for over an hour about everything and anything, and Amy couldn't believe how easy it was to talk to this boy she hardly knew, had never thought much about, and, in fact, disliked for his actions in Dr. Savin's class. By the end of their conversation, she knew he was going to ask her out, and she knew the answer would be yes.

When she got back to her room, she could hardly believe it. He was good looking and popular. Why had he asked her? Maybe college men were different after all, and she pushed his behavior towards Dr. Savin to the back of her mind and decided to go with the feeling, whatever the consequences.

Initially, the consequences were that most of her spare time was spent with Jack. They met between classes for coffee; they saw each other almost every night or talked on the phone for hours; they went to Woody's Bar where she no longer sat in the back with her friends, but stood at the bar with Jack and his buddies in a loud, boisterous elite group. She often missed the dorm sessions too, protesting that she was too tired or had homework to do late into the night after having been out with Jack.

Her Friday nights with the Savins became nonexistent. At first she cancelled, offering various excuses. Then when it became apparent that the standing invitation had become a standing refusal, both sides dropped the pretense. She knew Dr. Savin disapproved of Jack. He was, after all, a class trouble maker in his eyes. He thought him cocky and pretentious.

One day when Jack was absent, Amy and Dr. Savin had coffee after class.

"There's a whole world out there, Amy," he said to her with frustration on his face and in his voice, "with many fine, intelligent men more deserving of your time than that ignoramus."

Amy felt offended by his assessment. She found Jack to be very intelligent, more so than she, but he just wasn't about to give *Old Savin* the satisfaction of witnessing it or to desert his buddies by suddenly becoming a class participant.

Her indignation must have been evident on her face. Dr. Savin looked in her eyes and said, "I'm sorry, I shouldn't have said that. I can see you care for him and I don't want to lose a friend. Just be careful." He touched her hand, almost in a farewell gesture, and from that time on they only spoke of the assigned class literature or her grades.

But Amy was painfully aware that her new and exciting life at Woodland brought on unexpected change. Tina's good-natured teasing turned pointed and critical.

"Out with the super-star again tonight? No time for us peons any more, huh?"

Amy knew in her heart that Tina's ego had been dealt a blow by their sudden change in status and part of her wanted to go back to being *Little Girl* to Tina's experienced *Big Sister*. But she was in love, and nobody knew how lonely she had been or how she had longed to be important to someone. And so again she pushed Dr. Savin, the dorm girls, her roommate, and even her studies to the back of her mind to make room for Jack and his ever-expanding demands on her time, her personality, her principles, and even her body.

"Have a few more drinks and you'll have more fun."

No matter how she tried, she didn't seem to measure up to the abandoned behavior of the elite crowd, and she was aware that often Jack was disappointed in her socially.

"This is *Old Savin* going mental over Shakespeare's soliloquy," he'd joke, turning his eyes up and raising a trembling head and arm heavenward in parody of Dr. Savin in class, where he often waxed dramatic in appreciation of the literature he so loved.

The group had busted out laughing appreciatively, and so had Amy, when she saw Jack's eyes on her, even though she felt her friend's acting was one of the things that made the subject live for her.

"That little deception did more for Woodland College than all your snooty, Ivy League *Super Jews* or boring classes," Jack asserted pointedly when Amy had ventured that the football ringers at Homecoming didn't exactly demonstrate traditional sportsman-like fair-play. In response, she quietly acquiesced, feeling like a traitor to both sides of the controversy, but mostly to herself.

"I'm in love with you, and if you loved me you'd be willing to show it!" he said.

The physical side of Amy's relationship rapidly spun out of her control. Jack was obviously worlds ahead of her in experience, and the sweet kisses and hugs had advanced to intimate caresses and what the dorm girls had warned her about, *French kisses*. One night parked on a dark, side road and without fanfare or reasonable contemplation, she had lost her sacred and much touted virginity in a rushed, heated and almost violent encounter that left her feeling unloved, uncertain, and ashamed.

When she got back to the dorm, she longed to unburden herself to Tina but took a long, hot shower and later pretended to be asleep on her side of the room when Tina got home. *We're in love, and Jack will surely ask me to marry him now,* she thought in the dark, as she stared at the wall and longed for sleep.

Then Christmas vacation came, and Amy was almost in a frenzy about leaving Jack for two long weeks. She had to admit that she often felt the need for breathing space. He demanded more attention than anything or anybody ever had in her life, and she was exhausted with weighing her words to prevent offense, laughing loudly and drinking too much in order to fit in with his friends and rearranging her time to be at his beck and call, even though he often cancelled on her, many times by just not showing up for a meeting or date. Even so, lately he seemed to be distancing himself. And though he protested irritably that, *'nothing is wrong'* when she questioned him, too often she knew.

She sensed that he might be interested in another girl, even more so when a couple of the dorm girls hinted at having seen him out and about when he'd broken a date with her.

"Who was he with?"

"Oh, just his friends. You know, *the group*." They averted their eyes and pretended pressing business, hurrying away with the promise of talking more later. But Amy hardly attended the pillow-talk sessions any more and was torn between wanting to know and prolonging her fantasy of a sweet love affair culminating in a *lived happily ever after* scenario. They had been intimate, and for her that meant commitment, even though she knew in her heart that he didn't adhere to the same moral code as she.

They went to a movie the night before she went home for the holidays. He was attentive but quiet and nodded without comment when she talked of what they'd do when she got back in January. As was their custom, they'd made love in the car parked on a lonely road that led to a park closed for the winter, the engine idling to keep the heater humming and the windows steamy.

When they got back to the campus, he hadn't walked her to the door of the dorm, mumbling some excuse about having to *'clock in at some family thing.'* But he kissed her goodbye and, almost as an after thought, opened the glove compartment and took out a gift wrapped package which he pressed into her hands as she got out of the car. She was touched with the gift and wanted to open it in his presence and thank him properly, but he leaned to pull the door shut and drove away abruptly, leaving her standing on the snowy sidewalk with the tangible, beribboned tribute of his affection held reverently in both hands.

She took the package into a bathroom booth for privacy and perched on the edge of the stool to open her first Christmas present ever from her lover. It was a book of poetry by an unknown *beat* poet named Roger Lee Cerioni. She turned the cover slowly and read the inscription in the corner, "To Amy, wherever you go and whatever you do, remember our time here at Woodland."

It was like a message in a yearbook from a little known classmate. She could tell it was a dismissal, a termination, a farewell. Amy wanted to cry, but she put the wrappings in the wastebasket and took the book to her room where she read it from cover to cover, noting with her newly acquired knowledge of literature that it wasn't even very good poetry. But maybe he had carefully chosen the book because some of the poems spoke to him of their relationship, of his love for her, of their future.

The vacation was a disaster. She was exhausted, nervous, and irritable. She didn't hear from Jack, and when she brazenly called him at his home, his mother would sweetly reply, "Oh, I'm sorry dear, you just missed him."

She read the book of poetry and the inscription over and over, but it was not comforting. She tried to put a good face on their last night together. Why would he make love to her and give her a gift if he meant to break up with her?

When she got back to Woodland and the taxi from the bus station stopped at the dorm, she noticed his car at the curb and breathed a sigh of relief as she abandoned her luggage on the sidewalk and rushed to open the door. She longed to have his arms around her and thought they would park and he would show her that everything was all right. But he drove around, exchanging pleasantries as the heater hummed in the background.

"How was your Christmas? Did you get this last snow storm down there? Suppose you're all ready for classes tomorrow?"

When he finally did park the car, Amy noticed with surprise that they were back in front of the dorm, and instead of reaching for her, he turned to her and proceeded to break her heart.

"Listen, you must know things haven't been working out between us lately, and we're just not that compatible, socially or physically, and well, over Christmas I kinda got back with my old, high school girl friend and…"

"But you said you loved me and we were intimate. What is it you don't like? I can change. I've changed so much already, and I can change more. What…."

"Look, you're a nice girl, and we've had fun. But I'm just not interested anymore. Everyone says you haven't had many boyfriends, so let's say I provided you with some experience and part friends, okay?"

The sting of the rejection was momentarily overcome by embarrassment at the knowledge that she and their relationship had been discussed. And with whom?

Who was *everyone?* His friends? The dorm girls? Was it so obvious that he had been her first? Did her inexperience exude from her pores and hang about her like some thick aura?

She flung open the door and escaped from the car. Jack sped away before she bent to collect her belongings, still on the sidewalk, and began to maneuver the icy walkway to the front door.

When I First Saw You
By Roger Lee Cerioni

I knew not hour, time nor space
When I saw the beauty in your face.
The moments seemed to linger in a way
That your presence spoke eternal day.
It was hard for me to thus part,
Having to leave only my heart.

Hard Lessons

Amy had known tough winters before, but January 1951 would always stay in her memory as a month that advanced slowly, day by painful day. She thought of leaving college, but couldn't face the questions and disappointment of her family and friends back in New Scandia.

And what would she do if she quit? Try to get work? Where and how would she live? Go back to Ma in disgrace? Had all her well-constructed plans and goals come to depend on one man she had known for a matter of months?

In a moment of saner thought, she became her old practical self, remembering that she had paid for school through the spring term. She would stay at Woodland until the beginning of summer vacation. That would give her time to plan, and she wouldn't be wasting anyone's hard-earned money, mostly her own.

What to do about her broken heart, not to mention her lost virginity, wasn't as easy to factor. She suspected that much of the boastful sexual experience the dorm girls professed was merely bravado that made for lively conversation at *pillow talk*. She further suspected that most of them, like she herself, might agree with Ma when she'd cautioned Amy during some long ago attempt at a sex talk: *'Nice boys won't respect you if you have relations before marriage.'*

And so she decided to throw herself back into her classes. She spent the occasional Friday night with the Savins, worked her jobs, and gradually resumed her pre-Jack life, all the while in her mind dramatically resigning herself to becoming a spinster school teacher or librarian, having long ago deemed herself already unfit in many ways for the original ministry plan and, of course, *spoiled* for marriage.

Harder to rationalize was her abandonment of her friends during her brief love affair, which she perceived now as almost like a serious illness that had isolated her, sapping her time and strength. The dorm girls were forgiving, as were the Savins and the cafeteria crew. She even began to spend some cautious time with Frank, although she was still in love with Jack and girlishly thought she always would be.

So with time, life did return to some semblance of normalcy. Unfortunately she wasn't ever able to regain her close, sisterly relationship with Tina, but that wasn't altogether her fault. With the beginning of the second semester, a new girl moved into the dorm and occupied the one remaining room on their floor. Joy was pretty and feminine with a trusting and almost child-like nature. She was the perfect foil for the assertive Tina, as once Amy had been, and soon Joy and Tina were inseparable.

By the beginning of February, Tina had moved into Joy's room, and although she and Amy remained friends, the sisterly intimacy was gone. Amy had come to understand Tina's need to be dominant and didn't blame her. Sometimes she missed that shoulder to cry on, but had to admit that having a room all to herself was a new and enjoyable experience.

One evening while doing homework, she remembered some information in one of her textbooks from a last semester class that she thought she could use in a current paper. The book wasn't in her bookcase, and thinking that Tina had maybe mistakenly packed it with her things when she moved, she went down the hall to inquire.

There were no locks on the doors; most of the time they were left standing open. If they were closed, the usual procedure was to rap first, then walk right in, never bothering to wait for an answer. When Amy knocked and opened the door, the room was in darkness even though it was only early evening. She saw them standing in the light from the window locked in a tight embrace and kissing on the lips. Hastily she murmured an apology and backed into the hall, closing the door quietly behind her.

Back in her own room, Amy wondered if her eyes had deceived her. It was very dark and maybe they were just hugging, as all the girls were wont to do when comforting or complimenting. But she now had enough experience with passionate kissing to recognize what she saw. She knew nothing about Joy, but she certainly didn't think Tina was a *fairy*. What about her all-consuming interest in men and dating?

There were no explanations, much to Amy's relief. All three girls acted as if it hadn't happened. And since Amy and Tina weren't alone anymore, there was never a need to mention it, and Amy certainly didn't feel the need to tell anyone. It wasn't her business in the first place; and besides, Amy felt she owed Tina so much for initially introducing her to this life she now valued, her silence was but a small offering of gratitude.

Second Chances

The winter wore on—a winter of severe snowstorms. *Whiteouts* enveloped the campus buildings, walkways, and trees in swirling snow. Late one stormy night, Amy stood looking out her window when a deer materialized out of the maelstrom, leaning into the wind--starting and stopping as if unsure of its direction. She thought to do something but, at a loss, just stood and watched as it disappeared into the wildness.

Somehow she identified with the hapless animal, wondering to herself if she would find a way out of her personal storm.

Classes were cancelled the following day, mostly because the campus was snowbound and the teachers couldn't get there. It was like a party atmosphere in the dorm: a reprieve in the monotony of everyday schedules. Even the campus cooks couldn't maneuver the roads, but since the cafeteria was in the dorm basement, the girls had access to supplies and took the opportunity to whip up some breakfast. They ate sitting around the tables family style, exchanging good-natured insults and compliments on the food and generally enjoying the camaraderie.

Suddenly an outer door burst open, and blowing in with a considerable accumulation of snow were a number of boys from the closest dorm, driven to bearing the elements in search of food. Of course the girls were delighted, and a number of them, Amy included, went to refill the griddle with pancakes, all having previously observed the male appetites. Amy manned the griddle with her back to the door. When she felt a touch on her elbow, she turned to find Jack smiling sheepishly behind her, holding his empty plate.

"Hi, kiddo! How ya doing?"

She had of course seen him around campus, but only at a distance; she made a point of avoiding him. Now she muttered a response, transferred a few cakes to his outstretched plate and went back into the dining room.

He pushed a chair up to her table and proceeded to make small talk with her and her friends. The casual atmosphere had suddenly become tense, and Amy excused herself and went upstairs to her room.

She sat on the bed and tried to regain her composure, vowing that she wouldn't cry. She was startled out of her self-pity when her buzzer sounded, announcing a phone call in the lobby. When she got downstairs, she found it wasn't a call, but Jack standing in wait.

"I thought maybe we could talk?"

They found a couple chairs in the deserted dorm parlor and sat awkwardly silent for a few seconds, each of them wondering what to say and how to start. Amy felt she couldn't breathe, and her heart beat in her ear drums as she gripped the arms of her chair and looked at her feet. She so wished she'd had the courage of her convictions and rejected his request without explanation, as he had done to her outside the dorm that night months ago.

"I've missed you," he started "and I realize now I made a big mistake."

"What happened to the high school girlfriend?" She tried to

sound sarcastic, but already her heart had started to sing in spite of her mind shouting for it to stop.

"It didn't work out. She couldn't compare to you. I was a jerk and I know it, but I thought maybe you'd give me a second chance." He put his hand over hers. "We were good together and had fun. It's a shame to deprive ourselves of that."

"But you said we weren't compatible..." She wanted to hurl his words back at him, but they came out weak and faltering, almost a whisper.

"Look, I don't expect you to just take me back, even though I know you still care for me." He tightened the pressure on her hand and gently lifted it so he could hold it in both of his. Amy had all she could do not to jump into his arms right there, and she sensed that he knew it. "Think about it and I'll give you a call later."

Even now he was in control, and as he turned to leave, she wondered if maybe he were smiling. She kept her eyes on his back as he walked to the front door and left without turning.

He made it look as if he were acting out of consideration, when in reality, he was once again making her wait. She was alternately elated and furious. She recited his character flaws over in her mind, hoping to render him undesirable. She could think of nothing else for the rest of the day. But as the short hours of winter sunlight faded away and another snowfall began to blur the campus lights, Amy stood at her window and silently mouthed to another gathering snowstorm, *"Please let him call....Please.."*

Second Chances......Granter and grantee vow that everything will be different, and at first it is. But change requires so much effort, and gradually, imperceptibly, both parties fall back into the same comfortable and predictable behavior, and in a way it's a relief.

One night as they drove back to the dorm, Amy held her breath several times as the car swerved on the slushy road. Jack had been drinking too much. She usually looked forward to their tender farewells when the evening was over but recognized that on this particular night he was in an argumentative mood. As she turned to go, he caught her by the elbow.

"What's your hurry? You got a private session with the dorm broads? Do you tell them everything we do? Is it sort of like second-hand thrills? "

"Of course I don't. You know how private I am."

"Maybe we should try something shocking and really get them going." He tightened his grip on her arm, and Amy realized that to placate was the only way to avoid an ugly scene for her as well as for all the other couples in the process of coming home with dates at that moment.

"Some other time," she laughed. "I have to get in now. Remember my hours?"

"Maybe you're a fairy. Maybe you're all fairies, always hugging and holding hands. I hear Tina and Joy kiss just like you and I do. I'll bet you see it all the time…"

"Of course not, just that once.." As the words passed her lips, she wanted to sink into oblivion. What was wrong with her? Does being in love force you to abandon or bend all your principles, your loyalty? But Jack had seemed not to hear, and released her arm to fumble with his keys.

He won't remember, she thought, breathing a sigh of relief and getting out of the car.

But it wasn't a week later that Jack questioned her with a half smile on his face. "So, did you really see them kissing?"

Don't believe drunks when they explain away their bad behavior by vowing they didn't know what they were doing and couldn't remember a thing, thought Amy. The lessons seemed to be coming at her faster than she could absorb.

"I didn't think you'd remember that," she said. "It was just a slip of the tongue, and you were so drunk. Please don't mention it to anyone else. I'm not even sure that's what I saw, it was so dark in the room." It wasn't as if she had initiated the gossip she rationalized. Jack must have *had wind* of it from someone else first.

But she had all but confirmed it.

We all have two sides to our personalities. To survive in society we have our social side, but we also are aware of the person we see in the dark of our souls when we admit to our true feelings, opinions and selfishness....the side that's behind much of our public action and personal agendas. Fortunate is the person whose two sides coincide for the most part.

Homosexuals in the fifties must have lived constantly fearing the exposure of their alternate sides, which would result in extreme prejudice. Unless they were unusually strong, or a little stupid, or desperately craving attention, they lived with their secret, suppressing their urges, going to great pains to convince others they were heterosexual by dating the opposite sex and even getting married and having children.

How could Tina cope with this, she thought worriedly. *Who would have thought that I'd be the one to destroy her carefully constructed facade? I like her! She's like a sister. No, she means more to me than a sister. Maybe I'm a fairy too. Better that than a disloyal backstabber.*

Should she go to her and confess?

Her quandary became a moot point when a girl from Jack's group slid into the seat next to her at chapel one day and whispered conspiratorially, "Did you actually *see* them kissing?"

Amy was sick to her stomach. It now became not only her betrayal of Tina, but Jack's betrayal of her.

"Oh come on," Jack defended when she confronted him, "what's the big deal? You guys talk about JoAnne and Carol all the time, and if you want to know, I was saving *your* reputation. After all, you were her roommate first. And think about *my* reputation! I don't want people thinking I go out with lesbians!"

More and more, Amy was glimpsing a side of Jack she found unacceptable and unattractive, although at least he was honest, she allowed, as she guiltily acknowledged having joined in the jokes about JoAnne and Carol behind their backs.

Losing Love but Finding Self-Respect

She didn't see Jack again until the day of the memorial service for Dr. Savin.

Amy sat in the front row with Mrs. Savin, so deep in despair that she thought she could hardly be of any comfort to her friend.

She remembered vividly the dorm buzzer she decided she wouldn't answer, thinking it might be Jack trying to talk her out of her anger. When it stopped, she breathed a sigh of relief, having not yet decided how to handle the *Jack problem,* as she had come to think of it.

Then there was a knock at the door and the Dorm Mother came in.

"I'm sorry Amy. I know you were a close friend of Dr. Savin, and we've just had word that he died after being taken to the hospital last night."

Amy ran down the stairs as her buzzer sounded again and found Frank waiting in the lobby.

"I just heard," he said, as he caught her by the elbows. "I've got my car outside. I'll take you to their house."

When they entered, Amy forgot her aversion to hugging and enveloped her grief-stricken friend in her arms.

"What happened?" she cried, finding it difficult to speak.

As they sat at the dining room table where they had spent so many pleasant evenings, Mrs. Savin related the story of her brave, beautiful son who had come to the cultural outpost of Woodland to die.

"He had inoperable liver cancer," she explained, "and he didn't want to burden his friends and his fiancé with having to watch him deteriorate and die. I brought him life and I was there at his death. It was how he wanted it, and he was happy with his teaching."

"I wish I'd known," Amy sobbed.

Mrs. Savin took her hand in comfort. "He didn't want to spoil your friendship with pity. He wanted it to be because you truly liked and respected him. You were his prize student."

Amy remembered the later comment as a repetition of what she had said the first night they met, and wept anew that he had had so little to comfort him in his final days.

It was like a Shakespearian tragedy, Amy thought, *the star-crossed lovers, his sacrifice to spare others, his bravery in the face of death.*

He was to be buried back East, so none of his family or friends came for the service. It was a cold and brief tribute, since no one knew him well or even liked him much, because he had been too outspoken about many college shortcomings. But the whispered benediction was shaken by Mrs. Savin's unexpected and loud wail, *"He's left me here like a stone!"*

After Mrs. Savin had been handed into a car for her ride home, Jack approached Amy and almost formally expressed his condolences. Her heart softened toward him until he added conversationally, "How about his Mother? Leave it to Jews to be so dramatic!"

Amy turned and walked away without a word, ruefully thinking that when all was said and done, the Savins had solved her *Jack problem.*

Within the week, Chester Rilke was given the task of driving Mrs. Savin to Minneapolis, where she caught a train home. Amy made the uncomfortable and quiet trip with them, and assured Mrs. Savin she would supervise the packing and shipping of the few items they had brought from the East. They parted with the promise to keep in touch, but Amy never received an answer to her notes and learned several months later, through a college announcement, that her friend had died only weeks after getting home. *Her life's work being done,* Amy thought

The winter days crept by. Amy worked with a sense of relief and a feeling of satisfaction. Tina and Joy remained friendly but didn't really associate with the other dorm girls. Amy wasn't aware of any organized hazing of the couple. Surely they had been subject to slights and comments, but there was almost a taboo against talking about it, even during *pillow talk.*

The exuberant Tina was, however, a changed girl, keeping to herself, talking little, and seeming to have lost that zest for life that had made her so popular and endearing. Amy was sorry about that, but considered perhaps this was the new, true Tina and she hoped she was happy in this role. There had been no confessions, and Amy never knew whether Tina was aware of her role in *the outing.*

Amy began seeing Frank and they studied together, went to

movies, and occasionally to Woody's. Amy didn't receive any more calls from Jack and said hello only politely if she met him.

A Glory in It All

And so the winter wore on in the piney woods until one day, after spending the morning in Old Main for classes and work study, Amy emerged to a warm, blue sky and strong sun. Water dripped from the icicles on the roof, and streams of melting snow ran in the streets. Amy had been through these Wisconsin springs before and knew that, in spite of Ma's rejection of the returning sunshine on the spring of Wendel's death, this day heralded the lengthening and strengthening of the warmth and the return of life to the world.

She felt giddy and skipped around the puddles calling impulsively, "It's spring, Stewart!" to the figure that lurked in the basement doorway.

"Spring...and the voice of the turtle is heard in the land..."

Stewart replied loudly, and he followed the skipping Amy with his eyes, vaguely smiling as if trying to resurrect more words of a poem or capture a fleeting memory of some long ago spring on a different, far-away campus.

"You can say that again," she playfully replied and continued her skipping, leaving a puzzled and mumbling Stewart in her wake.

Although there was more snow and cold winds still blew, there were enough of those promising days to invigorate the whole student body, and everyone seemed free to anticipate the end of the school year and, eventually, the long days of summer.

But Dean Herregen's second triumph was upon them, and he was determined that the long-awaited and planned-for inauguration of Woodland's new president would be another *grawhnd* occasion that would reflect once again on his expertise.

The entourage was seen everywhere: conducting meetings, conferring on menus with the cafeteria cooks, and boring the chapel audience with his endless talks on the *protocawhl* of the ceremony and the *grawhvity* of the occasion.

Amy now spent most of her work-study time typing letters of confirmation to colleges that had agreed to send representatives, and she was amazed to realize that it was going to be quite a distinguished crowd.

You have to hand it to him, she thought, *he surely knows how to stage an event.*

He, himself, would of course represent *Hawhvawd*, proudly wearing the colors. Everyday the mail was full of letters from the full gamut of post-secondary education, from Ivy League to state schools to small private institutions (like Woodland), either sending regrets or naming an attendee. Amy read them all in order to sort them into two piles and send the appropriate form letter to each.

When she started work one day, the first letter she came across was from McGill University in Montreal, Canada. Even Amy was excited about this one.

Please let it be an acceptance, she thought, as by now she had become quite fond of the Dean and knew that this international recognition would please him.

The letter began formally and predictably,

Thank you…an honor….wish you well… Then Amy read the last line.

We are happy to inform you that we have a McGill graduate living in your community, Mr. Stewart Bailey. We will ask Mr. Bailey to represent McGill at your inauguration and hope that he will be able to comply..etc., etc.

She sat in stunned silence. Surely there were many Stewarts in the community, but Amy had a premonition as she placed the letter carefully on the acceptance pile. And it came to pass that Stewart of the furnace room was indeed Stewart Bailey, McGill Graduate of 1940. Amy wondered if Dean Herregen would honor McGill's appointment.

Mrs. Simon fussed and fumed. "Such a dilemma, really. What will the poor Dean do? He can't be expected to have Stewart at the banquet, really! Maybe Stewart won't understand."

But not long after, Stewart appeared in front of Mrs. Simon's desk, clutching a wrinkled and smudged paper in his hands.

"I guess I'm supposed to attend a banquet," he started, handing the letter to Mrs. Simon. She took it carefully between thumb and forefinger, and Amy, watching from her typewriter, thought for a minute she was going to deposit it directly into the wastepaper basket as if it were an unclean piece of trash. The silence loomed as Mrs. Simon scanned the paper, obviously looking for some disclaimer. When she found none, she handed the paper back to him.

"We'll have to talk to the Dean about this, really." Her tone was almost that of a mother threatening a youngster with punishment as soon as his father came home. Nevertheless, she led Stewart, letter in hand, into the Dean's office and exited, closing the door firmly and taking her seat behind the desk.

"Really!" she exclaimed to no one in particular.

Once again there were many meetings and clandestine conversations. Amy heard bits and pieces:

Can he be made presentable?

What if he causes a scene?

He is subject to outbursts!

She didn't dare inquire of the tight lipped Mrs. Simon as to the final decision, but as she took her place in the serving line on the night of the banquet, she searched the assemblage for Stewart, finding him at last at a table in the back of the cafeteria, strategically placed close to an exit door and flanked on either side by Mrs. Simon and Chester.

Amy was stunned! Stewart's hair and beard had been trimmed neatly and washed to a silky, wavy brilliance. He wore the proud kilt and sporran of a highland chief, topped by a tweed jacket that looked very familiar to Amy. The wildness in his eyes was absent and he looked serene, comfortable and handsome, unlike his dinner companions, who fidgeted with his tie or straightened his silverware and constantly looked at the door, as if making sure the passage was clear for a quick getaway should everything go horribly wrong. When Amy brought Stewart his dinner, he looked up, winked and said softly, "And the night shall be filled with music, and the cares that infest the day…"

"Shall fold their tents, like the Arabs, and as silently steal away…" Amy responded equally as soft.

"Really!" said Mrs. Simon. And Chester scribbled furiously in his notebook.

Dénouement

Now spring was everywhere, causing people to be giddy with anticipation. Amy thought it was a little sad also: friends would be graduating soon, others would go away for the summer and not return in the fall. She expected that she might never again see many people who had been prominent in her everyday life in the past year.

As for the dorm girls, they were determined to have tanned, glowing bodies for the end of the year events and spent every sunny afternoon behind the dorm on an equipment shed roof, hoping the reflection from the metal would guarantee them a change in their winter white skin.

Amy knew it was futile for her, cursed with a light complexion, to think about color, but climbed a ladder at the side of the low building to align herself in rows with the others, like sausages on a grill, to roast and sizzle, rubbing baby oil laced with iodine on their skin and raising their heads only to quench their thirsts from the ubiquitous Coke bottles.

Nighttime was ideal for sitting out, in Amy's mind. Many a warm spring evening when a slight breeze kept the newly hatched mosquitoes at bay, she would climb the ladder to the roof and spend some time alone, with the moon and the stars and her thoughts.

Some of her dreams had been fulfilled this year. If not wildly popular, she felt warmly accepted, drawing strength from the friends she had made, and she realized she didn't obsess about her popularity any more. She was happy with her classes, and now truly thought of the college as *Dear Old Woodland*. But, as with all dreams once come true, some seem to morph into something entirely different and not at all acceptable.

Jack was a disappointment as her first romantic lover. But in spite of the elder generation's warning about lost virginity, Amy had talked herself into viewing the encounter as valuable experience and vowed never again to be taken in by charm and outward appearances.

Tina and Joy had told her they wouldn't be back to Woodland but had decided to move to Minneapolis and 'become working girls together,' as Tina put it. Amy couldn't bring herself to ask if there had been discrimination and unpleasantness, or to what levels, and still couldn't admit to her part in the whole affair. It was a time when such things were swept under the rug, phrases like *better left unsaid*, or *let sleeping dogs lie* the usual response. Through the years, as Amy reminisced about her college days, she still felt guilt and often wondered if those *sleeping dogs* snarled with betrayal in Tina's college memories.

Her dear Dr. Savin loomed large in her evening reverie under the stars, and she vowed to try and live up to his expectations. She had known him such a short time, but he had set an example of what she hoped some day to be: knowledgeable, intelligent, kind, and above all, true to her convictions.

She would also remember Dean Herregen, *Dear Old Woody* himself. She had to admit there was a kernel of truth in what Jack had said about his doing more good for the college than teachers or classes. Winning that homecoming game would be an occasion remembered for years to come by every student at Woodland, whether or not they ever graduated. She also remembered the resurrected Stewart, who was allowed proudly, if briefly, to return to a life lost in the turmoil of his mind. The Dean was a survivor and an expert at *making a silk purse out of the sow's ear* he had been given.

The dorm rang with shouts of "Goodbye, see you next year!" Suitcases bumped and trunks scraped against the stairwell walls. Amy stood at the curb waiting for a taxi to take her to the bus depot. Frank pulled up in his rusted-out Ford and jumped out to load her luggage without even asking. The radio sputtered and crackled as they drove down the now familiar elm-lined street from the college. He ignored the static and casually asked, "You coming back next year?"

"You need a dance partner at Woody's?" she replied.

As if by magic, the static suddenly cleared, and Kay Starr was belting out, *The wheel of fortune keeps spinning around...will it ever smile on me? Will this be the day?*

Hopes
By Roger Lee Cerioni

I threw my hopes into the sky
Gleaming brightly in the sun,
Those wishes dear to the heart
Of things I wanted to be done.

One by one my hopes came back,
All fitting into some dream,
Not the wishes that I had planned
But wishes fitting into a scheme.

XII.
A Woman's Place

The afternoon sun warmed her. As she walked to her car, she concentrated on the quaint but hazardous main street laid with bricks arranged in zigzag patterns, carefully avoiding those that had worked loose or protruded. Traffic was constant, and pedestrians were hurrying purposefully without pausing to enjoy the unusually warm and sunny, late June day.

A majority of the vehicles lining Second Street were pick-up trucks piled with sacks of feed, complicated-looking machine parts, and rolls of baler twine. Farm families were using the previous day's rain as an excuse to enjoy a respite from their seasonal sentence of labor, and had collected the needed accouterments of their profession for tomorrow's assault on the brief but feverish northern growing season.

She climbed into the car, inserted the key, then paused to watch a woman expertly maneuver a large truck into a parking space in front of her. Two teenage boys jumped out of the back; a girl of about twelve sat in the cab with her mother.

Amy waited and watched, bemused by the almost military precision with which the woman walked to the sidewalk organizing her keys, purse and slips of paper, doled out money with obvious instructions to each of the children, who disappeared rapidly in three directions, instantly produced the exact amount of meter change, and mechanically patted her hair in four predetermined and predictable spots. She walked away, lean and brown in red polyester slacks.

Amy felt a pang of envy! Oh, to be that organized and decisive and to know exactly where you were going - no dithering, no wasted movements.

I'll bet she runs her whole life with lists, Amy thought. *Grocery lists, up-to-date address books, weekly work schedules, neat financial ledgers, a balanced check book...*

Any emergency could be tidily inserted into one or more of these lists and absorbed with a minimum of emotion and uncertainty.

'You're either in charge of life, or it's in charge of you,' Frank was fond of pronouncing. Amy had always argued that life was too short to spend time preparing for always-impending disaster. 'The substance of which ulcers are made,' she'd quip.

Unfortunately, that laid-back attitude didn't seem to surface for her when life's *little* disasters struck. Absently, she wondered if her red polyestered friend had ever lain awake worrying over a cat that hadn't come home by dark; under which list would that dilemma fall?

She turned the key and the motor started.

"This is ridiculous," she scolded herself aloud, "I can't just sit here wool gathering." That's what Ma used to call her frequent spates of day dreaming.

All the store fronts on Second Street were the same as they had been an hour before. Marla's Dresses still featured a big window of print skirts she had admired. The ice cream shop glass was still dominated by a glossy colored poster of a 'Super Chocolate Ice Cream Soda, complete with cherry on top!' As she turned onto a pretty residential street, she saw that the houses and lawns were still as neat and inviting as they had been a short time ago when she had dropped off her daughter to visit a friend.

But everything had changed for Amy in the space of about fifteen minutes, and she felt stunned and somehow removed: watching her hands on the steering wheel and automatically slowing for corners, as if by remote control.

She eased to the curb, waited a moment, then watched fifteen-year-old Wendy run toward the car. Her long hair rose and fell, the bangs blowing back from her high forehead. Amy anticipated and could almost repeat Wendy's breathless, hopeful greeting, "Can I stay and have supper with Pam and get a ride home with Dad later?"

"Not today," Amy replied, with no explanation.

Wendy hesitated, as if about to argue, thought better of it, turned to her girl friend waiting expectantly on the porch and called, with just a touch of mimicry, "I can't today," then she flopped onto the seat next to Amy, leaning against the door in order to put as much space as possible between her and her mother.

Amy glanced at the profile of her *baby girl*. The face was basically the same as it had been fifteen years ago. The chubbiness was gone, but her skin had retained that porcelain, pink look that had always been her best feature. Her eyes were the same bright blue behind too much makeup, although their look had become increasingly hostile of late.

'It's a phase,' Frank would comfort, 'In another two or three years you'll be friends again.'

But Amy missed that sweet and cheerful little creature who colored Easter eggs and picked wild flowers with her. Two or three years loomed like a long sentence of, if not hatred, at least disdain from the person she loved most in this world.

They drove without speaking for a couple blocks.

"Have a nice visit?" Amy ventured, not wanting to let the silence turn a small disagreement into yet another major battle.

"There's nothing to do out in the country alone," she accused, keeping her face turned away from her mother and staring out the window. Her bottom lip pouted slightly.

They had moved to their dream house in the country the previous September and belatedly realized that Wendy hadn't shared the dream. She had been occupied with school all winter, but Amy knew the summer was beginning to bore her. She was a completely social animal, who missed being able to meet her friends on a street corner to walk for blocks in the twilight or share a box of gingersnaps while sitting on the school yard swings, talking endlessly about boys, sex, cheerleading and any girls who weren't with *them.*

Amy suddenly wished she'd let her stay with her friend. Why had she wanted her home? It might have been better if she could talk to Frank alone, as a matter of fact. She wanted to tell her daughter that she understood feeling *stranded* in the country, but today she couldn't face the recriminations and accusations of the already well-argued discussion.

Instead, she smiled. "Let's stop for a chocolate soda!"

Wendy's glance was surprised, but she quickly resumed her sulk. "What about your diet?"

Amy shrugged and felt Wendy's manner soften a little as she wise-cracked, "Can I have your two new blouses when you outgrow them?"

Taking that for assent, Amy pulled into the ice cream shop. Their young waitress was eager and efficient. Her back as she bent over her order book reminded Amy of their white Christmas angel, her thin, sharp shoulder blades emerging under her white, dacron uniform like fledgling wings.

Wendy displayed a long suffering glance as Amy cautioned, "Don't forget the cherry on top!"

That night Frank was late for dinner. When he came home he was hungry first, and then full of talk about the day's meetings, triumphs, and vexations. She was usually interested in his stories, but listened with half her mind that night. He chatted enthusiastically, and she realized he had forgotten about her doctor's appointment that afternoon.

Suddenly it became important that he remember without coaching. It was a game; How long before he remembered and inquired about her health? She always eagerly awaited the outcome of *his* checkups, and this fact caused her to fume inwardly.

Maybe she was being too touchy about it. Her appointment was prompted by a weary and out-of-sorts feeling the last couple months. She was convinced it was menopause and voiced this opinion many times.

'It's probably stress now that you're an executive type woman,' Frank would tease.

At any rate, it was never a big worry to either of them, so why *should* it be on his mind? But her defense of him was half-hearted; she still felt wronged.

The phone rang, and as if by a prearranged signal, Wendy jumped to answer.

"Debbie'll come pick me up if I can go to town for awhile," she pleaded.

"Okay, but remember the ten-o'clock curfew." Suddenly her best friend again, Wendy patted Amy's head playfully as she ran to refresh her eye makeup.

"Thanks mom, and thanks for the soda this afternoon too."

Damn, Amy thought. Wendy had inadvertently given her father a clue. Now he had an advantage in the game. Although it didn't matter; he had already lost, she decided.

"You go to town this afternoon?"

He *still* didn't remember! It was time for the big play, with just the right amount of sarcasm - not too much so that she looked like she was playing the martyr, but just enough to make him realize he had been inconsiderate.

"In case you forgot," she sighed. "I had a doctor's appointment."

"Hey, that's right; what did you find out? Healthy girl?"

He wasn't contrite.

"I'll tell you later," Amy responded, shrugging towards the upstairs, where Wendy was noisily completing her beauty regimen.

Frank looked at her, more puzzled than concerned. She clearly had his attention now and was almost enjoying his discomfort. Then suddenly the game was over and she didn't care about his insensitivity. The important thing was giving the problem to him – saying it out loud to someone.

A car horn sounded and Wendy was gone in a flurry of sandals and hooded sweatshirt.

"Well?" He looked slightly worried, but more inquisitive. Amy struggled to be composed, but couldn't keep the tears from welling in her eyes. "What in hell is it? Do I have to play twenty questions?" He sounded irritable, causing her reply to take on a more biting edge.

"Oh, nothing serious...I'm pregnant!"

Mind over Motherhood

"Take a week to think this over," the doctor had said. "You know there is much worse news I could give a woman at age forty-four!"

Why were men always so logical about decisions that affected women?

"But it can be terminated," Amy stammered.

"Or you can have the baby. Nowadays many older mothers have perfectly normal babies. You must think it through and talk to your husband."

He made it sound so simple; weigh the pros and cons: baby? No baby? It's really simple, if you're devoid of any human feelings. *(Or a man...)*

Amy was ambivalent. She had begun to think of herself as a semi-liberated woman—not of the bra-burning, *sisterhood* group certainly, but she voted intelligently, voiced her opinions, and for the past four years, had held a job she enjoyed immensely. What had started out as a need for extra money to pay bills and save for Wendy's college had somehow burgeoned into a frenzied return to school to finish her degree. In relatively rapid succession came the luck of stumbling into a career instead of wage earning employment, and a self-improvement program that had left her thinner and feeling more confident.

'I know what I'd do.'

Her own words drifted back to her as she recalled a morning coffee discussion she'd shared with girlfriends, the topic being midlife pregnancy.

"After all," she'd argued, "we're progressive thinkers, supported by new laws enacted by other progressive thinkers who happen to believe that women have a choice as to how their bodies and lives are used."

How smug she had been as she mouthed the familiar rhetoric that swirled around the battle for the passage of the abortion law. *Get on the bandwagon women! This law is for you!*

But now Amy wished she could go back to those women who listened with her resolve and say, "Wait! It isn't that easy. It's not that black and white. Take a week to think it over, or maybe a lifetime!"

She and Frank had wanted more children; but when it didn't happen, they'd been content with pouring their efforts into Wendy, an activity they both thoroughly enjoyed. But Wendy was growing up, becoming her own person, and in the process (Amy had to admit it) temporarily less lovable and needy.

Then there were the heady perks of her job. She was respected for a certain amount of ability and could converse with authority on a few subjects besides Band Mothers and lasagna recipes. And, of course, there was the money. *The root of all evil* was a necessary evil, and factored hugely in most decisions.

"Maybe I could do *both*," she thought. "Women nowadays don't bury themselves in motherhood. They work, they go to school, they become active in politics. They separate the essential and important time with their children from the tedium."

But with a new baby?

Amy remembered the sleepless nights and overwhelming work load.

Over the course of the week, she lurched from one scenario to another. She'd been given a second chance to relive a portion of her life. *Like the plot of a B movie*, she'd muse. Then again, she couldn't quit her job, there were the new country house payments to be made, and besides, she didn't want to quit.

She wanted to keep the new person she'd become.

Did that mean she didn't want to keep the new person inside her?

At times the fervor of women's rights and choices seemed to pale under the protective instincts of impending motherhood.

The week of decision was passing quickly. At first they skirted the subject by mutual, but unspoken, consent, each thinking privately. One night the discussion could no longer be postponed. They went for a ride, driving down one winding back road after another.

"I'm surprised you're considering going through with this." He was speaking incredulously. "I mean, I know how you feel about babies, but this isn't a baby yet. Do you realize how old we'll be when it's a teenager? You think we're having trouble understanding Wendy now? Take that fifteen years down the line when we're fifty-nine!"

"Have you ever known a kid with old parents?" It seemed to Amy that he was relentless. "They're too tired to discipline or even be interested, and the kid usually ends up being ashamed of them. The way I see it, for the first time we have a choice in the matter; we don't have to be victims of fate."

"Is that what it's called? Being a victim? I thought it was called being a parent!"

Sadly, the discussion had digressed, and there was that damn word 'choice' again. The very thing women were fighting for – that she had espoused – was being used to unmask her. Did she really feel her ability to reproduce was her most unique and important feature, her *destiny*?

"It's up to you, of course," Frank said finally, "but I guess you know how I feel."

She stayed up late that night watching television, but really only seeing her own thoughts as they paraded through her mind. It was going to be difficult enough without trying to go it alone. If Frank wasn't one hundred percent on board with this, then she really had no choice after all. Abortion was the only logical next step.

The next day she called her doctor and told him her decision. He seemed disapproving and gave her the telephone number of a doctor in Minneapolis. He didn't wish her luck, ask to see her afterward, offer any comfort or volunteer to call and make the arrangements.

Times had changed, but not all of society had changed its thinking on everything.

Getting Through It

It was a gorgeous July day. The sun was warm but not hot, and the sky was blue. Amy decided to imagine they were off on a shopping trip and dispense with the intense agony of her conflicting thoughts. After the long days and nights of soul-searching and indecision, she felt relief. She kept telling herself she was doing the right thing. Frank reached over to squeeze her hand. He looked sympathetic, and she managed a weak smile to reassure him. By tonight she'd be home and everything would be back to normal.

The gynecologist was pleasant, soft spoken and gentle; the office was cheerful and quiet, except for the faint, taped music that played incessantly, blending one song into another.

The receptionist didn't flinch when Amy stated her business.

"Why should she," Amy reasoned, "I'm only exercising my right to reject an unwanted pregnancy." *(Or do I want it?)*

She took her chair in the waiting room. Several women in various stages of pregnancy read magazines while they waited for their appointments. Amy remembered their placid expressions and watched with a certain envy as they absent-mindedly rested their hands on, or gently rubbed, their bulging bellies. It made Amy feel more comfortable, oddly, knowing that her doctor was engaged in initiating life as well as terminating it.

The examination was quick but thorough.

"Everything seems fine. You can get dressed and stop at the receptionist's desk for your documents and directions to the hospital."

Amy wasn't aware that she was crying again until a tear rolled down her cheek. The doctor took her hands and looked in her eyes. "This is not your baby," he said firmly. "Don't confuse it with your pregnancy. This is merely a gynecological procedure necessary for your personal well-being."

It sounded like a mantra: sentences carefully designed to be repeated and embraced.

It's his reason for offering this service, Amy thought. That did make her feel better, and she repeated it to herself often over the course of the afternoon.

At the clinic, it quickly became apparent that this was going to be a group endeavor. Tough looking girls in too tight jeans sat smoking cigarettes (still allowed in most places, even hospitals, at that time) with *nothing fazes me* expressions on their faces. Others were just young and frightened, looking quite fazed. A few clung to boyfriends who looked squeamish and uneasy. Still others argued in whispers with tired-faced women, obviously their mothers.

Amy sat alone. It was also before the time when husbands accompanied their wives to the delivery room, and Frank was of the generation of men who busied themselves elsewhere at a safe distance and waited for results provoked by that most perverse of female organs, the uterus. Truthfully, Amy was relieved that he wasn't there, and hadn't encouraged him, although he had gamely offered. She knew he was worried, but she wasn't sure she felt up to the added burden of offering *him* assurance as well as herself.

All the girls, ranging in age from sixteen to near thirty, and Amy, forty-four, sat on chrome chairs in the laboratory waiting for tests. Each in turn was weighed, blood typed and sent to the bathroom for a specimen. All very impersonal and sterile.

She sat on the stool, willing herself to produce the requisite few drops. Lately it hadn't been a problem, but suddenly she was absolutely dehydrated. Perhaps she was concentrating too hard — if she could just think of something else. Her eyes scanned the walls and detected faint writing towards the top of the stall. She strained her eyes to read it.

For a few brief moments of happiness, I have to go through this. Underneath in different pen and hand, Amy read, *Anyway, everyone here is nice.*

This was not graffiti! These were expressions of fear, desperation, and disappointment. Amy wondered which of the sallow little girls with the tough faces had given script to these emotions. Maybe they were from a different group, but all so alike in their demeanor and problem. Which of them had found in the cold, toilet stall the anonymity necessary to allow a tiny crack in their shells of self defense, for a little emotion, a little light, to shine through?

Amy's resolve wavered back and forth. All afternoon waiting for one test or another, she entertained thoughts of getting up and leaving, which continued even as she felt the anesthetic relax her body.

Then it was too late.

Finally, the worst was over. Or was it the best? The baby was no more.

The heavy dose of valium made her float, as she lay stretched on a recliner. There were many of them in recovery, and they lay in rows like products from an assembly line, finished and waiting to be packaged. She struggled to focus her eyes and her brain and settled on the recliner next to her.

A slim girl who looked no older than Wendy, lay on her side, curled in a tight little ball. She looked like a child who had just been punished and sent to her room. The angles of her body were tight and guarded, and she sniffled quietly.

Amy leaned forward and touched her knee. "Not much fun, huh?"

She started slightly and raised her tear-stained face from her arm, immediately regaining her belligerent expression.

"It's not so bad. It's just getting through it!"

Just getting through it! The same could be said for birth, death, love and hate, all of life. You just have to *get through it.*

Frank took her in his arms when the nurse brought her to the waiting room. He really was such a good guy. She felt a tremor run through his body as he held her, and she desperately hoped he wouldn't cry. She could not have endured that. They drove the seventy miles home in silence with her sleeping off the anesthetics most of the way.

For the rest of her life, Amy followed the on going debate over the abortion issue. Aging politicians professed to know what was in the best interest of women. Various religious leaders and their followers branded her and all her young friends from the clinic murderers. Pro-life zealots blew up abortion clinics, killing in their efforts to protect life.

As time went by, she thought she had made the right decision; other times she wasn't sure. One thing she did know: no right thinking woman would ever use abortion as a means of birth control, as some right-wingers cautioned.

Amy thought less and less about it as the years passed, but she was occasionally burdened with a recurring dream: she would hear crying and find a crib that held a tiny emaciated and filthy infant. Without being accused, she knew the infant was hers and that she had somehow forgotten to care for it. She would waken awash in perspiration and guilt. She guessed it was her legacy.

One more thing she had to *just get through*...

XIII.
The Tomato Patch

Spring was late that year with wet, slushy storms well into May. But around the middle of the month, unwarranted by the weather, the trees and perennials began to sprout pale, tight buds proving that the rhythms of nature are oblivious to adversity. Several late May and early June frosts further punished the struggling greenery, and yet it persisted. Once again, spring *would* come to the Northland.

One early morning in June, huddled in a heavy sweatshirt with her stiff fingers gratefully encasing a cup of hot coffee, Amy stood and solemnly surveyed her tomato patch. She had set out twelve plants in time to provide for the ninety-day growing season specified in the seed catalogues. She had faithfully covered them against the cold every night, lifting the plastic sheet in the morning as soon as the sun was high enough to produce any warmth. She had fed them water enriched with unnaturally blue crystals, which were supposed to provide amazing growth and a heavy fruit yield. Each plant was surrounded by its own fortress of half a milk carton, to fend off attacks by underground pests.

But in spite of all her ministrations, they were a sorry lot. Their leaves were a sickly yellow-green, and some of them curled and wilted as if they had felt the frost through their thermal shield. Their stems seemed too weak to hold their sparse foliage, and they leaned against the milk cartons in strange stances, not unlike the spindly, young trees in the forest that bordered the yard, leaning for support against the full-grown parents that deprived them of enough sun and air to grow straight.

She set her coffee cup on the fence post and carefully folded the plastic cover for the last time that summer. "You're on your own," she spoke to them. "The pampering is over. From now on, it's survival of the fittest."

The kitchen was warm and smelled of coffee.

"Rough night?" she asked. A shrug answered the question; it was a subject beyond discussion. There had been too many dark nights spent in discussion, and the following cold mornings had dawned with no solutions...Eventually, the hope of a reprieve grew dimmer, and each day they awoke with fear and regret lodged in their chests like the beginning of nausea, repressed and denied in the hope that it would pass.

"I don't know if those tomatoes are going to make it; they don't look good."

"They'll be okay," he answered. "It takes them a while to acclimate, and we're due for some warm days. After all, it's the middle of June."

As if on cue, the weather did turn warm and sunny, and her tomatoes took on a brighter aspect. One morning they seemed straighter; the next morning their color had improved. She watered, fed, and weeded them, but, true to her resolve, she didn't cover them.

Sometimes she'd wake in the night to labored breathing and the fretful mumbling of his dreams. Uncertain and bothered, she'd stand by the open window, and sometimes she even donned her sweatshirt and went to stand by the garden. Sometimes she wondered if she should resurrect the plastic sheet, but she never did.

As the summer wore on, Amy's gardens seemed to make up for the lost spring. The bearded irises challenged exotic, tropical orchids in size and color, producing large hour-glass shapes in variations of purple and garnet, their spiked leaves spread like fans. The daisies swayed on their long stems and leaned their heavy heads into the neighboring bed, complementing the red phlox. Even the hydrangea bush, which had never blossomed, produced one large, magnificent flower of the deepest blue, which remained, unfaded, until late autumn.

The kitchen was hot and muggy and smelled of coffee as she came in from her morning inspection.

"Rough night?" she asked.

After the usual shrug, he said, "How do the tomatoes look?"

"They look healthy -- lots of leaves but no flowers yet. I'm afraid they won't have tomatoes in time to ripen before frost." *(Had she always been this pessimistic?)*

"They'll come around. You can always pick them green and ripen them by the windows."

"Provided we get any green ones."

"We'll get green ones. We always do."

Every February, as the house groaned and creaked with cold and the snow lay deep on the gardens, the seed catalogues would begin to arrive with their exaggerated pictures and outlandish promises. Amy would look longingly, but skeptically, and wonder aloud as to the practicality of planting a vegetable garden.

"Vegetables are so cheap that time of year. Lots of people even give them to you."

But he'd always argue, "Just a few tomato plants if nothing else."

As his mobility decreased, his car became the key to his prison. He'd pivot on his one sound leg, fold his wheelchair and throw it into the back seat. He went to the library, to his favorite bar and often on unadvised trips that could have proven treacherous to a person in his condition. But he loved to drive, and he made the most of each venture, never knowing if it was his *last hurrah*.

During past years, late summer Saturdays provided him with a mission to seek out area farmer's markets. Their postage-stamp garden never yielded enough provender for him, and he'd return with beets, cucumbers, bunches of assorted herbs, maple syrup and other such treasures. If it was a truly successful mission, he would have found vine-ripened tomatoes, his favorite vegetable.

Recently, stacks of books and magazines around his recliner replaced the road trips. He cut articles or excerpts that interested him, and often this collection included recipes he wanted Amy to try. Consequently, pages of bright pictures depicting everything from gazpacho to spaghetti sauce with directions calling for exotic herbs and spices accumulated in the kitchen, awaiting the bountiful harvest.

That year, as sometimes happens in the North near the big lake, the late spring predetermined an early autumn. The vast expanse of water didn't have time to really warm, and the nights turned cold by the beginning of September. Amy began to cover her green tomato-laden plants in order to extend the season.

The kitchen was warm and smelled of coffee those mornings, but he didn't come there for his breakfast any more. She'd take coffee and cereal to his living room chair, where he often spent the night propped up to ease his breathing.

"Rough night?"

The shrug.

"Any ripe ones?"

"Not a one! I'll bring them in today."

Amy spent the morning picking the hard, green vegetables that had begun to take on a whitish caste. Spreading newspapers on the floor, she laid the tomatoes in rows in front of the double glass doors with the southern exposure. Her hands were redolent with the sharp smell of the leaves, and her fingers were a bruised green from the excess chlorophyll hastily stored in the foliage over the short growing season.

Her hothouse was complete.

He had slept in his chair while she worked; and when she took a bowl of soup to him at noon, he was not interested in eating. She noticed that the grey from his hair had seeped into his face, making the line of separation barely perceptible. They both knew, without voicing it, that another hospital visit was inevitable. Later that afternoon, they made the trip.

It froze hard that night. The next morning, Amy's breathe hung whitely in the air as she surveyed the blackened, shriveled clumps that were her tomato plants. No need now to cover, feed, water or weed. Her cheeks felt suddenly colder, and she was surprised as she touched unexplainable tears.

Perversely, once it had frozen hard, Indian summer returned, and each day seemed mockingly more crisp and beautiful than the last. Amy cleared the ruined vines and cultivated the vegetable garden while the tomatoes ripened safely behind the glass. She reported their progress as she stood by the hospital bed. At first, he was interested, but gradually he stopped asking. Still she reported.

Late one night, the phone rang. When she stood by his bed, she asked, "Rough night?" He tried to shrug, but his chin shook, and he held her hand tightly.

"Get me home!" he said hoarsely. And she promised him she would.

After that he didn't talk any more.

Amy selected the largest, ripe tomato from her window hot house and brought it to his room. It was blemish free and perfectly shaped, truly worthy of representing its strain in any boastful catalog. It lay on his bedside table, but he couldn't eat it or even acknowledge that it was there.

As the days went by, it began to lose its luster, but Amy insisted that he would be getting better and want it for lunch. Finally, at the nurse's suggestion, she agreed to store it in the ICU refrigerator.

Eventually they all stood as a family around his bed and watched a monitor count out his life in digital numbers. After, when Amy was alone with him, she told him she was sorry she hadn't kept her promise to get him home and that the tomatoes were all ripe.

XIII.
The Love Letter

Ma had been dead for almost thirty years when her old, battered trunk surfaced in John's attic. It had been put there when the Grady children cleaned out her apartment, and forgotten as they rushed to lavishly spend their lives. Now that they were old and desperately trying to save their days and slow the pace of their passage, there was, at last, time to sort the contents and officially close the book on the Grady household of the 1930s.

There were only four of them now: Of course, Wendel had been gone since the war, and Harold had died several years ago at 70, an age that surprised the rest of the family who expected his tortured life would be much shorter.

The girls had married and raised families, though none had more than two children. After experiencing Ma's struggle to raise her brood of six, they'd felt neither equipped - nor desirous - to follow her example. John hadn't married, but remained the figurehead of the family, never intruding on anyone's life, but ready to extend physical or monetary help if any of the Gradys needed it. Amarantha sometimes wondered how different things would have been for him if his conscience had been less developed, if he'd not felt honor-bound at age 18 to postpone his personal life. She had not forgotten his long-ago words to Elsie: 'I can't leave now. Not while Ma needs me!'

And it seemed as if Ma had always needed him.

They were all quite elderly now; even Amarantha, the *baby*, was 70. The two prominent Grady trademarks they all sported, red hair and freckles, had both faded, the hair to grey and the freckles reduced to wrinkles or melted together into age spots. Amarantha smiled as she looked at them — *like an AARP meeting*, she thought, as she noted the thick glasses, hearing aides, and sensible shoes. *We all live alone, though,* she thought further. *Independent as ever or as Ma would say.*

Fending for ourselves.

Ma had accumulated few worldly goods. Her children lived more elaborate lives than she and, after her funeral, rejected the remaining remnants of her household...a sagging sofa, mismatched dishes, a black and white TV....preferring to give them to the other residents of the *Senior Apartments* where she had lived or haul them to the town dump. Nevertheless, someone had decided to save her old trunk, and now they had wrestled it down to the living room and arranged their chairs around it, the requisite coffee cups in hand, the contents were to be examined.

It had been a pleasant reunion, and Amarantha looked forward to the stories that the contents of the trunk would recall.

John snapped the latch, and as he raised the lid, they all leaned forward, their faces as expectant and apprehensive as archeologists opening a royal tomb. But it wasn't hidden treasure they expected to find. The treasure they hoped for was a glimpse of the past - to relive *the old times* they had been so anxious to leave behind once, to remember the events and relationships that had influenced their lives.

As with all old trunks, the top was a compartmentalized tray meant to hold small items. Ma's was completely covered with a multi-generational photo collection which contained both studio and *snap* shots. Some were of people they didn't know, even after they'd read the captions on the backs. *Raymond and his Pa having fun. Ha! Ha!*

Some pictures were familiar: Grandma and Grandpa Person, both old, standing in front of the *summer kitchen* which had been the first home they'd built in their new country. It was strange that they hadn't chosen to stand by the new farmhouse, a symbol of their success. An old-fashioned well, complete with bucket and winch stood to the right. Amarantha had always loved this picture, not because of the grandparents she barely remembered, but because on the lower left was a rogue chicken that had escaped the barnyard (and temporarily the stew pot) to be memorialized for generations to come in this photo. To her it always symbolized the happenstance in life, things that maybe even God couldn't control.

Amarantha held up a picture of Ma and Pa. He was seated loosely, as if barely perching on the edge of a stool. He wore a small pork pie hat pushed to the back of his head, and smiled lazily. Ma stood behind him with her hand on his shoulder. To Amarantha she looked quite familiar, with the thin line of her mouth and the hard eyes when she was angry.

"Look at our Father! How relaxed and handsome he looks," she said. "But Ma looks mad about something."

"He's got a snootful! I know that look all too well!" John was speaking, and there was a slight tremor in his voice. After all these years, his father could still evoke fear and anger in him, even from the grave.

Then there was Wendel, dressed in his sailor's uniform and grinning into the camera, those *butter spreaders* still much in evidence. He was so young! Amarantha could still see him as a little boy, galloping around their farmyard on his imaginary horse, slapping his hip and simulating the hoof beats with his voice—*pa-pum, pa-pum!* There was a long silence while the Grady girls dealt with their tears over the brother who was still missed after fifty years.

There was the familiar picture of Harold in his overseas cap, and though they shook their heads and speculated silently as to what demons had possessed him, there were no tears.

He had exhausted their tears long ago.

"He's in a better place," concluded Jenny.

Fleetingly, Amarantha thought of *the coach ride* and contemplated a belated confession. But what was the use. *He's dead and gone now,* she concluded in her mind, but just the recollection had caused an odd sensation to well in her throat and she colored slightly. No one noticed.

They spent a long time on the pictures.

I remember this day. We all went swimming in the river and had a bonfire afterwards.

There's that old cat you were so crazy about, Amy. What was her name?

How could you forget Tilda. She was named after our old grandmother.

Who's this with you and Ma, John?

The dialogue went on, as each photo brought people and events to mind. It was almost as if they were all together again in that farmhouse, and as Amarantha watched them, the wrinkles and magnified eyes disappeared, and they seemed young again if only for an instant; or maybe it was just the dim light.

When the pictures were exhausted and the tray lifted, there were artificial flowers sculpted with fine wire, each petal wrapped with human hair, and labeled with some of their uncles and aunts names: golden hair from Ma's baby brother John; a soft brown labeled *sister Jenny;* and so on down the line. Some members of the family weren't represented in this somewhat gruesome collection. Maybe a traveling hair artisan had changed his route before all the tresses could be collected.

Who knew? A lot of life was happenstance.

There were a couple blouses that must have been bought when Ma worked as a maid in St. Paul before she was married. They had seen pictures of that era....her jaunty hats, fitted coats....She was earning her own money and looked stylish and pretty. Amarantha never remembered her looking like that (faded house dresses and a battered hat for church were what always came to mind). Obviously, these delicate, lace-trimmed garments, now yellow with age and fragile, had been put away with that other life, long before their time.

Dozens of greeting cards containing handkerchiefs, sent to commemorate long past birthdays, littered the bottom of the trunk. Cloth hankies had been replaced by tissues. "But Ma couldn't throw anything out!" said Elsie, shaking her head as she sorted the envelopes into piles for burning.

Then, almost at the very bottom, they came across a yellowed envelope addressed to Ma and postmarked from a nearby town that was the county seat. It contained two sheets of lined tablet paper and penciled writing that was nearly too faded to read.

"Your eyes are younger than mine," Jenny joked as she handed the letter to Amarantha. "You read it!"

The pages were coming apart, some words lost in the disintegrating folds. They could tell by the greeting that it was from their Pa.

October 23, 1927

Dear little wife Minnie,

I will drop you a line just for pass time. Well Mama I am so glad you are going to move up here. It will be lots of fun and it sure will be a great big help to me. And dearie do the best you can and come as soon as you can and we will soon be happy again. I don't care about money any more. I am going to look for a happy home and live happy again and happy you will be. I ain't goin to get in debt any more and have so much to think about. Well Mama do you remember when you and I were sweethearts? Well we are going to be the same again, fix things up nice and cut out the booze. Well, Dearie I will close for this time and hope to see you soon.

From Your Hubby and Daddy,
OOOOOOOOOOOOOOOOOOOOXXXXXXXXXXXXXX

The Os and Xs went on for half a page.

Amarantha looked up puzzled. She was a little embarrassed at reading what was obviously a love letter, to say nothing of a personal declaration, meant only for one pair of eyes.

That's the trouble with committing your emotions to paper, she thought, they could always fall into the wrong hands.

What was this all about? Where was Pa that he had to write?

I didn't know our family had ever moved anyplace!" Amarantha remarked to the group.

Obviously, a whole chapter in the family history had eluded her for all these years, and she felt cheated or excluded, since this was the first she had heard of it.

"That must have been written when Pa was in jail," Elsie speculated. "I've never read it before. He sure was a con man. all those promises and *sweet talk.*"

"He could always talk his way out of anything when he was cornered," John said.

Jenny said, "Well he must have been sober when he wrote that, and maybe he honestly thought he could change and make life better for us all."

"He didn't, though, did he? He wasn't home two weeks before he was drunk again! It was always about him!"

John was not a talker. He had never developed the so-called *art of conversation* and usually asked or answered questions after a period of thoughtful consideration, and then with as few words as possible. Amarantha was surprised at his sudden vehemence.

She had always attributed this Grady reticence to their Scandinavian genes, but once Wendel had said that none of them talked much when Pa was around for fear of getting a slap to the side of the head.

"It was just a habit we all got into."

A young and insensitive Amarantha had laughed and teased him that he must have gotten a lot of slaps.

"Is anybody going to tell me what this is all about?" Amarantha demanded, waving the brittle pages back and forth like a flag.

Elsie answered, "I thought you knew this, but I guess there were a lot of things nobody wanted to remember or talk about. I was about eight or nine at the time..."

She proceeded to tell the entire story.

"I remember Ma and I were making bread. We had just made the loaves and put them in pans when Pa came in the back door. We could tell he was drunk. His eyes were squinty and he sort of fell against the door when he slammed it. He was roaring mad!

"'The yard's full of weeds,' he said. 'Where's *Basic*'? You remember how he called you *Basic* when he was drunk?"

She looked at John, who remained seated with elbows to his knees and his chin resting on his hands balled into fists. A muscle worked at the side of his chin.

"None of us knew why he did that, but from the way he said it you knew it meant stupid, lazy, or something else that meant a bawling out or worse punishment was on the way. Ma said John was working up on Grandpa Person's farm and was getting paid for it, but Pa was determined to find something to rail about.

"'There's plenty to do around here. It wouldn't hurt you to get outside and do some real work!'

"He poked me in the ribs, and I moved over behind Ma.

"She said to him, 'You sit down now and I'll get you something to eat.'

"That was Ma's ploy. If he would eat, he'd get tired and sleep it off without causing trouble. I remember Wendel was in the kitchen too and he ran right up to him and waved his skinny arms around and yelled, 'You sit down and eat!'

"If I hadn't been so scared, I'd have laughed at the way that little guy stood up to him." Elsie stopped to wipe her eyes. "But Pa just roared, 'I don't have to eat!' And Wendel moved fast to avoid the slap.

"Then Pa started throwing things around the room. He threw the tins of bread dough against the wall and turned the table over in what seemed to be one motion. We all scattered. We knew it was going to be a bad one, and Ma whispered to me to go get the neighbor who lived about a half a mile down the road.

"I ran 'til my side ached and I was gasping for breath. I burst into the Clemence barn. Old Bill Clemence was forking hay down from the loft. I wondered if he could be of any help against our Pa, him being older and not as strong; but even when Pa was drunk, he backed off if strangers were around.

"'Ma says come quick,' I told him. 'Pa's drunk and wrecking everything.'

"It almost seemed to me like he was moving in slow motion. He stuck the pitchfork in the hay pile and climbed slowly down the ladder. He motioned for me to follow and walked to the house where he fumbled in a kitchen drawer for keys to that old model A of his parked out in the barnyard.

"'I gotta go over to the Gradys,'" he said to his wife. "'Tom's drunk again and knocking up the place.'

"I felt so ashamed 'cause she just looked disgusted and shook her head, and said, 'You watch yourself now.' Then she muttered to herself, 'Somebody should put that sorry excuse for a man in jail or put him out of his misery, one or the other.'

"'Oh, he's hard-working enough when he's sober, he just can't leave the booze alone.'

"I was too scared to tell them to hurry, but I was imagining what was going on at home and was worried for Ma and Wendel. I told them I'd run on ahead and got to our house a couple minutes before that old Ford of his came *putting* into the yard.

"When I ran into the kitchen, Pa was alone, standing behind the door."

"'Where you bin?'

"I told him I ran to the Clemences. Then he reached out and grabbed me by one arm and threw me across the room, and I bounced off the wall. Just then Bill Clemence walked in the open door.

"'What's goin on Tom?'

"You could tell Pa was still plenty mad, but he set up a couple chairs and motioned for him to sit down.

"'A man can't even expect a little help from his family without getting all kinds of backtalk,' he said. 'It's no wonder I drink now and then!'

"He'd gone into the second stage now and was crying and feeling sorry for himself. Then he yelled for Ma.

"'Can't we even get a cup of coffee for a neighbor when he comes to visit!'

"Ma came around the blanket that hung to separate the kitchen from the bedroom. She held her hand over her mouth and turned her face aside until she stood with her back to the rest of us. She tried to measure some coffee into the pot, but her hands were shaking so hard that the grounds were spilling all over the top of the stove. Then I saw there was blood on her hands, but she kept her back to all of us.

"Pa made a motion to get up and said, 'Can't you even say hello to Bill here?'

"But she just shook her head and kept her back to us. Pa got up and grabbed her arm and turned her around.

"'Why do you act like this, you dumb Swede?'

And then he stopped and looked shocked at her as if he didn't know what happened, and we all stared, mostly at Bill Clemence, as Ma tried to cover her mouth with one hand, and Pa held her other hand at her side.

"Tears were running down her cheeks, but she wasn't making a sound. When she moved her hand to grab a dish towel to cover her mouth, we saw that her top lip was split open in several places and a couple teeth were hanging by threads of skin. Her whole mouth looked just like chopped meat."

Everyone stared at the floor. Amarantha had trouble controlling her emotions. Each word of Elsie's story was like a blow delivered across time, and she felt bruised and pummeled, her horror turning to anger as she assimilated these seventy-five year old revelations that stirred in the air around them like an ugly fog, invisible but fetid and clinging.

Suddenly, and oddly, she remembered reading about the holocaust after the war was over. How she was shocked and repulsed by pictures of naked, skeletal bodies and cringed inwardly at unspeakable acts of brutality. Being a thirteen-year-old girl at the time, she was just beginning to be self conscious about her looks, and stared with horror at the pictures of the empty-eyed women with shaved heads and facial wounds. She tried to imagine how she would feel with a bald head and a misshapen face.

Now she thought of her dear Ma and how she had been beaten, disfigured, and terrorized much as the holocaust women, not by Nazis, animalized by war and a world in chaos, but by her own husband who then signed his name with rows of hugs and kisses and promised they would be sweethearts again. No magazine covered her degradation. There were no glossy, enlarged photos of her *mouth like chopped meat.*

Amarantha covered her face with both hands, letting the pages of the *love letter* float to the floor. She realized, to her own shame, that she had never asked Ma how she had become toothless, just assumed it was the result of neglect. It was not until the early forties when Ma got steady work that she could afford false teeth, after having gone toothless for nearly fifteen years.

Amarantha hadn't noticed, or didn't care, that Ma's diet was restricted during that time. Now she remembered her eating mashed potatoes, cooked fruit which she called *sauce,* and dicing her meat into tiny cubes. She knew it was because she didn't have teeth for chewing, but didn't dwell much on how it affected Ma physically, not to mention mentally, or how her appearance must have lowered her self-esteem.

She did remember the day that Ma came home from the dentist with her new teeth. Amarantha was reading, and when Ma smiled, revealing the even row of white *choppers,* Amarantha placed the open book over her eyes and pretended to be repulsed at the sight. They laughed together then, and Ma opened the grocery bag she carried and placed several apples and a bag of unshelled walnuts on the table, evidently two foods she had craved all those years, and the two of them sat together with each a paring knife, cutting slices of raw apple and prying the walnut shells open with the tips of the knives. It was no big deal to Amarantha, who would rather have had candy or those marshmallow covered snowball cupcakes; but now she remembered the relish with which Ma chewed those formerly impossible fruits. Amarantha further remembered that Ma had overindulged and her unsophisticated stomach had rebelled later that evening.

Maybe that's why each Christmas I buy a bag of unshelled walnuts, even though the prepared nutmeats are much more convenient, she thought.

Amarantha shook her head to dispel her daydreams and forced herself to return to their circle around the trunk, which had lost the congenial, reunion feeling.

"Is that why Pa went to jail?" she asked. "Because he beat Ma?"

John took over the story. "I don't think it was exactly because of that. A man could beat his wife in those days, it was a privilege that came with the marriage vows. But it just so happened that Aunt Alma came to visit shortly after, and when she saw Ma's face, she raised a stink! She told our Grandpa, and about a day later he and Willie and Otto paid Pa a little visit in the barn."

John obviously enjoyed this memory, as he smiled a little and lifted his brows as if in anticipation of what he was about to say.

"I hid in a cow stall and listened. Grandpa told him in his broken English, 'You ever lay a hand to your wife again and you'll answer to us.'

"Pa tried to weasel around, whining about how hard it was to make a living and what he had to put-up with, but they just stared at him, then turned around and left. In a couple days the sheriff came to the house and arrested him for something I was never sure of."

Both Elsie and Jenny shook their heads in agreement.

John continued, "You know our old Grandpa Person had some *pull* in town. He was on the County Board and had all that virgin pine on his land. I always thought he laid some charges and tried to get rid of Pa. It would have worked too, if Ma had cooperated." Over this, John sounded disappointed.

Jenny spoke up now. "I remember when Aunt Alma came to the house and argued with Ma.

"'Our Pa will help you,' she said. 'Tom's never gonna change and he'll just beat you up again. You can get some work cleaning and ironing around town and be better off without him.'

"But by then, Pa had already written Ma to move up to Cedar Lake near the prison, and her mind was made up. That *love letter* must have come later to make sure she made the move."

John said, "I think Ma's decision to stick with the jailbird was the reason that Grandpa and the rest of the family up on the farm sort of gave up on us. I don't remember any of them ever intervening in our family affairs again. Oh, *the boys* used to come for coffee once in awhile and they brought treats from the farm: salt pork or some first milk for *kalvdanse*."

"Ma never went back on her decision, though," Elsie said. "She never asked for any help again, and they never gave any. Even when Pa died, those old Swedes held their grudge. Remember the funeral?"

Amarantha was barely four when Pa died and didn't remember much about it, but she had heard the story, told often with a bitterness that didn't lessen over the years. Ma's family had always been Lutheran. Pa was a *fallen-away* Catholic. The Grady lifestyle didn't much lend itself to church attendance: their clothes weren't presentable, they had no money for the collection plate, and their father's antics left them unacceptable to most of the upstanding church members. Besides, Pa wouldn't have stood for it. It was one of his favorite topics when he was drunkenly cursing everything and everybody that, *held him back.*

'Those hypocrites do everything I do on a Friday night," he would rail at Ma, implying that somehow it was her fault for being related to certain mainstays of the local Swedish Lutheran Church. 'Cheat their brothers on Saturday, but show up all holier than thou on Sunday morning.' In later years Amarantha tended to agree with his assessment, but couldn't see why it should affect his behavior.

When Pa died, however, Ma went to the Lutheran minister to arrange a burial, trusting that her family's membership entitled her to the Christian comfort of this last rite, and he turned her down. Not only did he cite the fact that Pa wasn't a bonafide member, he made mention of unforgiven sins and lack of support for the church as well.

John said he knew the county would bury Pa, but Ma was determined that he was to be given the respect in death that he hadn't earned in life. She went from parsonage to parsonage until the Congregational Minister agreed to conduct a funeral; and, meager though it was, Ma would spend many months cleaning houses to pay for it rather than accept the charity of the county.

And so they had gathered on a raw, March day. The minister, his wife, the musicians, and Pa's ancient great uncle and his

daughter no one knew were the only attendees besides the immediate family. Amarantha remembered the organ and a tremulous-
voiced soprano offering their renditions of *Old Rugged Cross* and
Beautiful Isle of Somewhere. She could not remember being upset
over the loss of the father she scarcely knew, but worried over the
tear-stained faces of her sisters and Ma.

But what stuck in her mind about the day, was when the old
uncle myopically mistook the basement stairs for an aisle and fell
to the bottom amid the screams of his daughter. So much for Ma's
dignified service for the sinner. The old uncle was only shaken-up
a bit, but they left immediately, to everyone's relief, and were not
heard from again.

Afterwards, there was no lunch in the church basement, as was
customary in those days after the service, and no relatives visited
with dishes of rice pudding or casseroles of Swedish meatballs.
This was a comparison Amarantha made years later, when she and
Ma attended the funeral of an uncle, who had in later life become
the town drunk, and she witnessed the traditional amenities
afforded his demise, sins and all.

After the drive to the cemetery, the funeral director dropped
the Gradys back at the church, and from there they walked the two
miles home to their farmstead. John carried Amarantha most of the
way. In spite of her tender age she sensed the desolate mood that
prevailed even when John had started a fire in the woodstove and
they sat together in their warm kitchen.

Amarantha's detailed reverie took only a few seconds and she
started out of it when Jenny said, "Yes, we all remember the funeral; but Rose Person told me years later that they all felt bad that
they hadn't come or done more for us then."

"That's easy for them to say now!" Elsie cried, almost throwing the words at Jenny, but catching herself quickly and concluded, "I guess hind-sight is always better."

"Why did Ma stay with him?" Amarantha blurted.

In an effort to dispel the bad feeling and regain their former
camaraderie, Jenny laughed, "You're just lucky she did. Otherwise
you wouldn't have been born."

"I'm not so sure that was lucky," Elsie countered, with a poke to Amaranthas's ribs.

Ultimately, however, too much talk about Pa meant the reunion had been spoiled; they were all quiet after that, making polite comments about the remaining mementoes of Ma's life, but unable to recapture their former enthusiasm.

John carried the trunk to Amarantha's car for her safekeeping and though they hugged and promised to get together again soon, Amarantha knew they all felt the relief of getting away and breaking the spell. They had separate lives. All they had in common now was the past, and that proved too painful to share.

Amarantha knew they wouldn't see each other again for a long time.

The long drive home was made amidst a swirl of questions and sound bites from the previous conversations. Why didn't she leave when she had the chance? Why was she strong enough to stand up to her parents and her whole family and not to an abusive husband?

Her face was like chopped meat!

Why do you have to act like a dumb Swede?

Hind-sight is always better!

Ma always wanted to fend for herself!

Amarantha's own comfortable, little house was a welcome sight when she spied the driveway, and the business of unpacking the car and tending to her animals gave her a temporary reprieve from her thoughts. But in bed later, sleep eluded her and she found herself going over it all again.

Was it merely Ma's determination to accept the consequences of her decisions that made her stay, even when it would have been better for her and her children if she had left? Was she too proud to accept help, to the detriment of her family?

Was she just a '*dumb Swede*' after all?

Then Amarantha thought of the love letter, and the allusion to, '*how it was when we were sweethearts.*' She remembered the promises and how he called her, *My Dear Little Wife.* Their courtship and marriage must have been what Ma considered a chance of a lifetime for a lonely country girl who worked as a domestic in the big city fearing the years would pass her by, and she would become an *Old Maid*. Here was a handsome Irishman, so different from the Scandinavian farmers from home, and he was interested in *her*, of all people.

Then it dawned on Amarantha like a new day.

We only remember and talk about the bad times when Pa was sick, she thought. *Ma remembered the good times when they were sweethearts; when he had delivered her from spinsterhood; when they had worked together on their farm in South Dakota, laughing as they tossed biscuits, hot from the oven, from hand to hand as they shared a snack before starting the evening chores. She remembered their first born that they proudly named for his father and the other babies that they welcomed before they began arriving too fast to fully appreciate.*

She remembered the night he gave her the garnet ring with the two tiny seed pearls on either side of the stone. She knew him before alcohol and mental illness had made him the man that John hated beyond his death. She knew him before he was cruel and violent, and she wasn't about to desert him in his time of need.

She loved him.

Amarantha had never been religious, but the release she felt at letting go of Pa's dark side was like a benediction. Her father wasn't an evil man, and her mother wasn't *just a dumb Swede.* Maybe if there was a heaven, they were together in that *Beautiful Isle of Somewhere.*

The cat jumped up on the bed and nudged Amarantha's hand, looking for a caress. She rubbed the soft fur and whispered into the small, leather-like ear, "It's a good thing Ma didn't leave Pa, or I wouldn't be here."

The cat flicked her ears several times, but she didn't move away and continued to narrow her eyes in contentment, purring loudly. Gradually, with the feel of soft fur on her hand and the soothing hum of a loving spirit in her ears, Amarantha drifted into the restful sleep that only forgiveness can provide.

XIV.
Return to the Wild

Cervidae

A sharp wind was driving the snow. She couldn't see if she held her head up, so she bent into the gale with her eyes on the *way to go*, trusting that the leader would alert the followers to unexpected danger. The snow lay deep in the woods, making it difficult to walk unless she kept to the much trodden ways. The winter was young, but already they had to reach high into the cedars for bark, the dormant grasses and shrubs lying too deeply covered to even be exposed by scratching the snow away with their hooves.

They wandered restlessly. It was the time to *walk this way*, but it was also a time when a curious urge drove them to leave their shelters to seek mates. It was an urge stronger than the search for food or water. It was an urge that often drove them to ignore signs of danger in order to fulfill their role in the survival of the species.

Amarantha

It was six o'clock, but already the night was dark, and even deeper so, since it was moonless. It was November 20, and the hours of dark and light were almost equal. Amarantha rested her forehead on the porch window, her fingers making a frame for her eyes to shield them from the kitchen light. She could see their phantom shapes in the yard, not so much shapes as slight accumulations of darkness that moved slowly and, occasionally, the flash of a white tail. She knew they were taking their usual trail across the clearing to the woods on the other side, and she had kept her harmless but irrepressible dog, Buddy, in the house to ensure their safe passage.

She smiled a little, as in her mind she heard again the long-ago, excited voice of her granddaughter.

'They're coming, Gramma, just like you said they would! Come quick and see.'

Laura's nose was pressed against the pane, and her eyes danced with the adventure of witnessing the wild and unknown.

"I see! Look how they march in single file across the same path at the same time every night. They've used that path ever since I've lived here."

"How do they remember?"

"It's called instinct or intuition." There was a question in her eyes. "They don't think things through the way we do, they just have a sense or feeling about where to go, what plants are poison to eat, when a storm is coming, what happens in certain seasons. All wild animals have it. Humans used to have it, but we lost it when we became civilized."

The clear little brow furrowed, prompting Amarantha to attempt clarification.

"We banned together in one place, planted gardens, made machines, started schools. Life is better for us, but we've forgotten how to live in the wild."

Laura still didn't quite understand the concept, but chose to push on to more interesting areas of exploration. The word *season* popped out of her Grandma's explanation as a point of interest.

"Do they know it's going to be the Christmas season? How do they know which plants are poison?"

"They don't know it's Christmas, but they know instinctively that it's the time for them to form families so they can start new fawns to be born in the spring. And some people think that certain plants look or smell differently to them, so they know not to eat them."

"I wish I had *stinct*," Laura said wistfully as she resumed her watch at the window.

Amarantha smiled again at the memory and shook her head. Funny how she could repeat every word of a conversation that took place so long ago, yet forget to turn off the burner under the tea kettle and sometimes even forget what day of the week it was.

Such a long time ago......Laura used to love to spend nights with her Gramma, tucked into the big, old bed in the loft with the flowery, flannel sheets and the down quilt. She used to argue that she even remembered sleeping in the loft crib, which Amarantha had set up for visiting babies.

But Laura was grown now, off on her own and busy with her life, as it was meant to be. She remembered telling her about how the mother deer and their yearlings separated and forgot all about each other, not even knowing if they met in the woods.

"I'll never forget my Mom and Dad," she vehemently vowed, "or you either Gramma."

The latter pronouncement was accompanied by a hug around the neck so tight that Amarantha's glasses had skewed to one side.

It had been a long time since anyone had hugged her that way, as if they really meant it.

She also remembered once telling a pouting and sullen young Laura how fawns are taught for their own safety to mind their mothers.

"Once when I went to toss some weeds onto the compost heap, I found a tiny, spotted fawn lying in a depression at the top. It was so still I thought at first it was dead. But its head was upright and a small spot of reddish fur on its chest moved the slightest bit with its breath. I didn't touch it, because you don't touch wild animals, but I came back several times that afternoon to see if it was still there. Toward nightfall it was gone. Its mother had come and gotten it. But it was told to stay very quiet and not run, and through instinct it knew to obey its mother."

The story had served to keep her independent little granddaughter obedient for a long time. But then, she was always such a good, little girl.

Such a long time ago...

Amarantha still kept the little pink, striped apron in the

kitchen drawer, though, thinking someday, if she were lucky, she'd bake cookies with a little great-granddaughter.

She rose from her seat at the window and went to the kitchen for her tea. She'd abandoned a newly brewed cup to watch the deer crossing, and now it was cold. *Probably shouldn't drink more anyway or I'll be up all night.*

Then she'd shrugged and laughed as she poured the tepid liquid down the drain.

I'll most likely be up anyway.

She used to be able to sleep through the night hardly moving from one spot, and now she found herself up prowling around in darkness a couple times, checking the weather, sitting by the window to watch the fireflies in the summer.

It was peaceful, though. The old house spoke to her in creaks and groans that she couldn't hear in the daytime, and had she lain unknowing in her bed, she would have missed entirely the starry skies, the phases of the moon, the northern lights, the isolated but cozy feeling of an overnight snowstorm, and the sounds and visits of the nocturnal animals.

Other nights she'd drift to sleep watching the stars through her bedroom window and woke only when Buddy stood by her bedside to nudge her awake with an insisting nose. She could never seem to identify the cause and effect of her sleeping habits.

She'd been in the country for over thirty years now and pretty much practiced a live and let live policy with the wild animals that shared her five acres. Oh, she had difficulties with deer and rabbits eating her perennial gardens, but learned to choose flowers they didn't like: foxglove, marigolds, and daffodils. Plants like lilies or roses she'd string nets across or spray with something objectionable to the noses and pallets of would-be marauders.

It was more a battle of the minds: she and technology against the deer and their instinct for survival. Her number one general in this war was her faithful Buddy. He patrolled the perimeter of the yard several times a day, barking a warning to would-be trespassers, and he was effective, although some of the more daring does sometimes stood their ground just beyond the *Maginot Line* and stamped their hooves in the ground, emitting a sharp sound similar to the releasing of an arrow from a bow. Buddy usually retreated a few feet to resume his barking at a safer distance.

Her fluffy, white cat was another matter. Frosty was one of those cats, and there are many, that considered herself rightful ruler of the universe, or at least of the household (*her* universe), and she had a strut that always reminded Amarantha of Marilyn Monroe's exaggerated and provocative walk. The deer that happened into the yard when she was outside displayed an overwhelming curiosity about her. Amarantha once sat quietly on the porch steps and watched a sleek, red-tinged doe approach a wary but unmoving kitty to the point where they touched noses. It was a beautiful moment broken only when Frosty, not willing to tempt fate for too long a time, bolted for a tree and climbed to observe from a low branch.

This almost imperceptible flow of life around her was what kept Amarantha in the country long after her family thought she should move to the city. The changing of the seasons energized her; the dark, quiet nights relaxed her; and the antics of her pets and habits of the wild animals amused her.

What more could you ask in life?

She stirred from her reverie to peer again into the darkness. The last of the phantom deer moved slowly into the trees.

"Hide and good luck."

Amarantha silently mouthed the wish, as if releasing it only to the cosmos would somehow carry it into the minds of the deer and serve them well. For tomorrow would begin the annual ritual of deer hunting.

She didn't allow hunting on her land, but lived next to the national forest where the deer roamed. Tomorrow she could expect to be awakened at daybreak by distant sounds of guns and would often see groups of orange-clad hunters on the roadside or driving down the forest lanes. An encounter of the worst kind, however, was to walk through a parking lot in a gas station or grocery store and come upon a vehicle that held the lifeless, gutted body of a once beautiful animal, its graceful form stiff and awkward in

death, its spirit and dignity replaced by clouded eyes and protruding, purple tongue. Then she would silently wonder if the
hapless animal had been one on the trail a few hours ago.

Survival of the fittest they called it. But the hunters always survived, fit or not, and often *harvested* the fittest deer for their antlers
or pelt or size. She had stopped railing against them, it did no
good. And maybe there were too many deer, with their predators
fleeing deeper into wilderness areas to escape civilization.

So why didn't the deer flee? Some people fed them through the
winters. Some hunters baited them. Both these groups treated
them like domestic animals, with the pleasure of observing them
in the wild and/or butchering them when hunting season came.

Perhaps, then, they were adapting to civilization, finding the
succulent, domestic gardens too convenient to abandon. Maybe
they were slowly losing the natural instincts of wild animals and
succumbing to the lure of abundant food, trading their intuition
for their freedom.

Cervidae

She half sat-half crouched, legs flayed but positioned for flight
if the need should arise. She could feel her heart pulsing against
her ribs and concentrated to slow the beat and ease her breathing.
Their footsteps were all around her, and their smell made her nostrils twitch in revulsion, but she remained still in a copse of scrub
oak behind a log.

She should run, she knew, but a pain in her shoulder had
impeded her progress and her eyes were blurring. She struggled to
keep every appendage at the ready and every sense open and alert
for any near and sudden movement. If she could not run, she
would lash out and kick and hiss deeply through her nose, trying
to keep them at bay.

Instinct told her to summon the immobile state she practiced
when small and in need of hiding from predators. She fell back
into it now, her eyes glassy and expressionless, every muscle quiet.
She needed to rest, perhaps even sleep, so she could renew her

fight for freedom.

She longed to crawl under a cedar tree onto a soft bed of pine needles and fallen leaves and moss with the branches drooping close to the ground, hiding her body in their dark fragrance.

Even in her stressful condition she could faintly feel age-old stirrings in her body and knew that it was the time for mating. But it was also the time for the woods to be thick with predators. They had drifted away from her hiding place and she cautiously allowed her breath to come more freely.

But then, some of them were upon her again.

Amarantha

It proved to be a hard winter for humans as well as for deer. Neither she nor Buddy was able to take their accustomed walks, due to deep snow and treacherous ice, and road conditions discouraged many trips to town. Amarantha had begun to feel listless and overly tired around the middle of February. At first she thought she had that Northern Wisconsin disease jokingly referred to as 'Cabin Fever.' But toward the end of February she caught a bad cold and for a while spent both nights and days sitting in her reclining chair in order to deal with congestion, the ever-faithful Buddy at her side with a look that seemed to say, *I'm feeling poorly myself.*

He was almost 15 in human years, and Amarantha often hugged him and voiced aloud the regret that they were both growing old, and that sooner or later either he was going to break her heart, or she his.

She'd always prided herself on enjoying her own company, but lately she'd rest her book or crossword puzzle in her lap and wish to hear a car in the driveway and someone at the door dropping in for a visit. She was in just this position one afternoon when she felt a sharp pain in her back that couldn't be assuaged with the shifting of her body. Later in the day it eased, but she didn't feel like eating and settled for a cup of instant cocoa.

Gradually, Amarantha fell into this scenario: sharp pain then slightly nauseous stomach, occurring intermittently, with a feeling of complete lassitude.

"You haven't eaten any of the food I brought you last week!" The accusation was flung by her daughter, Wendy, while making her weekly check-up visit to her mother.

"Haven't I? I must have eaten some of it." Amarantha couldn't really remember if - or what - she'd eaten. "I just haven't felt like eating, I guess."

"You've eaten almost a box of cornflakes!" cried Wendy. "Is that all you've had this week? You can't live on that! They're not even good for you. Well, I'm not going to buy any more cereal, then you'll have to eat all this good food I bring you!"

Wendy continued to stalk angrily around the kitchen, muttering about all she had to do and then *people* not even appreciating her efforts.

Amarantha felt confused. She'd obviously done something wrong, but she didn't know what. She felt her eyes fill with tears and she tried again to explain, "I've been getting this pain, and I don't want to eat then."

But Wendy didn't listen and continued to harangue about the food.

The God-damned food, Amarantha thought. Suddenly she was angry: at herself for being old and having a pain, at Wendy for not listening and accusing her. So with all the force she could muster, she walked into the kitchen and yelled at Wendy, "Go to hell!"

Wendy stopped short and looked at her mother astonished. This was uncharacteristic behavior, to say the least. Buddy, sensing his mistress's anger, chose this moment to direct a couple sharp barks in Wendy's direction also. But Amarantha's rage subsided almost as quickly as it appeared, and she took her daughter's hands in hers.

"I'm so sorry, but I'm trying to tell you about this pain I've been getting."

"What pain, what are you talking about?" Wendy was instantly alert. She had let her concern for her mother become clouded by her own stresses and issues and now realized she'd been harsh.

The upshot of the whole encounter, was a visit to the local clinic preceded by a long conference between Wendy and the doctor, to which Amarantha was excluded.

"She's very tired, she won't eat, and she's irritable. She even swore at me the other day, and she's never done that before! She says she gets a pain in her back."

Then came the hospital stay and a series of long tests performed with Amarantha inadequately clothed, on cold metal tables, in undignified positions. Nurses called her *dear*, and doctors jovially referred to her as *young lady* and Amarantha tried very hard to not tell them all to go to hell.

It was at this time that Amarantha began to notice that certain of the staff seemed to have auras of color around their bodies and she even detected certain smells from some of them. The cleaning lady who visited with her while she mopped and dusted her room had a rosy glow about her and emitted a clean smell not associated with the antiseptic fluids incumbent to her job. One particularly sweet and cheerful nurse seemed to be enveloped in a rainbow of colors and Amarantha was always so glad when it was her shift.

Conversely, however, the head nurse (male) possessed an aura ranging from grey to black. It seemed to Amarantha that he was constantly poking her with needles and seemed loathe to touch her without first donning thick rubber gloves that reached almost to his elbows. There was a sharp, eye-stinging smell when he came into the room and he wore a sour expression too.

Eventually there was another *doctor/Wendy* conference, and Amarantha heard that the sharp pains in her back were small heart attacks of varying severity that had produced the symptoms and left her heart in damaged condition. They were assured that there was medication, however, and that if she were careful, she could live a normal life again.

"Don't you think she should move to an apartment in town?" Wendy urged. But the wonderful doctor with the bright blue aura said, "I don't see the need for that yet, if she's more comfortable in her familiar home. She has help, doesn't she?"

"Well of course we help as much as we can, but she's all alone out there…"

"Sometimes moving an elderly person signals the end of an era, and they just surrender. Attitude is very important in these cases. I suggest you see how it goes." Then he turned to Amarantha. "You're going to feel a lot better when you start taking this medicine. You'll want to go out dancing again!"

"That surely will be a miracle, since I don't dance."

There was an instant of embarrassing silence, as the doctor looked crestfallen and Wendy said (sotto voce), "See what I mean?"

But sensing that she had been rude, Amarantha quickly added, "But maybe I'll feel so good I'll *want* to."

And so she was returned to her country home, prescription bottles in hand, bags of *healthy food* for her new diet, and lists of instructions from both Wendy and the doctor with various telephone numbers printed in bold ink. And they were right. Soon the pain was gone altogether and she began to feel more energetic. The winter wore on, as northern winters will, but she enjoyed the birds in the feeder, made healthy soups, and relaxed by the window with a cup of tea each night to watch the deer crossing. It was considerably lighter in the evenings now, and she could see them clearly and was even able to assign identifiable characteristics to different animals. She knew from past experience that this was dangerous, since she would now be looking for certain deer and concerned if they were absent.

It's how some people live, she thought, *never getting close to anyone or anything for fear of being hurt.*

But she couldn't be like that.

She'd been embarked on her new healthier life for several weeks when she noticed one morning that Buddy's food dish hadn't been touched when she went to refill it.

"Are you off your feed?" she inquired, looking into the kind, brown eyes. She paid particular attention to him then, noticing that he wasn't his usual energetic self and continued to avoid eating. "Your turn," she told him as he lay on the back seat of the car on the way to the vet. "Now don't you break my heart!"

"He's old and has a heart condition, but I think we can give him some pills that will keep him going comfortably for a while longer." Amarantha laughed on the way home as she tried in her mind to separate Buddy's diagnosis from her own.

"We're just a couple *fogies* with bad tickers, but we'll be out dancing before long," she assured Buddy, who rose to put his chin on her shoulder in response as they drove.

Gradually, the cold and snow gave way to longer days and a sun that was higher in the sky. The snow line receded down the hill from Amarantha's house until it was just a white line at the edge of the woods. And in the middle of April came the familiar sound that marked the real changing of the seasons and always lodged thrills of relief, joy, and nostalgia in her chest: the sound of the first *peepers* of spring just waking in the pond close to the house.

Spring was Amarantha's favorite season, and each year she vowed to, "make every day count," only to suddenly find herself in summer without really noticing exactly when the buds had become leaves. She started early, however, to check the flower beds in the morning for new shoots and loosen the earth around them as they grew; she watched for the first dandelion, in spite of the fact that they became too plentiful later; she marveled at the daffodils and lilacs, and in spite of not being a religious person, could almost wax spiritual over the northland's incredible display of lupine.

Summer was warm and easy. The hard but invigorating spring work in the flower beds was over, and they were maintained by occasional watering and weeding. Amarantha had established a comfortable routine: breakfast for her and Buddy (oatmeal for her, *senior* dog food for him); the taking of the pills (she sitting in a chair with a glass of water, grimly swallowing and grimacing after each, he gamely accepting his fate after having his mouth pried open and his throat stroked); a walk on the beach, often with a pink and purple Lake Superior sunrise as their backdrop; chores around the house or a trip to town; lunch and a pleasant afternoon on the screened porch reading or doing crossword puzzles.

It was one such ordinary day that became memorable and tragic to Amarantha. She was having trouble with her puzzle and with
exerting the necessary amount of concentration required for any
headway. Her eyes kept closing and her head nodding until she
finally surrendered to leaning back in her chair for a pleasant nap.
The sun was warm across her lap and the birds sang in the trees
beyond the screens. She often thought that her best rest occurred
in this old chair with its comfortable head rest and nearby foot-
stool. Buddy was stretched out in a sunbeam at her feet.

She didn't know how long she had slept but was awakened by
a sharp breeze, heralding a cool evening.

She looked at her watch and rose. "Time to get up, Buddy, it's
almost supper." She walked into the kitchen. Frosty was there
meowing and looking meaningfully at her empty bowl, which
Amarantha busily filled before noticing that Buddy hadn't followed her. She called again, "Buddy, come on boy!"

But there was no response.

With gathering apprehension, she hurried back to the porch
and knelt by her still prone and seemingly asleep friend.

"Wake up, Bud!" she said, as she patted his head, giving it a little shake. "Don't do this," she spoke as she tried to raise him to his
feet.

But his limbs were stiff and only then did she see that his eyes
were open but clouded and his tongue protruded, purple and
swollen. A fleeting image of the many deer she'd seen strapped to
hunter's cars crossed her mind, and she laid her cheek against the
soft shoulder fur of her glorious, golden boy and cried softly for
him and all the deer.

But mostly for herself.

"He had a long and very good life with you, Mom," Wendy
comforted, but Amarantha felt old and disconsolate. Large chunks
of comfort and loyalty and companionship seemed to drop from
her soul with every clod of dirt her son-in-law threw over that
once handsome body that now lay at the bottom of a deep hole in
the woods beyond the yard. In the days after, she often forgot he
was gone, calling for him to go for a walk or waking from a nap

and looking for him at her feet. Frosty seemed to miss him too, continuing to vie for treats and attention while looking around to see if he wasn't going to challenge her.

Her routine didn't seem so important now, so she gradually lapsed into lazing around in her pajamas, often forgetting her breakfast and walk altogether. Taking her pills became an occasional thing, and one day she noticed that Buddy's pills were still in the cupboard and she absent mindedly gathered up all the bottles and deposited them in the garbage can, hers included.

The absence of the medication didn't dawn on her until she began having the back pain again and went to look for them.

"Did you move my pills?" she asked when Wendy next came.

"No I didn't. How long have they been missing?"

"I don't know. I can't remember. Someone has taken them, that's for sure." The last was delivered with emphasis in the hope that she wouldn't be blamed for losing them, since lately lost items seemed to be a common complaint of Wendy's.

And so they were replaced, and this time Wendy put them in a plastic container with slots for every day of the week. But Amarantha became confused with the days and the breakfasts and the little slots and took them only when she happened to remember.

One sleepless night she was sitting by the window when she noticed a small spot of light alternately glowing and fading at the edge of the woods.

"It's too late for fire flies," she thought, "it's already October."

She moved in the darkened room to get a better look, and the spot continued to glow and fade in the blackness of the night.

"It looks like a cigarette. Is someone out there smoking a cigarette?"

She was alarmed at this thought and went to make sure all the doors were locked for the night. *I wish Buddy were here,* she thought, *I always felt safe when he was around. He wasn't much of a watch dog, but at least he could sound an alarm.*

She watched the spot and gradually sleep overcame her fear, and she awoke next morning stiff and cold from spending the night in her chair. In the light of day her nocturnal panic seemed silly. Nevertheless, she walked to the spot she remembered and searched in the dry leaves for cigarette butts or evidence of footprints. She found neither.

She was tired enough to sleep soundly the next night, but the next found her sleepless at about two a.m. and sitting by the window, as was her custom. She had forgotten the light, but immediately remembered when she saw once again the faint glow and fade at the edge of the woods. She had never smoked, but now found herself gauging the time from the glow to the fade, imagining it corresponding to the disembodied lungs filling with smoke and then expelling.

As the days passed her lack of sleep and imagination worked her into a frenzy, and she called Wendy spewing her fear incomprehensively.

"You've got to move home with me!" she blurted. "There's a man in the woods. He comes every night and I'm afraid he's going to rob or kill me!"

"What man? What are you talking about? Now Mom, you know I can't move home. I have my own family now. You remember Jim and Laura? You remember *Laura* don't you?"

"Family? But you're just in school. You can quit and come home. I need you now!"

Later she walked with Wendy to the edge of the yard and watched her brush aside fallen leaves and dry grass in an effort to discover some evidence of the stalker.

"Maybe he was over further." And then they would search another area, Amarantha becoming more distraught with each attempt.

"You're just tired, Mom, and imagining things. You haven't been taking your medicine and you're forgetting so many things, I'm afraid you're going to hurt yourself or burn the house down." Wendy was talking softly and holding Amarantha's hand, but her mother's face was streaked with tears and her eyes were wild with fear.

"You just come home now. You've been away long enough.

He'll go away if you come home!"

Fortunately for Amarantha and possibly due to additional medication, she remembered very little of the discussions that led to the decision to enter a local nursing home.

She sat quietly, despair written in her eyes and on every line of her face, as Wendy sorted through her possessions, chatting and sometimes inquiring cheerfully, "Do you want to take this to *The Willows*? I think you're going to love it there, Mom. There are lots of ladies to visit with and everyone on the staff is so nice."

Occasionally, her mind would clear long enough to grasp at reasons why she should stay in her beloved home in the country.

"I think Buddy has run away and gotten lost. He won't know where to come if I'm not here."

"Buddy died, Mom, remember?"

"Well, what about Frosty? I can't leave her here alone."

"Frosty's going to live with a nice family on a farm. She'll be fine."

Amarantha remembered that standard story used to comfort children when a pet had died or had to be euthanized. She was sure one of those fates had befallen Frosty, and although she was too tired to protest, the tears rolled down her cheeks as she thought of her beautiful kitty that had walked like Marilyn Monroe and touched noses with a wild, forest animal.

Cervidae

She had mated during the last season, but she was old and had been weakened by the hard winter and a wound in her right flank that didn't heal but continued to bleed and ache. She had been careless while grazing in a meadow when coyotes attacked and almost brought her down. She remembered screaming in terror and sending her sharp hooves flying into their midst until they had retreated enough to allow her to bound away, they being no match for her graceful leaps and strides.

Food was hard to find, and towards the end of winter, the herd had crowded together, eating any scrap of bark or twig they could find. Many died, but for some reason she had survived until spring when her fawn was born. She'd torn at the tiny form's enveloping sack and licked the small exposed body vigorously as instinct had taught her, but it had refused to quicken and eventually she walked away, leaving her final effort at perpetuating the species as protein for the forest's scavengers.

After that, she traveled in back of the group, waiting to eat until the stronger had had their fill, often being kicked or chased away from the rest and growing weaker every day.

Amarantha

"She seems so out-of-it." Wendy was talking to the nurse outside Amarantha's room.

"We've had to sedate her. She cries so much, and sometimes she tries to hit us when we come to take care of her. We're just trying to make her more comfortable. It's for her own good."

Wendy found her sitting in a chair studying something outside her window.

"Well, you're looking more chipper today, are you feeling better?"

Amarantha answered without looking at her, gesturing toward the trees in the yard. "What kind of trees would you say those are?" She sounded lucid and so much like her old Mom that Wendy's eyes filled with hope.

"Oh, I don't know, they look like poplar to me." Wendy walked to the window to look at the trees.

"I believe you're right. Isn't this place called 'Willows?' Wouldn't you think they could have a few willows around then?"

Wendy laughed, and Amarantha laughed, and it was so good to be laughing together again.

"You are feeling better!" Wendy pulled a chair close to her mother and took both her hands. "I don't want you to be unhappy, Mom; and I know you blame me for bringing you here, but I didn't know what else to do."

"Has Buddy come home? Are you going to take me home with

you today?"

Wendy's face fell as she realized the moment had passed and repeated once again the answer that had begun to seem like a mantra. "Buddy is dead, and I can't take you home because I work all day."

She fussed with the few things she had brought her mother: some candy she'd liked, a bottle of lotion, a magazine. But the all too familiar phrases had rendered Amarantha uncommunicative and crying again, and Wendy quickly went to stand outside the door, her hand over her mouth to keep the sobs from erupting and causing a scene.

A nurse stopped to put her arm around her shoulders. "It's so hard, isn't it? It might be easier on you both if you didn't come everyday. You just remind each other of happier times."

"I can't do that. She's my Mom!"

Amarantha drifted in and out of the life around her at *The Willows*. Wendy and the nurses referred to her *good* days, when she recognized people and asked questions about her surroundings. Amarantha couldn't quite understand what made them *good*, since for her they were a time of confusion and realization that the world was up-side-down and she was lost. And when the frustration of the *good* days became too much, she often lapsed into the relief of crying or reverted to almost animal behavior, hissing and kicking out at those near. Of course, her *bad* days often ended with her in restraints or drugged in her chair, her jaw lax, her mouth drooling, and her eyes staring into nothing.

"It's for her own good," they all agreed.

Auras became increasingly important to Amarantha. She responded to the pinks and the blues and the cool greys, but the darker the aura, the more wary she became. She wouldn't eat the food brought by anyone with a murky aura. Obviously, they were trying to poison her. Sometimes she would push the food to the floor. And those who came with needles or medication were often subject to a struggle that belied the fragility of her wasted body.

Some of the staff teased her. One young male orderly insisted on calling her *Gramma*. If it was a *bad* day, Amarantha paid no attention, but if the title somehow made it through the haze, it would strike a chord in her memory.

"Are you Laura?" she'd asked one day. Everyone had laughed then, and there were choruses of,

Ya, he's Laura!

Geez, Dick, I told you that after shave was too strong!

But Amarantha had persisted. "You said 'Gramma." Are you Laura? Is Laura coming to get me? Where's Laura?"

Of course the whole scene ended badly, but just before the nurse with the dark red aura came with a needle, Amarantha heard the young man, now hostile and stung by the mocking of his colleagues, say, *that old coot's crazy. She belongs in the looney bin!*

And in an instant before the injection took hold, she had shouted as loudly as she could, "That's where I am! In a looney bin! So you can all go to hell!"

Amarantha had led a temperate life. She hadn't been much of a drinker; she didn't object to alcohol, it just didn't appeal to her. She'd never smoked; she tried it once in college but could never quite get the hang of it, so she didn't persist. She'd always bragged about her sturdy *peasant stock* (now labeled good genes,) which had protected her from serious hereditary diseases. Her love of the outdoors, with walking and gardening, had kept her physically fit well into her advanced years and, ironically, now made her cling to life long after her brain, for all intents and purposes, had died.

It was autumn again. Amarantha had continued to hover in her own purgatory for a couple years. She seldom had lucid moments any more, and Wendy had finally taken to heart the advice to not visit as often. But a random visitor had brought a nasty cold germ into *The Willows*, and it spread like wildfire among the staff and patients alike, finally manifesting itself in Amarantha's thin chest cavity as a wracking cough.

"We'd better put a humidifier in here to ease her breathing," said the pink auraed nurse. She stood at the bedside with a hand on Amarantha's brow. Wendy was visiting and sat on the opposite side of the bed. As an aide rolled in the machine, plugged it into the wall, and flipped a switch to send a fine mist into the air, she said, "Good! That's gonna help your coughing spells, Mom."

She took Amarantha's hand and stood to look into her eyes.

"I just came to tell you that Laura's coming for Thanksgiving, and if you're better we'll come get you for dinner. Oh, she'll come to see you anyway, so don't worry about that." Her voice was light and her manner exuberant. "She hasn't been home for such a long time, and I can't wait to see her!"

Amarantha lay propped on pillows, breathing heavily but turned to Wendy. "Laura? Is Laura coming? Where is she?"

"She'll be here tomorrow, and she'll come see you right away."

"She'll want to watch the deer crossing. Can she stay overnight. I'll put the flowered sheets on the loft bed. She always liked that." A coughing spasm occupied a few seconds, as Wendy supported and massaged her back. Then she relaxed back and closed her eyes as she whispered, "Laura's coming."

Wendy was pleased at the trace of a smile on her Mother's lips as she left her sleeping and happy.

Later Amarantha awoke to a darkened room. She was disoriented and didn't remember where she was. Her chest felt so congested, and she had to sit to ease her breathing.

"I'd be better off sitting in my chair," she thought, as she eased her legs over the side of the bed and felt the cold floor hit the soles of her feet. She was surprised at how weak she felt but hung onto the bed with one hand while she reached in the darkness for the arm of her favorite chair. "Are you there Buddy? Don't trip me now."

But as she rounded the bottom of the bed a hissing noise caused her to look to the corner of the room. A red spot glowed, then faded as the humidifier continued to pulse in the darkness. Instant terror gripped her.

"He's out there again, in the woods!"

She whispered so he wouldn't be alerted. She went to check the doors, and the first one opened at her touch. She was in a lighted hallway then and pushed on to check the front door. She must be quiet. The front door swung open heavily, but she felt strong and determined and burst outside into the cold, November air.

Cervidae

She half sat, half crouched, legs flayed but positioned for flight if the need should arise. She could feel her heart pulsing against her ribs and concentrated to slow the beat and ease her breathing. Their footsteps were all around her, and their smell made her nostrils twitch in revulsion, but she remained still in a copse of scrub oak behind a log. She should run, she knew, but a pain in her back had heeded her progress and her eyes were blurring. She struggled to keep every appendage at the ready and every sense open and alert for any near and sudden movement. If she could not run, she would lash out and kick and hiss deeply through her nose, trying to keep them at bay.

Instinct told her to summon the immobile state she practiced when she was small and needed to hide from predators. She fell back into it now, her eyes glassy and expressionless, every muscle quiet. She needed to rest, perhaps even sleep, so she could renew her fight for freedom.

She longed to crawl under a cedar tree onto a soft bed of pine needles and fallen leaves and moss with the branches drooping close to the ground, hiding her body in their dark fragrance. It was the time for the woods to be thick with predators. They had drifted away from her hiding place and she allowed her breath to come more freely. But then, some of them were upon her again!

Dark forms parted the branches and crawled towards her. She remained silent and unmoving until she could feel their presence on her fur, pulling at her. The smell was thick now, and panic took reign over any intuitive discipline. She snorted through her nose menacingly and kicked with her sharp hooves with all her strength. Then a familiar sound reached her and she ceased her struggle for an instant to prick her ears.

Amarantha

"Gramma! Gramma! It's Laura! Let me help you. Come with me now. It's so cold and you need to be where it's warm."

Warm hands chaffed her hands and feet, and evergreen branches parted as strong arms lifted her from the ground.

"Laura, are you here? Did you come for Thanksgiving?" They clung together and their tears mixed, then Amarantha looked toward *the way to go* and lowered her head and closed her eyes for a long sleep on the moss and leaves under the a tall cedar whose lower branches reached almost to the ground, hiding her in their dark fragrance.

Winter Trails

They come at night when I'm asleep
And leave their prints to let me know,
They came so near on freshened snow,
Their spoor-marked trails pass by my door.
Deer on the hoof, ermine that wore
Their winter coats, not meant to keep
When sunlight's strong and streams run deep.

They come in summer, I know that well,
But forgiving grass shows not a sign,
And they disappear into the pine
As if they hadn't paid a call
Or grazed beside the kitchen wall.
Who knows their journeys? Who can tell
When life was good? When darkness fell?

My winter's here, and there to view
Are all the trails I've made in life
As daughter, sister, mother, wife.
The twisting, turning, stopping gait,
The steps I took to shape my fate-
When spring returns and winter's through,
Let someone come to walk anew.

Many thanks to:

Jan Lee, whose support for this project
went far beyond encouraging words

Steph Winter, who read,
listened and edited

The Four Lovelies,
who are always in my heart

About the Author

As a wife and mother pursuing a career that spanned thirty years and in which she wore many hats (librarian, teacher, PR director), Laurie Otis delayed completion of her first book. Now, with discretionary time and the advent of the computer, all the stored plots and thoughts at last have been committed to paper. At seventy-five, she still lives in rural Wisconsin at the edge of the Chequamegon National Forest with her dog, Buddy, and her cat, Frosty. She's currently working on a second novel.